Patrick Gale

was born on the Isle of Wight in 1962. He spent his infancy in Wandsworth Prison, which his father governed, then grew up in Winchester. He now lives on a farm near Land's End.

Praise for *Dangerous Pleasures*:

'Nattily subversive, sexually ambiguous, intelligent and disturbing. The prose sizzles with acidic observation.'   *Sunday Times*

'Not one of these eleven stories is a dud. All of them are concerned with the fallout that occurs when soft-focussing fantasy collides with hard-nosed reality. The lingering after-effects "lie on the sweeter side of bleak". Witty, moving and very much alive.'   *Time Out*

'Patrick Gale revels in absurd risks. It's the promise of an unexpected, and potentially implausible outcome that entices you into his stories.'   *Independent on Sunday*

'Gale is a master of character, and he slips under the skins of his women protagonists with such wit that it's often hard to believe he's a man. From the misplaced passions of a jilted writer these fresh, clear-headed stories are reminiscent of Gale's back catalogue of acclaimed novels.'   *Elle*

'Gale pins down the pain of love and leaving and the no-man's-land between the apparently real and the illusory. He writes of uncertain memories and threatened loyalties and, in 'Dressing Up In Voices', of a couple whose passionate, inevitable break-up is traced with unrelenting accuracy.'   *Scotland on Sunday*

Also by Patrick Gale

PATRICK GALE

Dangerous Pleasures

A Decade of Stories

Flamingo
An Imprint of HarperCollins*Publishers*

Flamingo
An Imprint of HarperCollins*Publishers*
77–85 Fulham Palace Road,
Hammersmith, London W6 8JB

Flamingo® is a registered trademark of
HarperCollins*Publishers* Ltd

www.**fire**and**water**.com

Published by Flamingo 1997
9 8 7 6 5 4

First published in Great Britain by
Flamingo 1996

Author photograph by Aidan Hicks

ISBN 0 00 654769 9

Set in Bembo

Printed and bound in Great Britain by
Clays Ltd, St Ives plc

Author's Preface

The tales which follow were written over the last ten years, sometimes to commission, sometimes on a whim, sometimes in an effort to work a fit of bad temper from my system, but always with the entertainment of a particular friend in mind. Some have been published before, as detailed below, but to tinker is only human, so they now appear in a slightly altered form.

Wig – *His* (Faber and Faber, US)
Dressing Up In Voices – *Twenty Under Thirty* (Sceptre)
Borneo – *Whitbread Stories One* (Jonathan Cape)
Other Men's Sweetness – *The Ten Commandments* (Serpent's Tail)
Old Boys – *Meanwhile In Another Part of the Forest* (Flamingo)
The List – *The Faber Book of Gay Short Stories* (Faber and Faber)

Contents

WIG

☙

for Rupert Tyler

WANDA would never have thought of buying such a thing, never have *planned* to do so. In this case, however, her thoughts and plans were immaterial. She was put upon, the object, quite literally, thrust upon her. The salesman pounced as she was waiting for a friend and as soon as she had felt the thing's slippery heaviness between her fingers, her fate was sealed.

Wanda had never mastered the art of evading the attentions of department store demonstrators and had gone through life being squirted with unwanted scents. Where other women could stride purposefully by, freezing all overtures with a glare or a scornful laugh, she would feel coerced into buying small gadgets for slicing eggs into perfect sections or recycling old bits of soap into garishly striped blocks. On the rare occasions when she heard him speak of her to his friends, she gathered that her husband's image of her was coloured by this weakness.

'She loves gadgets,' he would say. 'If she thinks it saves her time, she'll buy it. When they invent a gadget to live your life for you, she'll be first in the queue and let herself be talked into buying six.'

In her youth she had become a not terribly fervent Christian in the same way – sold the idea by a catchy sermon involving some crafty use of props – until her faith went the way of the spring-loaded cucumber dicer and the Bye-Bye Blemish foundation cream, gathering to it a kind of dusty griminess that dulled her guilt at its under-use.

'Excuse me, Madam.' It was a less vigorous approach than usual, tired and mechanical. He was evidently too drained by a long day of false charm to be mindful of his commission. 'Would you like to try a wig?'

A chip slicer she might have resisted. She had one of those already. And a hoover attachment for grooming the cat

3

(not a great success) but the very strangeness of that little mono-syllable seemed to pluck at her elbow. She paused and half-turned.

'I beg your pardon?'

He was a nondescript, sandy man; the kind of man one looked straight through. She did not imagine he could draw in much business and yet, now that he had caught her eye, she perceived something confidential in his very nothingness. She felt an immediate sense that, in talking to him, she became invisible too, temporarily shielded from critical view.

'A wig, Madam,' he repeated. 'Would you like to try one?' He did not smile. His manner was earnest, even urgent.

'Should I be insulted?' she asked, touching her own hair instinctively. 'Why me? Why didn't you ask someone else?'

'I did,' he said, with a ghost of a smile. 'I've sold several.' He considered the small rack of the things ranged on polystyrene heads on the trolley at his side like the grim evidence of an executioner's zeal, and stretched one over the backs of his simian fingers. 'I think *this* one for you,' he said. 'Not our most popular model, because it's rather expensive. To be quite frank with you, designs from the cheaper range tend to go to people looking for fancy dress or hoping to cover the short term effects of medical therapy. Try it on. I know you'll be sur-prised.'

She took it gingerly, expecting the cheap sweatiness of nylon but it was pleasantly cool, sending a kind of shock through her fingertips. It put her in mind of being allowed to hold a school friend's angora rabbit for the first time; now, as then, she was seized with an immoderate temptation to hold it to her cheek. It was blonde, of course. To that extent he *was* like any salesman. He had assumed, quite erroneously, that being a quiet-looking brunette with a sensible cut she could brush behind her ears or tame with an Alice band, she harboured a secret desire for Nordic bubble curls. Obedient, resigned to humiliation, she pulled out her hair slides then slid the wig over her tingling scalp. Feeling

4

slightly dizzy, she bent her head forward – she was slightly taller than the salesman – and allowed him to tuck in any locks of her hair still showing.

For all its mass, it felt no heavier than a straw hat. She could not restrain a soft laugh; she knew she would not buy but this was amusement as harmless as raiding the dressing-up box and, smiling at her, he seemed to enter into her childish pleasure.

'Good,' he said. '*Very* good.'

'Quick,' she said. 'Let me see.'

He was stooping below his little trolley for the mirror when she saw her friend – one used the term loosely – returning from the haberdashery department with the shoulder pads and French chalk she had been seeking when they parted company. The friend was a conventional woman with a tendency to spiteful tale bearing when she caught any of her acquaintance doing anything eccentric or irrational. Wanda froze as the friend approached, suddenly aware that the salesman had frozen too, in suggestive complicity. It was too late to pull the wig off without hopelessly disordering her hair yet she could think of no plausible explanation as to why she was standing there trying it on. The friend's worst done, she would find herself receiving pitying looks as one bravely keeping a struggle with cancer or alopecia to herself or she would be scorned as the frivolous vulgarian they had long suspected her of being. The latter would be almost welcome. Her friends were merely neighbourhood women who had taken her under their wings; ambiguous controllers she would happily avoid. She could easily hide solitary days from her husband.

The friend passed her by however, without the slightest betrayal of recognition, continuing to look querulously about for her missing companion. Wanda looked after her retreating form in amazement. Had she a bolder appearance, she might have thought it miraculous. The salesman had found the mirror and was holding it out.

'See for yourself,' he said. 'Of course, it *is* beautifully styled, but the reason it's so much more expensive is that, apart from the basic skull cap, every fibre in it is human.'

She did not look directly in the mirror but, in the second before she tugged the thing free of her head in a spasm of revulsion, she seemed to catch a reflected glimpse of an angry stranger.

'Horrible,' she stammered. 'I'm so sorry. My friend's waiting for me.' And she hurried off for a reprimand from the friend and a dour, unfattening lunch.

When he first singled her out for his special attentions – fumbling trips to the cinema, long, circular drives in his car, hectoring sessions of golf tuition – her husband had praised her normality. 'The thing I really like about you,' he would say, 'is you're so normal.'

Delivered in lieu of anything more romantic, the praise warmed her heart and briefly convinced her that normality was indeed her special feature. Pressing through on his advantage, he wooed, wed and twice impregnated her. By some sleight of hand, he managed to do all four without once mentioning love. She did not love *him* – this had been one of the certainties that lent her courage in accepting his proposal – but she nonetheless hoped that he might love *her* and be holding something back out of manly reserve. This fond delusion evaporated shortly after the birth of their second child, when he passed on an infestation of pubic lice and blamed it, with neither apology nor embarrassment, on insufficient aeroplane hygiene. She had learned to live with the delusion's residue. She had a nice house, two clean, healthy children and a generous housekeeping allowance from which she could grant herself occasional treats without detection. Although she had only ever experienced orgasm by accident, her husband continued to grant her perfunctory sexual intercourse at least once a fortnight.

*

For most wives, that evening might have been a memorably bad one; for her it was much like any other. Their daughter, Jennifer, refused to eat supper, pleading incipient vegetarianism, and was sent to bed with no alternative. At several points during the meal, Mark, their son imitated Wanda's way of talking, most unpleasantly, only to be rewarded with her husband's indulgent laughter. When she had seen the children off to bed, smuggling in an apple and some cheese to Jennifer, he pointedly admired a Swedish actress's breasts throughout the thriller she had not wanted to watch. After that, when she was ready to drop with exhaustion, he made her sit up and play Scrabble. Scrabble, like her normality, had been one of the things originally to bring them together. He had made her play it the first time he took her to Godalming to meet his mother.

An inveterate snob, he had learnt from his mother that most card games apart from bridge were somehow common and bridge, he swiftly gathered, lay beyond his impatient understanding. Scrabble, however, appealed to him. He assured her it was a game 'smart' people played. When challenged he would never say why and she suspected he was influenced by the game's appearance in a hackneyed advertisement for chocolate mint creams. His mother claimed it was sophisticated because it came in a dark green box and anyone knew that all the best things came in dark green – waxed jackets, cars, Wellington boots, folding TV dinner tables and so forth. The problem was that Scrabble was one of the few pastimes at which her husband seemed dim beside her. In front of his friends he pretended to boast of her cleverness, her facility for scoring forty-five with a four letter word placed slyly across the ends of two others, but in private she knew it maddened him. She learned early on in their relationship to temper her glee at triumphing over him. She avoided forming words like gnomon or philtrum which she knew he would vainly insist on challenging and she tortured herself by passing up frequent opportunities to score Scrabbles. Try as she might, however, she could not let him win. It was a

game at which he could never excel. She hoped he would abandon
the challenge, dismiss the skill he lacked as being feminine and
therefore pointless but it was as if he wished to bludgeon the game
into submission the way he did the television, or the dog. He knew
he could beat her effortlessly at golf, drive faster and mow the lawn
better than she ever would but he would not accept that in this
one, insignificant area of their life, he had no mastery and was her
inferior.

As usual, tonight, she trounced him despite her best efforts to
help him win. She murmured soothingly that he had wretched
luck with the letters he picked up but she knew he was seething
from the way he splashed his whisky when he poured his night-
cap and the entirely unnecessary fuss he made over some small
item of household expense for which she had failed to obtain a
receipt during that day's shopping excursion. She was weary to
her very soul and knew she would have to make an early start
the next morning because it was her day to drive the school run
so she pointedly popped a sleeping tablet before pecking him a
placid goodnight.

He ignored the hint, however. The cheap posturing of the
film had left him restless and aroused and his humiliation at the
Scrabble board had stirred in him a need for vengeance. She knew
the warning signs of old. An unpleasant memory from when she
was once laid low with gastric flu told her he would not be denied.

'You only have to lie there,' he said when she demurred and,
tugging aside the pyjama bottoms she suddenly remembered she
had forgotten to include in that morning's wash, he thrust his
erection into her face. It bumped her nose once then she obediently took it in her mouth, remembering to keep her teeth out
of the way. She had once been ambushed by an article on oral
sex while waiting in the dentist's waiting room for her son to
receive some fillings. It had changed her life – at least, it had
changed a small part of her life – with the advice to make a
yawning motion so as to widen the entry to the throat and avoid
telltale, not to say unflattering, gagging. Tonight she found it

difficult not to choke. As he pumped back and forth, his thighs weighty on her breasts, his grasp causing the headboard to bang against the wall, she fought back spasm upon nauseated spasm, diverting her thoughts onto undone tasks, recipe cards, the alpine perennials she had yet to plant on her rockery.

'I bet *she* never has to take this,' he said, mentioning the actress. 'I bet no one ever does this to *her*. She'd be on top. She'd call all the shots.'

He spoke in so matter of fact a manner that she feared his mind was on rockeries too and the ordeal might be prolonged much further but suddenly her cheeks were filling with his vile, familiar jelly. Never one for delicate gestures, he heaped insult on assault with a comment about helping to wash down her sleeping tablets. As he rolled off her and walked to the bathroom, she took a certain pleasure in spitting out his juices into the back pages of some golfing memoirs he had been reading.

Her children were enrolled in consecutive years of the same school and she shared the school run with mothers of three of their friends. School runs were a far cry from the easy suburban slovenliness of dropping one's husband off at the station with an overcoat flung over one's nightdress. Other children were all too often hostile emissaries of their parents, spitefully observant as only children could be. Normally she presented them with as clean and careful a version of herself as she would offer her husband's colleagues at the Christmas party. This morning, however, she had dressed in a hurry, thrown into confusion by a bad night's sleep and the discovery that her son had unplugged the tumble drier so as to recharge some batteries, and so left in a sodden heap that day's blouse which she had planned to iron before breakfast.

'You were wearing that dress yesterday,' said her daughter's best friend in a tone of friendly astonishment.

'I don't think so,' she said. 'Hurry up and belt up or we'll be late.'

'Yes you were,' said the child. 'I'm belted now so you can drive on. Yes you were. I saw you when Mummy came to pick up Mark and Jennifer.'

'Really?' Wanda replied, pretending to frown at some road works. 'I really don't remember. Maybe I was. How funny. Now. What have you all got on your timetables today? Is it horrid maths?' Incredulously she felt herself break out in a nervous sweat. The girl had turned away, oblivious to the bright conversational gambit. 'Mummy changes at least twice a day,' she told the others. 'Three times if she's gardening or something. She says Daddy likes it.'

Wanda amused herself briefly with the image of the woman in question actually effecting regular bodily changes – new hair, new teeth, new leg lengths – with the restlessness of a dissatisfied flower arranger. Then the unnervingly self-possessed Morag, the next child they picked up, physically recoiled as Wanda laughed her hello in her face, and she realized she had forgotten, in the rush, to brush her teeth. She was caught out in her hasty rootle through the glove compartment for a packet of peppermints and, forced therefore to pass them round, had to admit to her lapse if she was to justify taking the last mint and thereby depriving Jennifer of one. Any ground gained by doling out sweets was doubly lost by this tasteless revelation. The girls shifted slightly on their seats and giggled except for poor Jennifer, who pressed her nose to the window and stared with forlorn fury at the passing houses, condemned now for a mother not only slatternly but unhygienic.

After seeing the children safely into the playground, Wanda drove directly into town, while she was still fired with humiliation and rage. Only half aware of why she was there at all, she found a parking space then half-strode, half-ran back to the department store. For a moment she froze as it seemed that the salesman and his trolley had vanished but then she saw with a start that he was only feet away, helping a woman peel a long, red creation off her own head of nondescript grey.

Instinct and a kind of warning glance from him told her to stand back until the woman had made her purchase then, as she stepped forward he greeted her with a blandly surprised, 'Ah, Madam,' and asked if she wished to try on the same model again.

'No,' she told him. 'It's perfect. I know it is. I was just being silly before. About the hair being human I mean. I don't know why. Perhaps it made me think of nuns. But now I . . .' She faltered, her mouth suddenly dry with nerves. His face briefly clouded by concern, he asked if she would like to wear it immediately.

'Oh no,' she said, scandalized. 'Wrap it up, please I . . . I'll try it on again once I get it home.'

He wrapped it in tissue then shut it into a bag so discreet it might have contained a roll of curtain-heading tape or a box of talcum powder.

Meeting the extravagant price with a handful of notes from the horde she had pared from her housekeeping budget, she experienced a dizziness that verged on the erotic and she had to hurry to the coffee bar to eat two slices of cake to recover her equilibrium. It was only as she sat there, terrible booty on the chair beside her, softly munching, reduced like the immobilized shoppers around her to a contented sugar-trance, that she noticed the bag was not one of the store's own but of a different provenance entirely. It was black with small gold lettering which boasted outlets in France, Luxemburg and Florida. *Silence*, the company appeared to be called, which put her in mind of libraries. Perhaps it was meant to be pronounced in a French accent to sound less an imperative, more a bewitching promise. In small curly letters beneath the title the bag whispered, *Your secret is our pride*. She wondered if the store's management knew the salesman was there at all or whether he slyly played on the employees' ignorance of one another's purpose and throve in their scented midst like a parasite on a sleek but cumbersome host. As if to confirm her suspicion, he had moved his trolley again when she glanced around her from the downward escalator. He had shifted his favours from foundation garments and hosiery to between costume jewellery and winter hats.

At first she only wore the wig at home, when she was safely alone, honouring it with all the ritual befitting a complex pornographic pursuit. She would lock doors and draw curtains. She took off all her too familiar clothes, the better to focus on the wig's effects, and wrapped her body Grecian-style in a sheet or bath towel, much as she had done as a slyly preening child. Every time she stretched it anew across her knuckles and tucked it around her scalp she felt afresh the near-electric sensations that had first surprised her in the store. She was fascinated by what she saw, transfixed before the unfamiliar woman she conjured up in the mirrored doors of the bedroom cupboards. If the doorbell or the telephone rang during the hours of her observances, she ignored them, although, lent courage by curls, she made a few anonymous calls to people she disliked, words slipping from her lips which the unwigged her could never have uttered. Had her husband come home unexpectedly, he would have caught her in as much guilty confusion as if he had surprised her in some rank adulterous act.

And yet with each resumption of blondeship she grew less timid. The woman in the looking glass would not be ignored, it seemed, and her influence proved cumulative. Wanda grew bolder. She began to make short daytime excursions in the wig and did things she imagined a woman with such hair would do. She drove to smarter districts than her husband's where she sat in pavement cafés and ordered a glass of red wine that brought a flush to her cheeks or a searingly bitter double espresso whose grounds she savoured on her tongue. She bought expensive magazines, flicked through them with a knowing smile as though she recognized the people within, then, casually profligate, left them behind on restaurant tables without even bothering to retrieve the small sachets of free samples glued to certain advertisements.

She had a pedicure at an elegant chiropodist's, which left her feet dangerously soft in the new black shoes she had bought herself. Then, inspired by the pleasure of watching a woman crouch below her working at her feet with little blades and chafing devices, she paid to have her toe and fingernails painted traffic light red. This last impulsive indulgence seemed a miscalculation at first since it could not be shut away in her wardrobe like the wig and the shoes or easily washed off like the new, distinguished scent, but her husband seemed to like her with claws. Or at least he did not seem actively to *dislike* her with them. A few weeks ago she would have thought them entirely out of keeping with her rather homely character and what she thought of as her 'look' but now they seemed no more than a newly exposed facet of her personality. Her fingers seemed longer and more tapering than they had before, her clothes less a necessity and more of a statement.

It was only a matter of time – two weeks, in fact, before she dared to leave the wig on when she picked the children up from school. As she waited by the gates, other mothers complimented her on her bold new style. She did not duck her head or offer bashful thanks and explanation as she might have done before but merely smiled and said, 'You think so?' for their opinions were now entirely unimportant to her wellbeing. The children, especially the other girls on the school run, usually so slack in their compliments, touched her with their enthusiasm.

'It's amazing!' they cried ingenuously. 'You look like a film star!'

She knew that children's ideas of glamour were hopelessly tawdry and overblown, that, in the undereducated estimation of little girls, anything forbidden them – lipstick, bosoms, cigarettes, false eyelashes – was of its very nature beautiful so that mere prostitutes acquired a near-royal loveliness for them. She knew she should not take their effusions as a compliment. She knew she should play along for a moment or two then expose the wig for the fraud it was. After all, she would still have shown herself to be that rare thing among mothers – a good sport with a potential for sexiness. But then she saw how her daughter was sitting, squeezed into her usual corner of the back seat, mutely glowing at the praise her mother was receiving from these all-important peers. She even received a rare gesture of affection from her son; a warm, dry hand placed on her shoulder as he boasted of the points he had received for a geography test. She imagined the disappointment, disgust even, on their faces if she suddenly tugged the wig off. They might not praise her as a good sport; they might simply declare her mad. She was not yet so far from her own childhood as to have forgotten that madness in mothers was even less forgivable than bad hats.

So she drove on. Wigged. A game, laughing lie made flesh. She laid rapid plans. If she could make it through the night undetected, she would cash in the rest of her rainy day fund, call at her usual salon the next day, throw caution to the winds and have her own hair dyed and styled to match the wig. At the thought that she would thereby become the woman in her looking glass, the stylish, effortless woman of her daylight excursions, she felt herself suffused with a warm glow that began in her scalp and ran down her neck and across her breasts and belly. She gazed at the suburban roads unfolding ahead of her and smiled in a way that might have scared the children had they been less absorbed in their own chatter by now. She dreaded her husband's return however. She dreaded his mockery or anger. Once supper was safely in the oven and the children were bathed, she locked herself in the bathroom to check with a mirror that no tell tale label or lock of her own hair were showing. The look was perfect however. She reapplied her new carmine lipstick, gave the back of her neck a squirt of scent then stood back to admire her full length reflection, stepping this way and that. He had a treat in store. He had a whole new wife.

Which were his own words exactly. At first he was perturbed. He wanted to know what had suddenly made her do it.

'You,' she said lightly. 'You said you wished I was blonde like that actress. So I am. I can always change back if you don't like it.'

'No', he said, looking at her in an uncertain, sideways fashion as he mixed his gin and tonic and poured her a sweet sherry. 'No. Don't do that. Was it very expensive?'

'Not very.'

He had no idea how much women's hair cost to fix. He naïvely thought it was maybe twice what he was charged by the barber in the station car park.

'Supper'll be about five minutes,' she said. 'I'm running a bit late. And I don't want a sherry. I want a gin.'

'But you like sherry. You always have sherry,' he insisted.

'I'd rather have what you're having,' she said. 'If there's enough that is.'

'Sure. Of course there's enough. There's always enough.' He tipped the sherry back into its sticky lipped bottle and poured her gin. 'I dunno,' he said. 'I go to the office and when I come back I find a whole new wife.'

She simply smiled. 'Plenty of tonic,' she said girlishly. 'Or it'll go to my head.'

Over dinner he admired her nails too, apparently only noticing them for the first time now that she was blonde. He tried not to stare but she felt him watching her whenever she walked over to the cooker or the fridge.

'What are you staring at?' she asked at last, amazed that he had made no comment on the unpleasantly chemical pudding she had made by whipping milk into the brown powdered contents of a convenient packet and tossing in a few biscuits soaked in cherry brandy.

'You've killed her,' he joked. 'Haven't you? You've gone and killed her and put her outside in the deep freeze or something.'

She paused at the dishwasher with her back to him and shuddered involuntarily.

Don't be silly,' she said as soon as she could. 'You'll give me the creeps. Coffee?'

'Please.'

'In here? Or are we playing Scrabble?'

'No games tonight,' he said, affecting a yawn. 'I thought perhaps an early night . . .'

She had always wondered how oral sex would feel when performed on her but in all the years of their marriage he had never offered and she had never thought it entirely proper to ask. Tonight, emboldened by the unprecedented interest he was showing in her hands, her feet and her borrowed hair, she realized that she needed no words to ask him. While he was giving her breasts more attention than the usual cursory lick, she simply placed a hand on his head and pushed. He hesitated for a moment as though unable to believe what she was suggesting so she pushed again, quite firmly, so that her wishes should be unmistakable. The surprising pleasure he proceeded to give her had little to do with anything he was doing to her and everything to do with what she was doing to him. She had always supposed that sex was a matter of submission, patience even, but now it dawned on her that it was eight-tenths power.

She woke with a headache. She wondered if it had anything to do with the gin then thought that perhaps the wig was too tight. Could her head have expanded? *Did* heads expand? Like hot feet? The headache intensified as she dressed. She scowled as she brushed her teeth and teased the wig back into shape on her scalp. Downstairs the pain broke out as sulkiness, when she complained about being expected to polish her husband's shoes, and naked temper when she shouted at her daughter – her beloved Jennifer – for complaining that there was no fat-free milk for her cereal. Where these displays would normally have been beaten down by louder ones from the offended parties, she was amazed to see her husband mutely take up the boot polish and her daughter reach for the gold top with something like terror. Landed with the school run again by some cooked-up excuse from another mother, she thought her head would burst with the added burden of the children's chatter. She paused at some traffic lights to rifle her bag for painkillers which she gulped down without water, heedless of curious stares from behind her. Odious Morag – whose favour her children only cultivated because her parents had a swimming pool and threw vulgarly ostentatious birthday parties for her – had already riled her by insisting on sitting in the front like an adult because she said the back of the car 'had a bad smell'. She then began to tease Jennifer for having a crush on a teacher.

'That's enough,' Wanda said, wincing at the pain her own voice caused, booming behind her eyes. 'Stop being horrid.'

'But it's true,' Morag insisted. 'She always tries to sit in the front row.'

'I don't!' Jennifer protested.

'She *does*. And yesterday she stayed behind to ask him questions before break.'

'I said that's *enough*!' Wanda said and found herself slapping Morag on her soft, pink thigh.

For a moment there was stunned silence as Morag looked from thigh to driver and back again. It had been a fierce little slap; Wanda's palm still stung seconds later.

'I'll tell,' Morag said at last.

'Good,' Wanda told her, giddy with the release of uttering words she had too long swallowed. 'Then maybe you'll get another slap for being a telltale as well as an ill-bred little madam.'

Morag made as if to cry at this but Wanda silenced her.

'Stop it,' she hissed, astonished at the scorn in her tone. 'You're too *big* to play the baby.'

The euphoria of the others was palpable behind their silence as Morag stifled her petulant sniffles. Pulling up outside the school, Wanda defied the pain in her head.

'Jennifer,' she said. 'I'm *glad* you're showing an interest in your lessons. I'm *proud* of you, darling.' Jennifer shone with pleasure even as Morag seemed to shrink in significance.

Wanda tore the wig off with a gasp as soon as she was clear of the area. Glancing in the mirror to flick her own hair back to a semblance of life, she saw a livid, purplish welt where the thing's netting had been grinding into her forehead. From time to time as she drove, she would rub hard at it with her fingertips. She had a tendency to raise her eyebrows when people were talking to her, especially when she had no interest in what they were telling her. Possibly this habitual action had made the wig's chafing worse, producing this shaming record of insincerity.

Back in her house, before she had even loaded the breakfast things into the dishwasher, she hurried to the telephone and called her hairdresser's. To her dismay, no one, not even a junior, could see her for anything more than a dry-it-yourself light trim for two days. She had a deep, almost pathological sense of consumer loyalty, never being lured by a bargain rate into forsaking the tradesmen she had always patronized without a commensurate sense of guilt which she felt obliged to own when she next entered her usual shop.

'I bought half a pound of these in that other place on the parade,' she would confide in a confused salesperson. 'I never normally shop anywhere but here but, well, you know how it is. I just saw the price and in I went.'

Often as not she would add some placatory lie about the bargain goods having proved inferior to those from her usual stockist as though the thought that her dereliction had been punished would comfort them over her momentary infidelity. It was with a heavy heart, therefore, that she reached for the *Yellow Pages* and looked up the numbers of rival salons. She would not tip, she told herself, however good they proved;

that way the disloyalty would seem less wounding. But neither Bernice of Bromley, Shy Locks or Louis D'Alsace could fit her in. After a few more, similarly disappointing calls, she gave up, called back her usual salon, and made a morning appointment for the next day. It was only another forty-eight hours, she told herself. If she had fooled her small world so far, she could fool it a little further.

To soothe her nerves she left the wig on the hall table for swift snatching up should there be any surprise callers then she threw herself into a satisfactory penance of housework. She scrubbed the bath, pulling a skein of matted hairs from the plughole, cleaned the nasty fluffy bit of carpet behind the loo, wiped the tops of the door surrounds and descaled the shower head with a powerful caustic she had recently heard of being used in a desperate suicide bid. Then, with no break for coffee, she set about taking every saucepan and labour-saving device from the kitchen cupboards, cleaning it, washing down its shelf, then putting it back again. She even wiped the sticky residue from jam and marmalade pots. The varnish on her new nails chipped off in places but she slaved on, taking a kind of delight in finding other unpalatable tasks to tackle. She skipped lunch, eating only aspirin because she still had the residue of her morning's headache, and forged on with polishing her husband's collection of silver plate trophies and the fiddly cake stand with matching slice which his aunt had given them on their wedding day. (Wanda had kept it in the back of a cupboard, polishing it still more rarely than she used it because it had too many little nooks and crannies and something in her rebelled at using even a discarded toothbrush to clean it.)

Suddenly she saw it was time to be picking the children up again. Cursing clothes, time, duty, she ran to the hall, tossing aside her apron and snatching up the wig. The wig no longer fitted. She glared at her pink-cheeked reflection as she stuffed her hair back behind her ears and tried again. She even checked to see if the label were the right way round. She glanced at her watch and let out a whimper. She caught herself toying with the possibility of driving into school as she was only with a headscarf on in the vain hope that the children would prove less sharp-eyed than usual. This was ridiculous! Wigs did not shrink. It was not in their nature. And heads, healthy adult heads, did not grow. Brooking no nonsense, she tried one more time.

Never had the saying that one must suffer to be beautiful been so rigorously brought home to her. She succeeded in donning the wig and styling it much as before but it might have been made of cheese-wire it dug so fiercely into her. The headache, which had never entirely left her all day, paled by comparison with such immediate pain. Driving to the school, she felt herself multiply martyred. She was not yet so vain as to have become irrational. She wondered if she were sick. Women such as she had become, women with scarlet nails and borrowed splendour, were never ill. They had everything organized, and disease was not part of their plan. They vomited with tidy aggression in other women's bathrooms then partied on, lips painted afresh. They scorned hospitals. Illness bored them and the surgeon's knife filled them with selfish fears. They died violently, she sensed, in a kind of anger at a world that had cheated them. Women who made love in blonde wigs and took pains to deceive their children died crushed beneath the wheels of trains or skewered by the steering columns of their lovers' cars. A trickle of warm moisture ran from under the wig across her temple. She glanced fearfully up at the mirror, half expecting to see blood, but it was merely sweat and she dabbed it away with a handkerchief.

She was one of the last of the parents to arrive but there was not a breath of complaint from the children and she remembered her show of strength that morning. She noticed its effect almost immediately; a change had come over the pecking order in the group. To her surprise she saw that it was her daughter who now held sway, telling people where to sit, holding power of ultimate disapproval or permission. And it was Morag, normally so haughty and spiteful who was now the po-faced wheedler and appeaser.

'Mrs Spalding, I know it's very short notice,' she began, with such soft shyness that Wanda anticipated mockery, 'but my parents are taking me to the cinema tonight and I wondered if you'd let Mark and Jennifer come too. We've all done our homework already. We did most of it in break and we finished it in the last lesson because Mr Dukes was off sick. Daddy would drop them off afterwards. So you wouldn't have to do anything.'

Wanda acquiesced so easily they seemed quite startled. Jennifer began to plead automatically before realizing her wish was already granted. Wanda could think of nothing but the cruel way their voices played upon the pain in her head. The possibility of emptying the car that little bit sooner and facing an evening of relative tranquillity was an unlooked-for blessing. Her immediate impulse on swinging clear of Morag's parents' long drive was to snatch the wig off but she checked herself with the thought that she would only have to pull it on again for her husband's benefit, possibly with even greater difficulty and pain than before.

When she reached home, she walked swiftly round drawing all the curtains and turning on a few lights to create a pleasant, welcoming atmosphere, then she kicked off her shoes and lay in the middle of the drawing room carpet, breathing gently. The scents of potpourri and cleaning products soothed her. The tang of carpet freshening powder was a reminder that she had not rested all day. She closed her eyes, concentrating on breathing slower and slower, counting to herself as she drew in the fragrant air. The pain in her head began to subside and, fancying she felt the wig loosen perceptibly about her skull, she slipped into a sensuous doze.

She had given no thought all day to what they were to eat for supper. Normally it was something she did after the children had been taken from her after breakfast. She would load the dishwasher then allow herself a cup of coffee and a couple of the biscuits she kept hidden inside the drum of the electric potato peeler and she would pore over recipe books and a shopping list. Given though she might be to the blandishments of kitchen gadgets, she had never been one of those modern mothers (slatternly mothers, she thought of them, lucky, happy slatterns) who contented themselves with a hoard of frozen meals and a microwave oven. Apart from *Instant Whip*, the nearest she had ever allowed herself to fast food was a pressure cooker, and *that* she only used for steaming puddings and root vegetables. When she woke to find her husband standing over her asking if she were all right and what was for supper because he couldn't smell anything cooking, she stared up at him and felt panic in her very soul.

'I . . . I fell asleep,' she stammered, climbing to her feet and padding, shoeless, into the supperless space across the hall. 'Morag's parents have taken the children to the cinema. I had a headache when I got back and I lay down and I must have fallen asleep. Sorry.' She looked about her. The lack of lights and steam, the lack of sizzle, formed a dreadful, silent accusation. She could not pretend that the automatic oven switch had failed to come on when there was palpably nothing in there waiting to be cooked. There was not even a piece of meat. She opened the fridge door then closed it again hurriedly as he came in behind her. There was nothing. No bacon. No chicken breasts. Not even some humbly reassuring mince.

'I work my guts out all day,' he was saying, as to some invisible jury, 'and it's been a bugger of a day too, and I come back to find you fast asleep, looking like nothing on earth, and the table not even laid.' She darted a hand to her head and was relieved to find the wig still in place. 'What's got into you?' he asked.

She decided to brazen it out. 'I forgot,' she said.

'You *what*?!'

'I forgot. I've never done it before and I won't do it again. But I forgot. I spent the whole day cleaning and scrubbing and I completely forgot about supper. And I've had a terrible headache. Why don't I fix us both a nice drink? Better still, why don't we live a little and go out. The children are safe with the Hewitsons until 9.40. If we went now I'm sure we could get a table. I've had a bugger of a day too.' From somewhere deep within her she found a reserve of flirtatious gaiety. 'Come on,' she said. 'You mix us both a nice gin and put your feet up while I go and put on something pretty then we can pretend we're young and free again and you can take me out for dinner. Somewhere cosy. Somewhere French with candles!'

There was a pause, perhaps for only a second, in which she was intensely aware that the fridge had developed a louder buzz than usual, which she knew was the sign that it was reaching its point of built-in obsolescence, then he began to shout at her. He called her filthy things – filthier things than he ever did when they were having sexual intercourse. He implied she was a failure as a wife, a mother, a woman even, and then he slapped her. He had offered her many insults in his way and in his time but he had never, until this evening, touched her in violence. She fell back against the sink. Then, all at once, the shock of his big bony hand against her jaw seemed the ultimate denigration and she took a knife from the wooden block beside the bread bin and pushed it into his stomach. It was a big knife, her biggest, and the block was a particularly cunning one with a discreet mechanism which sharpened each blade as it released it for use.

She had often heard of the similarities between pork and human flesh, in particular their skin structure and the thickness of their fatty deposits. After the initial resistance, which might as well have been caused by the starched cotton of his shirt as by any strength of skin and muscle, the knife slid in with appalling ease and swiftness. The sensation was not unlike slicing into a rolled pork loin. Her husband gasped and staggered backwards, then forwards, then slumped to the floor. Never having taken a first aid exam, he did not know better than to pull the knife out. She had punctured his liver. By the time he was writhing and coughing on the linoleum, his suit was turning purple with his gore. She tried to staunch the flow with tea towels, but he was beyond her help. He seemed to spit in her face as he died but perhaps he was only coughing.

She called for an ambulance and the police, telling them her husband had been stabbed but not by whom, then she looked up the relevant cinema in the local newspaper and telephoned to leave an urgent message for the Hewitsons that an emergency had arisen and they were to hang on to Mark and Jennifer until contacted by the authorities. Turning back, she saw the big red thing on the kitchen floor and was suddenly sick, just as she had imagined women with blonde wigs should be. She vomited nothing but acrid juices, having eaten nothing all day, but it ruined the parts of her clothes the blood had not already stained, and she determined to change into something cleaner before the emergency services arrived. Both hospital and police station were a good fifteen minutes' drive away. Skidding slightly, because her feet were wet, she hurried across the kitchen and up the stairs to the bathroom. She tugged her blouse over her head and stepped out of her skirt. She began to wash her bloodied hands in the sink then realized that there was so much of the stuff on her that a shower would do the job better.

Having been descaled only that afternoon, the jet was extra strong and she welcomed its buffeting. It was only as she raised her hands to her face that she remembered she was still wearing the wig. Blinking the water from her eyes, heedless now of how badly she treated the thing, she took a handful of curls and tugged. She recoiled with a gasp. Crying out as though the water were scalding her, she flung back the shower curtain and struggled to see herself in the looking glass. The mirrored surface had steamed up and her flailing hand could not reach it so she tugged once more at the curls and felt once more the unmistakable agony of her own outraged scalp refusing to yield.

DRESSING UP IN VOICES

for Jonathan Dove

THE ONLY TIME I ever lost control – I mean truly lost control,' he said, 'was with someone else's wife.'

'Go on,' she said and pushed aside the carcass of the small bird she had just eaten.

'Well he was some kind of financial genius. I met them through Flavia.'

She wrinkled her brow to show that she knew no Flavia.

'You know,' he went on. 'Flavia. The broker who used to lead Edward around like a spaniel.'

'Oh yes,' she lied, keen for him to press on.

'Anyway, the genius, who incidentally was ugly as sin, had to go away to Washington for some secret advisory mission and she turned up on my doorstep and we sort of fell into bed.'

'Goodness,' she said.

'Quite. I mean, she was dead sexy and all that but . . . Actually, now that I think about it she wasn't sexy at all. But that was just it, you see.'

'What was?'

'Why I lost control. It was all forbidden. She said she loved him, or at least that she had immense respect for him. There was something else too, because she forbade me to let on to anyone else what was going on.'

'So she turned up on your doorstep more than once?' she asked, for whom his doorstep was as yet no more than a dot lovingly marked on an *A–Z* page.

'God yes. Every day for a month.'

'No more?'

'A month was quite enough. Anyway, he came back. She seemed to be scared of him, terrified that he might find out. She wouldn't talk about it, but now and then there was a close shave – someone meeting her on her way to my place, that sort of thing – and I'd see the panic in her eyes. Smell it on her almost.'

'Goodness.'

'Of course, it was only the trappings I fell for; the secrecy, the air of the illicit and probably the knowledge that, all being well, I'd never have to take up any responsibility for her. Anyway, I lost control. Utterly. She would ring up at about six to ask if I was free and I would say yes, ridiculously excited, then ring whoever I was meant to be seeing and cancel. Even really good friends.'

'Didn't anyone suspect?'

'Well of course they did, but I blinded them with half-truths. There was a married woman, I said, but no one any of them had ever met. I think, when a month went by and no one had been introduced, they just assumed that I was ashamed of her.'

'Or that she was ashamed of you.'

'What?' He looked up from the napkin he had been shredding and saw that she was mocking him. He snorted. Their waiter took away his spotless plate and her bird carcass. Gus asked him to bring them both a pudding. He asked for it in fast Italian.

'What did you ask for?' she demanded, cross because she had wanted *zabaglione*.

'Oh, it's their speciality. It's a kind of ice-cream grenade, encased in white chocolate and dribbled with Benedictine.'

'Oh.'

'Sorry. Did you want something else?'

'No.'

'No, come on. Did you? 'Cause I can grab someone and change the order.'

'Well . . .' She looked across the candle into his pale green eyes. He wore the apologetic expression she had seen last night. He had been doing something delectable back and forth across her abdomen with his short, blond hair and small, pointed tongue. She had run a hand across the back of his neck, as much to feel the stubble there as to make some dumb show of gratitude, but he had stopped and looked up at her with that apologetic look on his face; a painfully proper child caught out at an impropriety. 'No. Go on,' she had told him then. Now she merely smiled and confessed to a hankering after a warm froth of egg and Marsala. He had the waiter at his side with one brief turn of the head.

'You do have *zabaglione*, don't you?' he asked.

'*Certo, ma è freddo*,' the waiter told him. '*Per i barbari americani*.'

'Oh no,' she burst out. 'Please don't bother. The ice-cream thing would be fine.' Cold *zabaglione* was like offering a virgin a bed with dirty sheets. She had wanted the world's most erotic food and they were trying to fob her off with a pornographic approximation. She loathed Benedictine, but now would suffer it meekly.

'But I'm sure they could heat it up for you,' he urged her, visibly embarrassed. 'They could use a *bain-marie*.'

'No, Gus, honestly,' she insisted and turned to send the waiter away. 'What he ordered will do beautifully,' she assured him. The waiter left them with a tinge of a sneer. Gus's ring hand lay on the table. 'Sorry about that,' she muttered and reached out to touch his fingers with her own. He let his hand lie dead beneath hers then withdrew it to effect a needless adjustment to his hair.

'How about you?' he asked.

'What about me?'

'When did *you* last lose control?'

'Oh,' she laughed. 'It's sad, but I don't believe I ever have.'

'So your books aren't autobiographical? All that rage? All those thwarted lusts?'

'Lord no,' she sighed, peeling a runnel of softened wax off the candle. 'I mean, of course I have to write about feelings I can sympathize with, but I couldn't begin to live such a violent life. The very idea!' and they both laughed. The very idea of such a sane animal running fabulously amok! How too absurd! How . . . How endearing! She felt herself grow dim before the massed jury of her heroines and continued, 'Besides, I don't think you can put real happenings into fiction. Not without toning them down.'

'Too wild?'

'Sort of. There are too many jagged, messy bits. Heaven knows, there's nothing more dead than a tidy story, but there needs to be some kind of perspective.'

'Oh look. *Perfetto*,' he pronounced as their white chocolate grenades of ice cream arrived before them. He attacked his at once with that same decorous greed she had noticed in bed. She sank a spoon into hers and watched the chocolate armour crumble into the alcoholic ooze below. She carved out a spoonful then let it lie.

'I'm not altogether sure that I've ever been in love,' she said. He failed to interrupt so she continued. 'It's not that I'm heartless, or even incapable. I've *thought* I was in love several times.'

'Tell me about it,' he said, eyeing her pudding as his own all but disappeared.

'I suppose you could call my attitude romantic insofar as I believe in the possibility of meeting someone with whom one could pass the rest of one's life and for whom one would be prepared to die.' She realized of a sudden that the man at the adjoining table was listening with keen interest so she paused to take a mouthful of her grenade and give him time to resume his conversation with the youth before him. The ice cream hurt her throat. Benedictine was as reminiscent of dry-cleaning fluid as the last time she had tasted it. Mutely she offered her plate to Gus.

'Are you sure?' he asked. She nodded. He accepted it and began to eat again.

'And each time I meet someone and they say they love me, I'm flattered, and usually for them to have got that far they have to be fairly attractive, so I'm excited as well. And, I don't know. The whole business is so very beguiling. Other people's bed-rooms and breakfast. Going through a day with that mixture of smugness and light-headed exhaustion . . .'

'Bliss.'

Was he, she wondered, talking about love or the pudding?

'So I throw myself into it, fingers crossed and hoping that this time it'll be the real thing. But of course that's stupid because, as I realize each time I bring something to an end, if it *were* the real thing I shouldn't have had to cross my fingers, or hope, or crank up my indulgence. If it were the real thing, I'd have lost control. Of course writers and films exaggerate no end but there's no smoke without a fire and I just know that, if I don't feel physically sick at separation and giddy every time I hear someone's voice or find one of their odd socks at the bottom of the bed, then I'm faking. Every time, after I've started faking and got myself thoroughly involved, there comes a sickening moment when some demonstration of theirs shows me that they've lost control and I'm still sitting there with fingers crossed and my spare hand firmly on the joystick.'

The man with the youth tittered. Gus quashed him silent with a sharp look. It was one of the unimportant things that made her sick at their every separation and giddy when she heard his voice. That and the wholly irrational whatever that caused her to invite him repeatedly to her bed while the furies of rationality keened a despairing no.

She had found him at an unmemorable dinner party three years ago with his pretty and seemingly vacuous girlfriend, Loulou. Gut-stabbed by lust, she had set out perversely to woo the girl rather than charm the man. Loulou proved far from vacuous, was calculating indeed, and she had been made swiftly a party to her ceaseless round of infidelities. They would ask her to supper and she would dutifully play the role of professional wit and novelist, gabbling away about nothing when she needed to take Gus by the lapels and scream about the betrayals that passed unseen beneath his patrician nose. More recently there had been a falling off in their meetings because the strain had been becoming too much for her. Also she had been busy convincing herself that she loved another man, who was yet too ghastly to trundle out for friendly inspection. Then, three weeks ago, a postcard had arrived.

'As you may have gathered from the radio silence, my life has been suffering a sea-change,' Gus wrote. 'Have severed communications with Louise and am anxious not to lose you in the ensuing drawing-up of ranks. Let's have supper. Soon.'

On one heady impulse, she sacked the horrendous man whom no one had met, and invited Gus round for supper and sympathy.

She had planned to borrow a leaf from Loulou's book. She had planned to question him mercilessly about his domestic disaster and shattered faith in love then offer a shoulder to cry on and a brave new bedfellow to help him forget. ('Poor Gus', *bang*). In the event, she sat back and watched the unfamiliar spectacle of herself losing control. After feeding him with what she knew to be his favourite dishes, shopped for and prepared with passionless care that afternoon, she started to tell the truth then could not stem the confessional tide.

'I want you,' she had told him, curled in her chair as he sprawled across her sofa. 'I've wanted you ever since I first saw you in Nadia's horrid green kitchen. And I hated Loulou because she had you and I only became her friend so as to find out more about you and get as close to you as I could. I thought she was vacuous and that you deserved better and then she started to . . . Gus, I knew everything. She told me everything and I didn't tell you because I wanted her to be as unfaithful as possible. I thought that the more she slept around, the less likely you'd be to forgive her if ever you found out. Sometimes, knowing what I knew and not telling you, was more than I could stand. But I couldn't tell you, you see, because I knew you loved her and that you'd hate whoever opened your eyes. So I couldn't come between you. I had to wait. And now you're probably wondering how best to extricate yourself from this appallingly tawdry little scene.'

But he had not left. Not until breakfast. And he had come back. Again and again.

As he drank cognac and she a small black coffee, she realized that they had made no plans for the night. Tomorrow was a bank holiday Monday, so there would be no need for him to get up early to be at his office. She had kept tomorrow free on purpose so as to share his day off but he had still said nothing. He talked about how depressing it was to watch one's friends marry off, settle down and revise their address book according to their partner's whims. She listened with half an ear, making sighed or chuckled responses where necessary, but she was thinking about that night, the next day and the following weekend. She wanted him to ask her back to the 'smallish place' in Islington that she had never seen. She wanted to wake up in his bed, feel his back beside her then fall asleep again only to have him rouse her later with coffee and a wet, late rose. (She watched the man and the youth leave. She saw the fleeting brush of his hand across the youth's own.) She wanted to explore Gus's bookshelves and record collection while he shaved. Would his flat be indescribably sordid, with a dirty frying pan on the stove and a mattress on a dusty floor, or was Gus hiding behind a landlord's furniture and non-committal colours? She drained her cup to the bitter dregs and slid her miniature macaroons across the table to his eager hands.

'Shall we, er?' he asked, when he had finished munching. She hummed assent and smiled until he had to smile back. She watched as he summoned the bill, and she reached for her wallet.

'Here,' she said, crinkling a note at him.

'No.' He waved it away, deftly handing back the bill to the waiter with a piece of plastic tucked inside it. 'You bought the tickets so this is on me.'

The tickets had cost far less, but she demurred for only an instant as his salary far outweighed her publisher's most recent advance. Proportionately, her concert tickets had cost her several of his grand meals.

'I'll wait for you outside,' she said and headed for the door.

'Your coat, *signorina*.'

'Of course. How stupid of me.' She had forgotten her coat. She stood awkwardly as the waiter insisted on helping her on with it.

'*Buona notte*,' he said and held open the door with a grin.

'Goodnight,' she replied and went out.

The pavement was nearly empty, although it was not long past eleven. She had forgotten how even the West End could become suburban on Sunday nights. Autumn was coming. The sky was cloudless and there was a chill in the air. She watched a woman dancing, drunk, with her reflection in a darkened hairdresser's window, then turned back, nervous, to see if Gus was coming. There he was, swinging into his cream mac with a frown, mildly irritated by a hovering waiter, and she knew that she would have to speak first. As he emerged on to the pavement he did not return her smile but the words were already on her lips. As good as spoken, so, '*Dove adesso*,' she asked.

'What?'

'How shall we get back?'

'Um. Look.' He drew her alongside him with an arm across her shoulders. 'We need to have a talk.'

We've talked too much already, she thought, panic clutching her from within. That's our trouble. We've talked everything to death. We should hurry home, hurry to either of our homes and make rapid, violent love without a word being spoken. Then again, slowly, still in silence. Then make ourselves over to sleep. Tomorrow all will be well. Then. For now.

'I'm all ears,' she said brightly, making as if to meet his eye but seeing no further than his coat buttons before cowardice drove her to look straight ahead. They began to walk.

'We've had a lovely time,' he said swiftly. 'A *good* time. And I'm very fond of you, but . . .'

'But,' she echoed.

Don't say another word, she meant to say. Least of all fond. Fond, with its connotations of passing folly. I'll find a taxi, leave you here and we'll never meet again. Oh Christ, Christ, Christ. This is going to hurt, whatever you say, and the least you could do is let me go without you making a little speech to make your suffering less. The least you could do would be to shut up and hurt; suffer a part of what I . . . We shall have to meet in hot Christmas sitting rooms and bray delightedly.

They came to a line of scaffolding poles ranged along a length of pavement. She slipped apart from him and walked on the pavement's edge so that the metal came between them. She was looking sternly ahead and felt that he was too. She pictured their two, pinched, white faces as an oncomer might see them. Second division terrorists trying to pass plans for an assassination without it being seen that they are known to one another. But the pavement was empty. They waited, obedient, at a crossing although there were no cars coming through the green lights.

'But I don't think we should carry on with the bed bit,' he said. She said nothing. They walked on and she could find nothing to say. 'Do you see?' he asked eventually, as they came into Trafalgar Square and waited at another crossing.

'Yes,' she said. 'It's just that I can't think of anything to say that isn't banal.'

'What a pity?'

'Yes. That would do.'

No more words. Leave me. Let me go home. I want so *much* to go home.

'How will you get home?' he asked.

'Walk in the right direction until I find a taxi, I suppose. What about you?'

'Can I walk with you until you find one?'

'If you like.'

Go away. Take your patrician nose and go away. No. No. Stay and get in the taxi with me. Come home. Unsay it all. Gainsay.

'I think the trouble was that I'd got so used to not thinking of you in, well, *that* way. With Loulou around and everything and you were so . . .'

'What?'

'So horribly clever.'

'That's *no* reason. That's a worthless thing to say.'

'Yes it is.'

'I moved too fast,' she cut in. 'I frightened you off.'

'No. Not that.'

'What, then?'

'I don't think it would have made any difference how fast you moved. I just wasn't ready. Not for you. Not for anyone. Anything.'

'I think I could tell,' she said slowly.

Of course she could tell. He had organized the entire weekend so that, while spending every hour together, they spent as many of them as possible out of doors, in public, away from any kind of bed. He had engineered the discussion over dinner. The disgusting, cold discussion. He thought he had prepared the ground so that it would be less of a shock for her. Well he made a lousy job of it.

'I suppose, if the chemistry is wrong, then no amount of good will can help,' she said, feeling cheapened by the words.

'Yup,' he said. 'And believe me,' this with an awkward little tug at her shoulders that made her teeter and graze one of her ankles on a heel, 'there was plenty of it.'

They walked the length of Whitehall in total silence. Three late buses sailed past them, buses she could have taken to escape him, but she needed to hurt herself. She resolved on taking a taxi or nothing, knowing that taxis on the route she would take were rare. They reached Parliament Square and she clutched at a straw.

'Look, Gus, this is silly. There are loads of cabs going in your direction. Leave me here. I'll be fine.'

'Are you sure?'

'Yup. Easier on my own. I'll be fine. But look, there's some stuff of yours in my flat; that black jersey and some socks and things.'

'Oh God. So there are. What are you doing tomorrow?'

'Nothing much.'

'Let's meet for tea and you can give me them then.'

Success!

'Where?'

'St James's. That funny sixties cafeteria place.'

'Okay. Fourish?'

'Make it five.'

'All right. But are you sure?'

'How do you mean?'

'Well.' She paused. 'I could always post them to you.'

'Don't be stupid. I still want to see you, remember.'

'Oh yes.' Silly me, she thought, I forgot.

'Here's a cab,' he said. 'I must run.'

They tried to shake hands but she missed and ended up with a fistful of mackintosh. She waited until she heard his taxi door slam then allowed herself a brief wave as he escaped her up Whitehall.

She walked home along the North bank of the river and over Albert's fairground of a bridge. Buses only passed her when she was between stops and taxis were either busy or going the wrong way and unwilling to turn back. She toyed with the idea of climbing the low railings into the small green space known as the Pimlico Shrubbery for a good weep, or abandoning herself to showier grief on a bench facing Battersea Power Station, but she preferred to walk and punish her elegantly shod feet. If she got home too soon, she would not sleep, thanks to the coffee she had drunk and the ideas circling wildly as to how she should approach tea-time tomorrow. A middle-aged black couple were having trouble starting their car at one point and she stopped to help the husband push it. When it started, he offered her a lift home but she said no thank you, she was almost there, although she had at least a mile to go. Pushing the car, she had broken the heel of one of her shoes.

Before letting herself in, she leaned into a neighbour's skip to vomit all she had eaten in the restaurant. This was easily done; there had been gobbets of blood around the small bird's bones and she had only to think of these. Sleep came, thick and dreamless. She woke with blisters on both big toes and fresh resolution in her heart.

She rarely wrote short stories. Her novels were fat, exhaustive expositions of character and possibility that drove critics to wield terms like *sprawling* or *magisterial*, and she found the smaller form unsatisfactory. The short stories she *had* written gained most of their poignancy from the fact of their being dismembered first chapters, and could not stand comparison with the more finished work of specialists. She had spoken truly in telling Gus that her novels made no use of autobiography. She left herself alone but, unconsciously, she did use her acquaintances, transmogrified with bits and pieces of each other. Her method resembled a child's picture book whose pages were cunningly split into threes, enabling one to join head of stork with body of rhino and mermaid's tail. Thus Janet's temper might join with Edward's charity in Susan's body. Susan's body was one of a kind, but neither she nor Janet nor Edward ever recognized their contributions to the hybrid result. Hardly surprising, since even the authoress frequently failed to recognize what she had done.

Though using real people, she had never drawn on real events. Real events were too hard to transplant; each had its peculiar logic and trailed sticky strands of cause and consequence that refused to adapt to the simpler systems of fiction. This morning's material was different, however, because she would treat it in isolation with the bare minimum of adaptation. At least, that was the idea.

She was in the bath inspecting her blisters when the thought came to her, so she went straight back to bed, her head turbaned in a towel. She always worked in bed in the winter months because she suffered from the cold when immobile. She kept the computer on a hospital table that she could swing over the mattress before her as she sat cross-legged and furled in a quilt. The green letters sliding across her glasses, she worked for several hours without answering the telephone or pointed beseeching of the cat, and told the truth.

She wrote about how she had met Gus and Loulou, how she had inveigled her way into their lives and eventually into Gus's bed. (Well . . . Gus into *her* bed.) She told how they had walked around Clapham looking at hurricane damage, how she had taken him to hear her favourite pianist playing her favourite Brahms intermezzo and how he had found her ugly after feeding her on a small, bleeding bird and hateful French liqueur. Ugly as sin. She told of her walk home. She changed the facts in only a few points. She had herself accept the lift from the middle-aged black couple, whose lasting devotion she then envied until they took her home for a drink and she saw their child's wheelchair. She turned herself into a scholarly lesbian and she switched Gus and Loulou's genders. Loulou became, with perhaps wanton cruelty, a philandering estate agent called Lucian, while Gus became Rose, an uncertain blonde. Gus had many faults, one of the more endearing of which was his failure to understand why lesbians should exist, much less to sympathize with what they might do. Even if she had herself and 'her' do exactly the same things in bed, he would never recognize himself in Rose.

She stopped writing towards three because it was time to feed the cat and dress for tea but also because she could not finish the story until she knew how their own would end. As long as she had been tapping at the computer keyboard, she had kept thoughts of the night before at a bearable distance, but as she

39

brushed her hair and chose her clothes, the hurt returned. She realized that she still had not wept. For all the fluttering in her chest and the returning tightness in her throat, she found herself yet capable of selecting clothes with an unselected look and of lending a mournful pallor to her make-up with a pale powder she had once bought by mistake. His black jersey (surely one that Loulou had given him), a pair of very unwashed socks and a tie that was rather too wide, were in a carrier bag near the front door. She had gathered and folded them last night apparently, in a daze between vomiting dinner and brushing teeth.

She arrived at the cafeteria far too early, of course. He was nowhere in sight, so she forced herself to walk over to the crowded bridge to kill time. Several nondescript women and an elderly man with a crutch were leaning on the eastern railings staring crazily at the sparrows that clustered over their crumb-filled hands, as though this minor miracle were not something they indulged in every afternoon. A few children shouted amazement and a youth in a Chinese revolutionary cap filmed them on a Japanese camera. She walked on, past the hideous Walt Disney candelabra and crouched a while to watch the aggressive patrolling of a black swan. She should have brought it something to eat. She wondered if she could remember to return with a piece of cake when their tea was over. She held out her empty hands to it, fingers spread.

'Sorry,' she told it, then saw a woman crouched, photographing her from a few yards away. She had on a brilliant white dress that looked far too thin for the day and she wore her armfuls of almost pink red hair in a mane. The woman lowered the camera and smiled, showing her teeth, then stood to show that she was tall and built like Juno. She could not smile back so she stared. Then Gus called her name and set her free. She turned and hurried to the squat, round cafeteria where he was waiting.

'There was a dreadful queue when I got here so I got us stuff without waiting for you. Do you mind?'

'Of course not.'

'Shall we sit in or out?'

'Oh out, I think. It's cold but the sunshine is so lovely.'

She led him to an empty table. There were no free-standing chairs, only circles of wood with fixed-on arms that splayed out from each central table column. It felt as if they were sitting at either side of some chaste playground mechanism; a miniature roundabout that, with a few thrusts from their short, childish legs, would set them gently turning, very safely, always equidistant.

'While I remember,' she said, and passed him the carrier bag.

'Oh. Thanks,' he said, feigning surprise then peering inside to make sure she had held on to nothing that was his. 'My favourite,' he said, inspecting the outside to see which shop it hailed from. 'How clever of you. You got home okay?'

'Yes. But I walked, like an idiot, and now I've got blisters on my toes.'

'Now look,' he said. 'I know you like fruity teas and they had a huge choice so I brought several bags and some hot water.'

'Goodness.'

'Cherry, mandarin or . . .' He exaggerated the need to peer at the third. 'Yes, or mixed fruit.'

'Cherry sounds lovely.'

'Pop the others in your bag.'

'Are you sure?'

'Yes. Go on.'

'How absurd we both sound; like maiden aunts stealing sugar lumps from Fortnum's.'

They laughed, uproariously almost, and she saw that he was wearing the tie she had given him two years ago, at Loulou's Christmas party. He had bought a plateful of cakes and proceeded to sink his teeth into a chocolate one. His nose just cleared the icing. She decided on the vanilla one for the black swan and set it aside on a paper napkin.

'What's that for?' he asked, dabbing crumbs off his chin.

'A black swan. I teased it by crouching down with nothing to give. Made me feel guilty.'

'Wouldn't it rather have bread?'

'Would you?'

'Point taken.'

'Bread or cake; they're neither of them exactly natural fodder for a water bird.'

She took a mouthful of a rather nasty, dried-out flapjack and dunked her cherry tea bag up and down. The water did not turn pink but became a disappointing, traditional sort of brown. Suddenly she saw the statuesque camera woman approaching and turned back to Gus.

'What are you up to this evening?' she asked.

'Nothing much. Tabitha's having a drinks party.' She wrinkled her brow to show that she knew no Tabitha. 'You know. *Tabitha*. She helps run the Burden Friday Gallery. Anyway, it's a choice between her or the reprint of *La Dolce Vita*. Want to come?'

'I don't know her.'

'To the Fellini.'

'No. I can't.' He looked a question at her and she thought quickly. Why couldn't she go? Would she not love to? Sit close beside him and be bombarded by glamorous disillusion in a darkened room? She met his pale, bland gaze and thought that on reflection she would not. 'I've a story to finish.'

'I didn't know you stooped to stories.'

'Actually it's a question of aspiring; they're far harder than novels. And yes, I do sometimes. This one's for a magazine. They pay absurdly well.' She saw that he was not listening to her but was smiling politely up over her shoulder.

'Can I help?' he asked.

She turned round to a warm, brown cleavage and what, close-to, proved to be pure white cashmere.

'*I thought* it was you!' The woman's camera – a large, professional thing – dangled from one hand. There was no time to make any kind of face as she bowed and kissed her warmly at the edge of each cheek. The brush of lip whispered in her ear and a scent of ambergris hung, delicious, after she had withdrawn.

'How *are* you? You look so *well*!' A long, smooth hand stroked her jaw and shoulder. The stranger laughed, brushing back tumbling hair. 'Sorry. How awful of me!' She turned to shake Gus's hand. 'Joanna Ventura.'

'Angus Packard.'

'I must run. I'm late again, but please,' she turned back and touched the shoulder again, 'ring me. Please?' As she vanished into the crowd, Gus all but gaped.

'Where have you been keeping *her*?'

'Oh,' she said drily, 'Joanna's hardly even in town so when she is I tend to keep her all to myself.'

'She looks like Anita Ekberg.'

'Who?'

'The one in the fountain in *La Dolce Vita*.'

'Oh.'

'I didn't know you knew any Americans apart from squat Jewish publishers.' Funny. She had not noticed the accent.

She finished the story swiftly, perched on the edge of the bed, her coat unbuttoned but still on. Her women in love held their last meeting over cheap Muscadet outside the National Film Theatre. The rendezvous was ostensibly held for Gus/Rose to return an unlikely black silk petticoat. She handed it over to the jilted heroine, wrapped in a used, brown paper envelope, then broke down. She begged her to forget the hasty words of the previous night then went on to make an absurd scene when her generosity was rebuffed. The heroine paused in her return across Westminster Bridge to open the envelope and send the petticoat dancing down to the brown waters beneath them, then laughed wildly in the face of a man in a suit who stopped to rebuke her for littering the city.

She pressed a button that corrected her typing then set the machine to print. As the daisywheel rattled away, she felt in her coat pocket for a handkerchief and found a ticket for the next evening's showing of *La Dolce Vita*. There was writing on the back. A woman's hand. She read it, turned the ticket over to check the performance time, then turned back to reread the writing. 'I dare you,' it said and there was a telephone number.

Suddenly the printer went wrong. There was a high-pitched bleep and a grinding sound as a half-typed sheet of paper was chewed up. She threw the ticket aside and, scowling, busied herself with freeing the page and returning the cursor to the beginning of her new text. The challenge was in red ink, however, and she could see it from the corner of her eye.

A SLIGHT CHILL

❦

for Francesca Johnson

'CAREFUL OF THE PAINTWORK, Harper!' Angel sighed. 'I said *careful*!'

'Sorry, Miss,' said the plump girl, labouring under the weight of her trunk. 'It's heavy. I slipped.'

'I know, Harper. Just go a little more slowly and you won't slip again. Girls have broken legs on these stairs before now. You might cause a serious accident.'

'Yes Miss. Sorry.'

Harper moved on down the stairs and banged the paintwork again. She did not care. Usually Angel inspired a certain sisterly respect among the girls, fear even but it was the last day of term so a spirit of barely subdued anarchy scented the air along with the usual, stouter smells of disinfectant, boiled greens and a particularly noxious *eau de toilette* the fifth formers had taken to wearing. There was no time for punishments or black house stars. Trunks had to be packed and trunk lists checked. There were beds to strip and books to return to the library. Lockers had to be swept out and inspected and there was the brief, rowdy ceremony of prize-giving to be got through along with the usual perfunctory speech and presentation to a retiring mistress.

Very few parents lived close enough to collect their girls by car – most of the school population would be evacuated to Newcastle and the London train by a convoy of buses after prize-giving – and yet girls were already drawing arrogant strength from the incipient resurgence into their lives of men. The mere anticipation of fathers, stepfathers, older brothers and, in some unfortunate cases, mothers' flash fiancés was already rendering the female rule of term time negligible. For a few brief, dangerous hours Miss Prewett, Miss Clandage and Dr Trudeau ceased to be terrible absolute rulers and became objects of mirth, even of pity. Angel always felt that the last day of term, more than any other, reminded one that the teachers were dependent on the girls for their livelihood. Girls returned to wealthy, even distinguished households for parties, new dresses, extravagant presents, a whole world of social advantage, while the likes of Miss Clandage would be spending Christmas visiting other, similarly frugal women or burdening families to whom they were not figures of awesome learning but unweddable sisters, ridiculous aunts. Miss Prewett would be earning her Christmas keep by executing tidy watercolours of her sister's children in distant Taunton. Dr Trudeau was leading a skiing and study party in Aviemore. Angel would be visiting her parents in Hampshire but before then she would be seeing Richard.

Richard! She stood back in her corner of the landing as the girls trooped past her from the trunk store to the dormitories and looked on them with a fresh benevolence. She was one of them, she knew. She was not born to be a teacher. She was only marking time here, a kind of skivvy doubling up as assistant matron and junior school English teacher. Times arose, had arisen often during this last, long term, when she feared the isolation of the place, its undiluted femininity, might be leeching away her youth and crusting her over. Matron or one of the older teachers would assume her complicity, envelop her with a deadening first person plural, and she would feel a chill across her heart. How many of them, she would wonder, had begun as she had, with no intention of staying much beyond a year or two only to give the place an entire life? At such times, however, she had only to think of Richard. His dog-eared photograph, used by her as a bookmark, was her passport to normality. She had even let some of the older girls glimpse it so they should know she was really one of them and a mere tourist in the common room.

The photograph showed him in uniform. He was a captain in the 17/21st Lancers and currently based at Sandhurst where he seemed to spend much of his time teaching mountaineering skills and planning the next expedition he would lead to the

Himalayas. He had seen no active service beyond an early tour of duty in Northern Ireland but still it worried her when he wrote her letters on regimental notepaper which bore the motto *Or Glory* beneath a menacing, winged death's head. (Dr Trudeau had been on the point of leaving the school for marriage when her fiancé's plane was shot down on a bombing mission.) Richard and his solicitor brother owned a small flat in Baron's Court. The brother was away at the moment so the first precious days of Richard's Christmas leave and her school holidays were to be spent in indulgent privacy at the flat before she joined her parents in the Itchen Valley. He had pressed her to spend Christmas with him too and she was sorely tempted. She was an only child, however, so subject to extreme parental pressure at this time of year. She was lying to her parents as it was, having told them she was spending a few days with an old school friend. They knew Richard existed, approved of him, indeed, as a future son-in-law but Angel sensed that they preferred not to think of her as a sexual animal just yet. She knew, from chance remarks, that her father, especially, liked the thought of her spending her days immured in this chaste, all-female institution rather than having her gad about town with her contemporaries.

The last girls, juniors mostly, struggled past her down the stairs with their empty trunks on their backs. The smallest helped one another out, bearing their luggage between them, grimacing at how strenuous the steepness of the staircase made this. Angel walked up to check that the trunk store was empty. One remained. She stooped to read the label and saw with a shock that it belonged to Kay Flanders. Kay, a cowering creature, unpopular for no discernible reason, had died suddenly in her sleep earlier in the term. In the rush to have the whole ghastly business over as soon as possible so as to cause as little distress as possible to the other girls, no one had seen fit to empty the trunk store to uncover her suitcase. Her uniform and sports kit had been donated to the school second-hand shop, her few remaining belongings – her 'effects' as the undertakers called them –

parcelled up and borne back to her family with the tiny, bloodless corpse. Angel locked the trunk store door and carried the oddly pathetic suitcase down to the sickbay for Matron to deal with. She paused on the way to tear off the incriminating label and crumple it away in her cardigan pocket. Ghoulish stories were already circulating in the dormitories that Kay's pale shade loitered in the blue washroom humming *I Can Sing a Rainbow* while she jabbed at her skinny limbs with a pair of carefully nametaped nail scissors. Angel wanted nothing to feed the myth. Girls would say anything to frighten one another. Girls' imaginations were flexible as the tiger in their cruelty. The suitcase always reappeared, they said, lying in wait for whichever junior was luckless enough to be last in the line to reclaim her trunk. It was neatly packed with Kay's dismembered body, they said. On quiet nights, they said, it could be heard shifting around in the crowded attic, twitching, hungry.

She found Matron taking a girl's temperature. It was Adams. Alice Adams, a wan, spiritless little thing, rarely without a runny nose or a patch of eczema. Angel found herself suddenly coy about drawing attention to the dead girl's suitcase, realizing that Alice Adams had subtly replaced Kay Flanders as the girl always on her own, in the corner, at the back, the girl nobody wanted on their team, the girl found indefinably unwholesome. Adams gazed up at Angel as Matron took back the thermometer to read it. As ever, her small eyes were dully reproachful.

'Guess who fainted,' Matron said. 'Set down her trunk on her bed then keeled over. Thank heavens she wasn't on the stairs or someone might have been hurt. Well Adams. No temperature. How do you feel?'

'A bit sick, Matron.'

'Well go and lie down in there for a bit, out of everyone's way, then we'll see how you feel in a little while. Have you fainted before?'

Adams nodded seriously. 'Last week,' she said. 'But not for long and I felt all right afterwards.'

'Hmm. Well go and lie down for now.'

Adams walked into the sickbay and closed the door behind her.

'I found Kay Flanders' trunk,' Angel said.

'Bloody hell,' said Matron. 'Stick it under the table and I'll get it sent home to the parents. Listen. I was going to come and find you anyway.'

'What?'

'You're going back to your parents for Christmas, aren't you?'

'Well yes. Eventually. I was going to spend some time in London first. With a school friend.'

'Ah.'

'There's a problem?'

Matron jerked her head towards the sickroom door as answer.

'She's not well. I mean, she doesn't have a temperature or any obvious symptoms but she's getting more and more weak and listless and I'm convinced she's anaemic.'

'Shades of Kay Flanders.'

'Well exactly. I don't want to start a panic about viruses or anything on the last day of term but I do want Adams checked out by the haematologist in town.'

'I could drive her in.'

'Bless you. The trouble is – God I hate to ask you this.'

'What?'

'Well there was never any question of her going home for the holidays since there's only the mother and she's out in New Zealand.'

'Ah.'

'She was going home with the Lloyds who'd offered to take her skiing with them but frankly I don't think I can allow it. She's far too weak. And I was wondering whether – I mean, I can happily take her on from about the twenty-eighth but between now and Christmas is simply impossible for me. Could you bear it? We'd all be so grateful, Angel. She's a sweet little thing really. Very quiet. Fond of books. I don't know why they're all so beastly to her.'

Angel cursed herself. If only she had told the truth from the beginning, if she had blithely admitted to looking forward to six days of uninterrupted Richard, lie-ins, romantic walks round Kensington, last minute Christmas shopping instead of repeating the virginal lie about the old school friend. Confessed now, the truth would sound like a sad, graceless little fiction, and the impatient, uniformed, mountaineering fiancé from Sandhurst, like the product of too many cheap romances read in a practical flannel nightdress.

'Yes,' she heard herself say without a trace of hesitation. 'Of course I can.'

'Count your blessings, Angel,' her mother was always telling her. '*Then* complain. There's always a bright side if you'll only look.'

Her mother would have been proud of her. Sitting at the foot of Adams' bed, explaining the change in holiday plans, she was rewarded by an enchanting smile from the child's bloodless lips. Skiing, apparently, would have been a torment to her, much less skiing with the Philistine Lloyd girls. 'Can we go to the British Museum and see the mummified cats?' she asked, excited. 'Can we go to the National Gallery, Miss?'

'Of course,' Angel told her, 'but only if you promise not to faint.' And she realized that her plans need not be wholly scuppered. Richard's brother was not there. Alice Adams could have his room and surely be bribed to say nothing to Angel's parents about the sleeping arrangements. Certainly, there could be little afternoon passion – unless, as seemed probable, the child could be exhausted sufficiently to take to her bed for an after lunch nap . . .

'Do you like animals?' she asked. 'Dogs and things?'

'Oh *yes*, Miss! My mother never let me have a pet because she thinks they make me wheeze. But they don't.'

'Well *my* mother has always preferred animals to humans,' Angel assured her. 'So you'll have a lovely time when I take you home. She has several dogs. Six I think.'

'Six?!'

'Then there are the cats and she looks after several ponies from the village, so you'll be able to go riding if you're feeling strong enough by then.'

Alice Adams' pleasure was cheaply bought. Angel foresaw an easy transfer of duties once they were back at her parents' house. There was nothing her mother enjoyed more than an animal-mad child; she liked to exploit their weakness in a kind of indulgent slavery. Alice would soon be set to mucking out stables, mashing dog food and wielding currycombs. She would love every minute of it, regain some colour in her soap-pale cheeks and prove no trouble at all.

Before prize-giving, all the girls had to gather in their forms to be set their holiday essays and to hear how well or badly each had done in the course of the term. The clamour from these traditionally rowdy gatherings followed Angel down a corridor on her way to call Sandhurst from the pay phone under the stairs. To thwart queues, the apparatus had been meanly rigged so as not to receive incoming calls. Because of this, most of her communication with Richard was by mail, her three or four pages of chat being met by his unvarying two sides of more buttoned-up reports of barracks life. On this occasion, her stock of change had almost run out by the time he was called to the phone so she had a scant two minutes of his voice. She blurted out about Alice Adams, fearing his disappointment, but he was sweet and funny and said it would be fine and could he see the mummified cats too. 'Christ,' he said. 'I'm horny,' just before they were cut off, so she was blushing as she emerged from the phone cupboard.

Angel relaxed again. She hurriedly finished writing the reports on her English class then combed her hair, repaired her lipstick and joined the staff at the back of the hall for prize-giving. By the time she was joining in the school song, *Fields of Honour, Chambers of Wisdom*, she had half-convinced herself that having the child tag along need be no bar to her enjoyment of time with Richard and might even enhance it. The time alone with him would be all the more precious for being the harder won. She had recalled, too, a dictum of her grandmother's that other people's children were a telling means of auditioning the prospective father of one's own. Would he play imaginatively with the girl without teasing her? Would he prove hard and impatient or would he actively enter into Alice's entertainment the better to woo Angel?

In the hour that followed, the school emptied with astonishing rapidity. Fathers and daughters carried trunks to cars. Mistresses, clutching travel bags, shepherded excited girls onto waiting buses for the trains south. There were hasty, tearful farewells on the terrace, rapidly swapped Christmas presents, a diminishing hubbub of greetings, promises, hearty invitations and sighed regret, then Angel found herself alone on the gravel, coat buttoned up against the icy moorland wind. There were no late parents, no missed trains. The evacuation was almost military in its precision.

She was not quite alone, of course. Adams, she knew, was still lying in the sick bay and the cleaning women had descended with mops, dusters, drums of bleach and carbolic and wax. She heard them chatting loudly as they worked and realized this was a last day of term for them too. Matron passed her on the stairs, jauntily got up in a lambskin jacket and vivid headscarf. She was carrying a tartan suitcase and a newspaper parcel of flowers from the garden and whistling at the pleasure of escape. Seeing Angel, she stopped whistling and modified the perkiness in her step, recalled abruptly to the responsibilities she was about to abandon.

'I've rung the haematology department and made her an appointment for tomorrow at ten,' she said. 'And after that you'll both be free as air.'

'Oh good,' said Angel.

'Yes and I've had a word with Mrs Brack to let her know you'll be staying on the extra night or two. She's cleaning out the freezers but she'll leave you bread and milk and eggs and so on in the pantry. If you have to buy anything, keep the receipts. Oh and you'd better give me your parents' number so I can sort out about picking her up after Christmas or you'll end up with her the entire holidays!' Matron laughed gaily and Angel smelled sherry on her breath.

Approaching the sickroom door, she heard one of the cleaners chatting to Adams then realized it was another child. Hurrying in, she saw it was Lotta Wexel. She was sitting at the foot of Adams' bed and chuckling at something. Hearing Angel, she turned, a smile still bright on her rounded face. Angel felt a stab of vexation.

'Wexel? Weren't you meant to be catching the London train? All the buses have gone!'

'Oh I know. But I couldn't go with poor Alice stuck up here on her own. And anyway, my parents don't come over from Budapest until Christmas Eve so I was only going to be staying in an hotel.'

'On your *own*?'

'Oh yes.' Wexel shrugged maddeningly, as though this were perfectly usual for an eleven year old. 'So I might as well stay on too and keep Alice company. Oh please, Miss. Say I can.'

'Well . . . I hadn't really planned on staying . . .' Angel felt even her modified plans under siege.

Newly arrived this term, Lotta Wexel was officially the nearest Alice Adams had to a friend, insofar as she spent most of her free time at her side demanding confidences and forcing them on the other girl in return. The bond was inexplicable. Where Adams was thin, pale and listless, Wexel was vigorously Central European. Pink cheeked and raven haired, she made up for the want of distinction in her looks with rude good health and a superabundance of energy. 'Paprika in her *blood*!' Miss Clandage would sigh.

Born in the saddle, apparently, she was one of several girls who rode with the local hunt during term time and was entirely without fear, riding at the front and taking hedges and walls in a frenzy of excitement. Her foreignness was untraceable in her accent, she was not too clever, her parents were well connected; she should, by rights, have been one of the most popular girls in her year, a natural pack-leader. However she elected to spend most of her time with the outcast Adams. Previously her closest attachment had been poor, sinister Kay Flanders. The other teachers thought there was something commendable in this and only Angel had found something faintly repellent in the India rubber cheerfulness with which Wexel had bounced back after Kay's sudden death.

What Alice Adams gained from such a high profile protectress would be hard to say. She was so quiet and mirthless by comparison. One might almost have fancied her a kind of parasite, battening on the other girl's hale ebullience. Looking at her now, her pinched face pale even against the pillows, Angel wondered if Adams were not a little reluctant, however, at having such a playmate thrust herself upon her. Then she realized the pleading in Adams' eyes merely stemmed from fear lest this change of plan might jeopardize the promise of time with her mother's menagerie. Angel mustered a reassuring smile.

'Well of course you can stay on, Wexel. I have to take Adams into the hospital tomorrow for a blood test. We can make a trip of it. Maybe go to the cinema in the afternoon. How would that be?'

'Oh *yes!*' Lotta enthused and slapped the mattress beneath her.

'But you're not to tire poor Adams out. She's not very strong at the moment.'

'I know. *Poor* Alice.' Wexel turned a sickly smile on her stricken friend.

Angel realized, bitterly, she would have to call Richard again. One juvenile invalid might not have changed their plans so very much but her tireless companion certainly would.

'Don't you need to tell your parents, Wexel?' she asked, clutching at straws. 'Won't they worry if they call the hotel and find you're not there?'

'Oh no,' Wexel insisted coolly. 'They never worry. They won't ring anyway. They're far too busy travelling around. My father's reclaiming some old estates of my grandmother's which the Communists stole. One was turned into a loony bin. Just imagine! And another one was turned into a horrid collective farm. They'll be fine, Miss. Don't worry.'

As Angel turned from the room, Adams went into a spasm of panic.

'Please, Miss. Where are you going, Miss?'

'It's all right, Adams. I just have to telephone my friend in London. To say we won't be coming to stay there now. I'm afraid we'll have to see the museums another time.'

'Museums are boring anyway, Alice,' said Wexel. 'We can play hide and seek. We can climb up on the roof and pretend it's a castle.'

'You most certainly may not,' Angel insisted.

'Please, Miss.'

'What, Adams?'

'Can't you call us by our Christian names now that it's the holidays?'

Angel sighed. 'Yes, yes,' she said. 'We'll have supper at six as usual then you can come up to the staff sitting room where it's cosier and we can watch television. How's that?'

'Brilliant, Miss. Thank you, Miss.'

'Lotta?'

'Yes, Miss?'

'Have you got change for a fiver?'

As Angel walked back to the pay phone, change bulging her cardigan pocket, she heard Wexel's laughter again and her low, insistent gossiping tone. She wondered what such inexperienced girls could possibly find to discuss at such length.

Richard was disappointed, of course, even a little angry. Why could she not just send this other girl packing, he asked. Why could she not assert herself for once. The questions were rhetorical, however. He knew Angel was not assertive. He suggested instead that he apply for a change of leave so they could meet up after Christmas instead. She could still see her parents, still maintain the fib about the school friend in town and that way they would enjoy time alone as planned, unchaperoned by sick children. His patience lent her heart and she unpacked her things again with a sadness on the sweeter side of bleak.

Wexel saddled up her pony and galloped off onto the moor for two hours before supper. Perhaps Angel only imagined Adams' relief, but the child certainly revived a little when left alone and came downstairs to nestle quietly in a window seat reading Edith Sitwell's life of Elizabeth I. The last of the cleaners left. Disinfected and aired, whole sections of the school were now closed off. As the afternoon drew swiftly on and rain clouds scudded across the moor, Angel busied herself writing letters and tried not to dwell on the acreage of dark and empty rooms stretching out around them. The temperature plummeted and they retreated early to the staff sitting room where Angel lit the gas fire and wound the clock. Darkness fell before Wexel returned. Hearing the clatter of hooves in the stable yard, Angel realized, with a guilty start, that she had quite forgotten about the other girl and should, by rights, have been worrying about her. Adams, too, showed a trace of surprise, starting from her book and hastening to draw the curtains against the night.

Wexel had evidently thrived on her ride. She had ridden miles, she claimed, taken several walls at a gallop, seen a fox and hawks and had great fun being chased by some young beef cattle. Her green eyes shone and her cheeks were scarlet from the cold. She was wet through but not even shivering.

Glad of an excuse to take charge again, Angel hurried her off to a hot bath and a change of clothes while she and Adams whisked up mushroom omelettes and a mountain of buttered toast for supper. The meal over, she sent Adams up for her bath and sent Wexel to watch the television and plan their evening's viewing.

When she followed Wexel up, she found the television playing to an empty room. Happy of solitude, however brief, she watched ten minutes of the news then began to feel uneasy and climbed the dark stair to the dormitory wing to check on them, feeling the chill from the great, black windows she passed on the way. The fluorescent light from the washrooms spilled out across the newly waxed boards of the upper corridor. A small cloud of steam was gathering outside the open door. She could hear a bath filling. One of the great advantages of institutional life was the quantity of hot water the furnaces churned out. Baths here filled in moments.

At first, all Angel could hear above the gushing water was whimpering. Then someone turned the taps off and she heard, with a shock, that it was a thin, pallid, girlish voice singing.

> '. . . *pink and purple and blue.*
> *I can sing a rainbow, sing a rainbow.*
> *Sing a rainbow too!*'

The voice was weirdly magnified by the washroom acoustic. Angel froze for a moment, thinking, despite herself, of Kay Flanders' trunk waiting below the table in Matron's consulting room. Then she pulled herself together and strode into the washroom where Wexel was crouched behind a bank of washbasins, singing into the steam overhead. Adams was huddled in her dressing gown in a chair beside one of the baths, wash bag clutched in her lap.

'Lotta, stop that nonsense at once and go downstairs to the television.'

Wexel stood grinning.

'Sorry, Miss. Were you scared?'

'Not a bit. Go on. Let poor Adams – I mean Alice – take her bath.'

Wexel came out and, with a parting grin at Adams, slapped down the stairs in her slippers. Adams slipped off her dressing gown, which she had held so tightly about her, and slid into the bath.

'I wasn't a bit scared,' she said wearily. 'I don't know why she bothers.'

She began soaping herself, briskly unselfconscious. Angel was shocked at how skinny she was. Her ribs stood out and her veins showed grey-blue against her translucent skin. She put Angel in mind of some eerily transparent fish she had kept briefly as a child, their visible internal organs in constant fluttering motion.

'Don't be too long,' she said, then paused. 'What's that under your arm?' There was a reddish patch in the girl's left armpit.

'Nothing.' Suddenly modest, Adams slapped a hand over the strange welt to hide it from view. 'It's just some eczema. Nothing serious. I often get it.'

Angel remembered seeing Adams adjust her shirt repeatedly at the supper table and realized the fabric must have been chafing her. Recurrent or not, the eczema was serious enough to have been scratched to the raw. She had glimpsed fresh blood, livid on its surface.

'I'll make us some cocoa if you like,' she said. 'Don't be too long.'

She made a mental note to have a word with the doctor about it the next day. When she returned downstairs, she found Wexel merrily making cocoa already, singing innocently to herself as she whisked the milk.

The remainder of the evening passed quietly enough once she had put the girls to bed in their dormitory. At one point she thought she heard weeping but when she stepped out onto the stairs to listen, found it to be only giggling. The school was a red brick Victorian monstrosity, surrounded by uninhabited moorland and windswept hills – the folly of a long since bankrupt mining baron. Even with all girls and staff present, there was room to spare. Left alone there, the three of them were preposterously isolated. As rain lashed the windows and draughts moaned in the chimneys and caused distant doors to slam, she had anticipated bedtime fears but found Wexel and Adams apparently fearless and herself far more disturbed than they at the prospect of sleeping adrift on such a remote raft of bricks. The girls at least had each other for company. She was alone at the other end of a long corridor and a flight of stairs. Aware of her own absurdity, she found herself going to bed with a light left on outside her door for comfort and even then she tossed and turned, watching the racing of moonlit clouds through a gap in her curtains and trying in vain to wrestle her thoughts into quiet moderation.

When she slept at last she dreamed, not of ghoulies and ghosties but, in exaggerated technicolour, of Richard. Nothing happened in the dream. He just sat on a rug in dappled shade and becoming battledress, talking contentedly in a language she could not understand and breaking off his monologue occasionally to smile at her and touch the side of her face with a roughly bandaged hand.

In the morning she realized she was not the only one to sleep badly. Wexel was up before any of them, taking her pony for a dawn canter, but Angel found Adams still paler and weaker than on the previous day. When she offered to drive into town and see if she could persuade the doctor back with her, however, the possibility of being left behind seemed to galvanize the child into action. Wexel returned before long, noisily full of the joys of the winter landscape and soon the three of them were crossing the moor in Angel's Morris Traveller.

They caught the haematology department on a miraculously quiet day. Samples were taken and Angel told that if she cared to return after three, results would be ready by then. In the interim, she took the girls for an improving walk around the castle ruins, followed by an indulgent trip to watch a deeply sentimental cartoon film at the cinema.

As they took their seats, Adams made a sudden apologetic darting movement past Angel so as to sit on the other side of her from Wexel. Angel was concerned that Wexel's feelings would be hurt but the girl said nothing of it, merely enthusing about how excited she was to be seeing the film, having heard so much about it from the others. Having made such protestations, it was strange therefore how often Angel looked about her during the film to find Wexel's stare fixed not on the screen but across Angel on Adams' obediently attentive face. Caught out a second time, Wexel turned hastily back to the film but now it was Angel who turned to stare at Adams, struck again by her air of mute parasitism, her excessive emotional hunger. The way she devoured the mawkish events on the screen was of a part with the way she had darted through to another seat so as to have unlimited access to an adult. Watching her, Angel felt two waves of revulsion, the first at the child, the second at herself for so easily joining the ranks of despisers and bullies.

The junior haematologist confessed herself confused.

'Could I have a word in private?' she asked.

'Of course. Alice, go and see what Lotta's up to in the waiting room. We won't be a minute.'

Adams left the room. The haematologist watched the closing door then turned back.

'I have to say that if Dr Murchison were still here we'd have sorted this out in a minute; she's the expert on things like this. Are you sure all these details are correct? Her blood type and so on?'

'Well . . .' Angel shrugged. 'I didn't take them myself. The parents supply most of them to Matron and each girl has a medical at the beginning of the academic year. Why?'

'Has she . . .' The young doctor frowned, picking at the

rubber on her pencil then looked up. 'Has she been abroad recently? To the Tropics, perhaps? India?'

'Not to my knowledge. Her mother lives in New Zealand. I don't know if that counts. Why?'

'Well . . .' The doctor tried to laugh. 'You'll think I'm awfully stupid but we took two samples and I looked at them over and over and got a colleague to check and, well . . . There's something not quite right.'

'Does she have a virus?'

'Not that I could recognize. It's more as though she has a whole new blood type. Now listen. There's probably no need to worry. She *is* very anaemic and that can be dealt with at once. I'll give you an iron prescription for her and you can make sure she eats plenty of iron-rich food. Meanwhile I'm going to send these samples on to London for a second opinion.'

It was agreed that Matron, who lived in Sussex, would drive Adams into London for a further examination after Christmas. Shopping for dinner on the way back to the car, Angel collected the prescription and bought spinach and steak. Wexel chattered all the way home about the film, about other films, about the Christmas lights in the department stores. Deaf to her prattle, Angel caught glimpses of Adams' listless face watching her in the rear view mirror and caught herself thinking that, far from being sick, the child was not even human.

'Look!' Wexel shouted in her ear as they pulled up the school drive. 'There's a man in the window!'

'Nonsense,' Angel said. 'It was probably just a shadow or a curtain.'

'There's a man. There. Look!'

Sure enough, as they pulled closer a man came out of the front door to greet them and she saw that it was Richard.

'It's a friend of mine,' she told them rapidly, suppressing a sudden urge to leave them locked into the car and lead him into the house. 'A good friend. He must have come to stay.' She felt herself beaming as she opened the car door. 'How on earth did you get here?' she asked him, aching to give him more than the perfunctory hug and a peck she allowed.

'Taxi from the station,' he told her. 'Emptied my wallet so I hope you're not going to turn me away. I found a back door unlocked and let myself in. What an old barn! So. Who's this?'

She introduced him to the girls who were staring, then led the way to the kitchen and food.

It had proved impossible to take his leave after Christmas instead because officers with children apparently took priority. Faced with the options of moping alone in Baron's Court or visiting his parents, he had decided to surprise her. While the girls took their baths, she showed him around and had the pleasure of defiling the tiny, old maid's bedroom that had been her cell these last months. They were both indecently excited at making love with the sounds of the girls singing and splashing in the washroom below, and at having to be quiet and quick. She bathed her cheeks with a flannel soaked in freezing water in an effort to still their burning while he watched from the bed, smug and smoking. The room smelled frankly male of a sudden. She tidied her clothes and hair and, fighting off further advances, slipped downstairs again to make supper and prepare the way.

Wexel was first down, cheeks even pinker than usual from her bath, and took an unsqueamish pleasure in slicing the three bloody steaks into pieces for a pie that would serve four. When some blood splashed onto her dressing gown she merely giggled. Angel had planned on bribing her, buying her discretion with treats, but found the girls' connivance offered without asking.

'Is Richard your boyfriend, Miss?'

'Yes. He's my fiancé.'

'He's very handsome.'

'Thank you, Lotta.'

'You needn't worry. We won't tell anyone he was here. Alice says she'll feel safer tonight having a man about the house.' Wexel laughed again at the smutty innuendo of what she had just said, or possibly at the absurdity of Adams' girlish confidence.

As auditions for fatherhood went, Richard's was a success. As if responding to careful gender programming, the girls took to him the moment they learned he was a cavalry officer. They teased him like an older brother, swung on his big hands as if they had known him all their lives and, it seemed, accorded Angel new respect by association. Richard appeared genuinely to enjoy their company – he had always had an immature streak – and could hardly wait until supper was over so as to play hide and seek and murder in the dark around the cavernous, empty classrooms. In this, however, he had the ulterior motive of ensuring they were thoroughly exhausted by nine o'clock and begging for bed so as to leave him the more adult pleasure of exhausting his appetite for Angel.

The next morning, conditioned by Sandhurst, he was up early and left Angel for a lie in while he thrilled 'the chubby Hungarian thing' by taking her riding. The weather was clear, even thinly sunny, by the time they returned so the rest of the day was spent in taking a long ramble across the moor, broken by a pub lunch and several stops for thermos coffee and custard creams. He tested their map reading, their knowledge of birds and geology and – supreme nobility – gave Adams a piggyback ride when she grew too tired to walk any further. Angel began to feel slightly left out of the fun and found herself planning that, as and when she *did* marry him, she would bring forth men children only. She reminded herself, however, that it was important to keep the girls sweet. One word of this escapade when they returned next term and she would be job hunting without a reference. Announcing that it was important to Adams' iron levels, she let Richard serve the girls red wine with their supper and knew their discretion was purchased for another night at least.

Letting him read them a bedtime ghost story was not such a good idea, however. Wine-doped, they seemed on the brink of sleep when Angel left them, but she and Richard had not progressed far beyond the slow unbuttoning stage, when the night was rent with distant screams. Cursing, buttoning her blouse up again, Angel hurried down her bedroom stairs and along the

dormitory corridor to find Adams almost frenzied with terror
and Wexel watching her with the same calm cheerfulness she
had brought to the slicing of steak and rolling of pie crust. She
calmed Adams but could not break her insistence that she sleep
with Angel and Wexel sleep elsewhere. Angel was secretly furious but sensed the child's implacability and knew the night
would be interrupted repeatedly until she gave in. Wexel was
curiously compliant.

'Poor Alice,' she said. 'If it helps you sleep. But honestly, it
was only a silly story. It's all right, Miss. You sleep here and I'll
go in the sick bay. There's still a bed made up.'

'Very well,' Angel sighed. 'This is incredibly irritating of you,
Adams. I hope you realize that.'

'Sorry, Miss.'

'I'll just settle Wexel in over there and I'll be back. Don't
worry. I'll leave all the lights on.'

'Sorry,' she told Richard, with a kiss. 'I think she's a bit drunk
actually. You'll just have to watch TV if you can't sleep. There's
a portable next door in Matron's room and she keeps her sherry
in the cupboard in her bathroom. Adams will fall asleep soon.
I'll probably be able to slip back to you during the night.'

'You'd better,' he growled and playfully nibbled the side of
her neck, 'or I'll get restless and come and find you and who
knows whose bed I might stumble into.'

Sadly, she proved as deeply affected by wine and fresh air as
her nervous charge and after five or so minutes of lying in the
dormitory listening to Adams' adenoidal breathing, Angel fell
into a slumber deep as the darkness around her. When she awoke,
with a start, the clock over the stable yard gate was striking seven.
For a while she lay there, assessing how her need for sleep
weighed against the pleasure of tip-toeing back along the corridor and up to Richard's musky bed. He would stir slightly in his
sleep, mumble faintly. She would rouse him slowly with small,
nuzzling kisses and the judicious touch of her dawn-chilled
fingers . . .

She rose and pulled her dressing gown about her. Adams was snoring, far from fear. Climbing the stairs to her bedroom, carefully avoiding the stair that creaked, Angel reflected that this was probably far more fun than Baron's Court. She opened the door as softly as she could, eager to surprise him by touch rather than sound. Then she froze, unable to believe what she thought she saw in the grey dawn light.

He lay spreadeagled on the bed on his back, one arm trailing over the mattress' side. His eyes were open but fixed dreamily on the ceiling. Lotta Wexel was crouched over his naked body, her back to the door, eagerly chewing at the bridge of muscle across his armpit. As Angel darted back from the doorway, he let out a helpless groan of desire.

Mind reeling through scenario after nightmare scenario, Angel walked swiftly then ran back to the dormitory. Adams showed no sign of waking at her approach. Angel lay on the bed without taking off her dressing gown. This was absurd. Ridiculous. It was unthinkable that he should do such a thing and unlikely that Wexel, for all her insufferable bumptiousness, would prove so pliable to his will. After five, maybe six, minutes of indignant soul-searching, Angel sat up and walked back along the corridor. Either she was seeing things, delusions brought on by too much rat-trap cheese at dinner and his flirtatious references to impatient bed-hopping, or she was compelled to act, however compromised her professional position already was.

Checking first on the sick bay, she almost laughed aloud with relief. Wexel was fast asleep there, one of her pillows tumbled onto the floor, one chubby foot protruding from the bedclothes. Vowing to say nothing to him for fear he should think her quite mad, Angel passed on to Richard, who was also deep in dreams, and woke him with teasing slowness, rousing him delectably as planned.

Angel was the last to wake in the morning, finding herself sprawled in bed alone and naked with a pleasantly bruised feeling in her groin to remind her she had not been alone for long. She packed swiftly and came down to find Richard frying up a hearty farewell breakfast for the girls. He led them in singing songs and playing games most of the way home, although Alice Adams soon retreated into a doze in her corner of the back seat. Angel dropped him off at his parents' house on the way, pausing for a lingering kiss in their shrubbery and a promise that he would ring her at her own parents' house that night.

It was already dark when she pulled the Morris up at a meter outside the Wexels' Mayfair hotel. Leaving Alice to sleep beneath a blanket, she ushered Lotta into the lobby while a porter unfastened the trunk from the roof-rack. She was surprised to find she had grown almost fond of the girl, intensely irritating as she was. The parents proved surprisingly elegant. The mother was sparely chic, with dark hair tied back and fat pearls glistening at her neck. Mr Wexel was taller and broader even than Richard, with bright eyes and a closely clipped beard. It was hard to imagine that boisterous Lotta could have anything to do with them. Then they kissed the child and Angel saw a strong family resemblance in the mother's profile and the father's busy glance.

'And this is Miss Voysey. She's given us *such* a good time.'

'*Enchanté.*'

Mr Wexel did not quite kiss Angel's hand but he bowed over it minutely and held it a fraction too long for comfort, raising his black eyes to hers and causing her a spasm of erotic perturbation. Mrs Wexel and Lotta had slipped outside to check on the trunk and say goodbye to Adams.

'Such a sweet child,' Mrs Wexel told Angel. 'But so thin and pale one could see moonlight through her,' and she laughed a well-bred phantom of Lotta's red-blooded guffaw.

Returning to the car, eager to make headway because snow had been forecast, Angel found Adams awake and trembling. She had locked all the doors from the inside.

'Let me in, Alice. Quickly. That's it.'

'Can we go now, Miss?'

'Of course. We'll be there in an hour. Really, what a performance! Did you take your iron pill?'

'Yes, Miss.'

'Good girl.'

Before they had reached the motorway out of Chiswick, Adams was already fast asleep again, her legs drawn up so that she was lying the width of the back seat. Angel reached back to pull the travel rug over her for warmth. It began to snow, just as Mr Wexel had prophesied. The flurries fell thicker and faster until Angel was half-blinded by the conical glare they made before the headlamps and was reduced to driving at a crawl. Desperate for coffee and something sweet to fortify her, and anxious to ring ahead to her parents and tell them not to worry if she was late, she pulled off into the motorway services at Fleet.

Turning round as she unfastened her seat belt, she tried to stir Adams gently and found that she couldn't wake her.

'Adams? Adams!' Fear made her reach instinctively to the formality of term time. 'Adams, wake up.'

She grasped at the girl's skinny wrist, felt the sides of her neck. There was a pulse, only a faint one but she was alive. Terrified that the child she thought was sleeping peacefully had slid into a coma, she locked the car and sprinted across to a bank of telephones outside a fast food restaurant to summon an ambulance. She was about to return to the car when a certain apprehension made her fumble in her bag for Richard's number at his parent's house. His mother answered and chided her for not having come in for tea when she dropped him off.

'Sorry,' Angel said. 'I'd have loved to but I was so late and I had some children to drop off too. Is he there? Could I have a word?'

'I'm sorry, dear.'

'Has he gone out?'

'Oh no. He's taken to his bed and he's only just managed to fall asleep. Nothing much wrong with him but he came over all weak and dizzy so I tucked him up with some hot whisky and lemon and the electric blanket. He's just caught a slight chill, I expect, walking on those moors.'

The ambulance was held up in the snow. Alice Adams was dead on arrival at the hospital. Angel arrived at her parents hours later, after a terrible blur of forms to be signed, calls to be made and statements to be given. Climbing from the Morris in her parents' garage, numb from cold and emotional exhaustion, she saw she had the girl's redundant trunk still strapped to the roof rack. The leather label flapped in the breeze that was flinging snow through the open doors and, watching its feeble motions, Angel thought of Kay Flanders and how she had died, as the letter to parents put it, quietly, in her sleep.

BORNEO

✧

for Nick Hay

BEE TOOK A SANDWICH, doing her best to fill the gap left behind, and opened the French windows onto the garden. She stood on the steps for a moment then saw that the whirligig clothesline was still out, laden with knickers and bras. Stuffing the sandwich into her mouth, she strode out to remove the wretched thing from disapproving view.

Tony had died on a draughty Sunday in late autumn. They had some friends to lunch after Eucharist, then the two of them had gone up on the downs to walk off the blackberry and apple crumble. The wind had been so strong that they played games, leaning into it, yelling to make themselves heard. Tony's deputy, Mike, was playing at Evensong so there had been no rush. When they came home, he had sat down to watch the new Trollope serial while she made a pot of tea. She had walked in with the tray to find him lying on the floor, his face twisted, dribbling at the pain. His hands had pressed at his temples as if his head were trying to burst. When the nurse had let her in to kiss her husband goodbye, Bee had seen bruises from the pressure of his own fingertips.

'Coo-eee.'

Bee spun around with a handful of knickers. Mrs de Vere was standing there in a tea cosy hat and second-hand coat. Sturdy, black NHS specs glinting in the sun.

'Mrs de Vere. How lovely.'

Mrs de Vere was not meant to be here. Thursday mornings were usually the time for Bee's Afghanistan bandage parties. She would pour out coffee for a collection of the more lonely or immobile women of the area (picking them up by car, where necessary) while they cut up old sheets into bandages for her to send to refugee camps. In fact, Bee had not got around to sending any bandages for months, and was stockpiling the things in a fertilizer bag in the basement. She thought she had put off all her regulars. Evidently this one had slipped through the diplomatic net. A pronounced outcast, on account of her thick Dutch accent, disgusting mothbally smell and jealous obsession with the Bishop (whom she was rumoured to have followed from post to post since his ordination), Mrs de Vere was not coffee morning material.

'I was not going to come this morning, on account of my arthritis you see, but I heard that you were having a coffee morning next week so I thought today I make a special effort for the little Afghans, yes?' she burbled.

'Of course. How kind. Actually, I'm giving a coffee morning today as well,' said Bee, hoping that her breathing through her mouth was not too evident. 'So I thought I could find you a chair near the fire and give you a sheet and let you get on with it. There'll be all your friends here. Let's go in, shall we, and find you a cup of coffee. You like it made with milk, don't you?'

Dinah had yet to appear with the rest of the cups and saucers. Bee prayed that the guests would not arrive in a rush. She ensconced her unexpected visitor in the gloomier corner by the dining room fire and found her a pair of scissors and an old sheet. Mrs de Vere would insist on humming Lutheran hymns as she worked. Perhaps the spitting of the logs would cover it.

Everyone had been marvellous, of course. They had all heard within hours, without her breathing a word, and for the next month she was surrounded by a cushioned wall of comfort. Bee had seen this in operation on others, been a press-ganged accessory to it herself. She had imagined she would react angrily, stifled by the crushing affection. Her submission, in the event, surprised her. The house had reeked of flowers. Every hour brought another fistful of cards and letters. She was honoured with gifts, as one miraculous; packets of home-made fudge, the solace of chocolate cakes, deep-frozen cassoulets for one, books of poetry with the relevant pages kindly earmarked. There was a small bunch of friends who had sent or brought something every day; a token of love. Once she started to venture out, she could subside into tears in the most unsuitable places, like the public library, secure in the knowledge that someone in the vicinity who *knew* would rush over with hugs and murmurings. She had never realized before how many of them had suffered. Tony's hideous death brought such a quantity of pain and doubt to the surface that the community had seemed irrevocably altered. Her affection for it was not increased, but she approached it with new-found respect. That they had all felt the agony of bereavement at first-hand was only natural, far more interesting was the chemistry in death that caused so many of them to lay bare the poverty of their faith. Not a batch of consolations arrived but contained one astonishing recognition of the insane cruelty of existence, of the seeming impossibility of any but a psychopathic deity. The strongest of the latter were written on diocesan notepaper. Bee was an atheist. It was her best kept secret. Only Reuben knew. She had meant to confess to Tony, but his cheerful faith had disarmed her, and then he had died. The spate of avowals in the wake of his death had implicated her in the community. This was the first cord that bound her in. The second had been their guilt.

The house in the cathedral close was a traditional perk of the post of Organist. Mike took over Tony's job. He had five children as well as a wife. Gently, shamefacedly, Bee was evicted. She had finished her teacher's training after meeting Tony, but had done no work since their marriage. The task of teaching the Baby Form at the choir school had recently fallen vacant and it came with a half-share in a pretty, Regency house just outside the Close gates. It was widely known that Bee got on well with children, probably because she was unable to have any of her own, poor thing, so the headmaster's wife was approached to approach the headmaster, who subsequently approached Bee who, to everyone's relief, accepted his kind offer. As the sole woman on the teaching staff, Baby Mistress shared number eight, Chaplain's Walk with the Assistant Matron. Jennifer was a cheery, horsy type, who lived happily alongside Bee for two years before following the custom of her post, getting herself impregnated by Stephen Simkins (PE) after being seen swimming with him in the moonlight and the buff. They were still on their honeymoon and Bee had the house to herself until Jennifer's replacement arrived.

She handed Mrs de Vere her coffee, then retraced the smell of hot lemon and spices to the kitchen. Her twenty-three-year-old brother, Reuben, was using a fish slice to slide some newly baked biscuits onto a wire tray. The frown of concentration and faint baker's flush only enhanced his vulpine charm.

'That's the last batch,' he said. 'How many d'you think'll come?'

'Oh, Christ. It could be forty. There are fifty local members. Twenty of them are in homes or bed-ridden, but the others all promised to bring friends. Oh Christ.'

'Have a gulp of my gin.'

'Rube, it's only ten-thirty!'

'So? Have a gulp of my gin.'

'Thanks.'

She took the flour-dusty glass, perched on the kitchen stool and gulped. He had descended on her five days ago, tanned, penniless and suggesting, by his echoing want of a future tense, that the stay was indefinite. The tan was Indian. He had been out there for nearly a year, making a small, shady fortune as a jewel dealer.

'I still don't understand why,' he said, arranging cupcakes in rings of alternating colours on a vast, borrowed plate.

'Because it's usually run by Miranda Cotterel, but she fell off her bike and did in her hip.'

He had woken one morning to find himself relieved of every

worldly possession, save the sleeping bag around him and a quantity of Marks and Spencer underwear. His copy of *India on a Dollar a Day* had also been left behind, apparently on a whim of superstitious benevolence. His escape involved a Foreign Office ex of his from school, then a certain amount of murkiness in Bangkok. Dear Rube was nothing if not resourceful.

'You're not on the committee, are you, though?'

'No. But Miranda Cotterel has some very persuasive friends who are.'

'An offer you couldn't refuse?'

'Sort of, only they think they do it to give me something to occupy my poor, bereaved soul. Rube, you're a saint. Can I do anything?'

'Don't you dare.'

He had dropped out of school at seventeen to enrol in life's university as, variously, masseur, waiter, singing telegram and escort; all activities pursued under the generic carapace of travel writer.

'Bee, do you even know where Borneo is?'

'No. But then, neither do they.'

'Have you read the charity's magazine?'

'Lot of smiley black nuns, isn't it? Look, let me take those through. I hate feeling spare.'

'Don't drop them.'

'I'm not incapable.'

She bent forward to kiss his gilded cheek and brushed her twinset on a plate of sieved icing sugar.

'Dolt.' He dusted her down and pushed her gently from the room.

The clock on the dining room mantelpiece struck eleven. In the kitchen, Reuben had two kettles, a preserving pan and a pressure cooker full of steaming water at the ready. The two thirty-cup teapots on loan from the WI had been scrubbed and contained equal heaps of Gold Blend. He poured himself another generous gin. Interleaved biscuits and radiating rings of small cakes waited on the sideboard.

'Will you have a biscuit, Mrs de Vere? Those ones are lemon. Very good. Freshly baked.'

Mrs de Vere lowered her busy hands to her lap and gave Bee a stare. Her lenses were thick, full of milky eye.

'I must not be eating biscuits or cake neither. They cause me to choke. I had an unpleasant experience as a child and have been prone to choking ever since. But you must have one, thank you all the same.'

'Oh dear. Yes. I think I shall.'

Bee bit off a piece of biscuit. It was still faintly warm and crumbled delightfully on her tongue, but the doorbell rang and she had to swallow the rest in a rush.

'Bee. Anyone here?'

'Dinah.' Dinah Stapleton, friend with cups and saucers. 'Thank God. No. They're all late.'

Dinah was the school secretary. Urbane and discreetly pagan, she survived on an illusory sense that her every pleasure was illicit. She conducted her friendship along conspiratorial lines, making a point of arriving among the first, whenever Bee was entertaining, so as to enjoy a snatched conversation, sotto voce, in the hall. She heaved her basket-on-wheels up the steps, scowling at each clatter of the school crockery within, then stopped dead and pointed at the alien coat hanging on a hook.

She mouthed her enquiry: 'Whose is that?'

Bee grinned and beckoned her into the kitchen.

'Hello, Dinah.'

'I say. Home is the sailor. Hello, Reuben. Have you been terribly busy? Don't answer that. Bee, who?'

'Mrs de Vere.'

'What? Why?'

'Quite. She's not meant to be here, but she didn't realize that the Bandage Girls were cancelled for this week, and she lives right up on Priory Hill so I couldn't very well turn her away.'

'Well no. Of course not.'

'Bless you for bringing all that.'

'Yes. We must shove it on trays for you. Come on. No rush, though; they'll be at least another ten minutes. Oh yes. I've got something horrid for the Bring and Buy —'

'Damn! The stall. I still haven't —'

'It's all right,' soothed Reuben, placing a slightly unsteady hand on her shoulder. 'I did it while you were boiling Dame Vermeer's milk.'

'Thanks.'

Dinah was clattering out a third trayload.

'Your stalls are always so well stocked, Bee,' she said. 'I don't know where you manage to find so many unwanted Christmas presents. Don't you ever get any you want to keep?'

'Not often. What did you mean about ten minutes?'

'They're all at the Deanery.'

'Why the hell? They know they're meant to be here.'

'Didn't anyone tell you? You picked an appalling day. *She* invited everyone to a rival do about a week before you did. Boat People.'

'Why didn't she invite me?'

'The crib gaffe.'

'I only gave it a bit of a dust and changed the dead flowers. You'd think she made the thing by hand, she's so prickly about it.'

'She did.'

'It was one of those plaster-cast kits.'

'Well, she made the manger.'

'Excuse my butting in,' said Reuben, 'But they're here.'

He had seen them walking up the drive. Bee hurried into the hall and opened the door as Mrs Clutterbuck reached for the bell-push.

'Daphne, how lovely.'

'Hello, Bee. You know Mrs Thomas. And this is my cousin, Jane.'

'Hello.'

'How d'you do.'

'Come in.'

'Hello, Dinah.'

'You've been terribly busy.'

'Is that the errant brother out there?'

'Look at all the biscuits.'

'Marvellous spread, Bee.'

'Oh. Mrs de Vere. How nice.'

'What are you doing with that sheet?'

'Rag-rugs? Oh I see. It's bandages. Lovely.'

'Milk, no shug. Perfect.'

'Wonderful bikkies, Bee.'

'Reuben's actually. Coming! Hello. Come in. I'm Bridget Martin,' said Bee.

'Hello.'

'Hello.'

Miss Trott. Miss Deakin. Mrs and the Misses Hewlings. Penny Friston. Marge Brill. Reverend and the Mrs Pyke. Reverend Yeats. Sister Veronica and Mother Lucy from that strange community at Perton Bagshawe. Rapidly the dining room filled and the temperature rose. The hooks were laden with tweed and scarves and a pile of coats began to form at the foot of the stairs. Bee stopped answering the door and left it propped open with the umbrella stand. She realized that she should have served coffee from a table in the hall for the dining room, and by degrees the drawing room as well, were becoming so crowded that it was difficult to manoeuvre a coffee pot, cream jug and sugar bowl simultaneously. Dinah had manned the Bring and Buy stall and was therefore cut off at the far end of the room. Bee stood, helpless, outside the dining room door, tray in hand, and made explanatory faces at Miss Wodding and Mrs Lloyd-Mogg who were staring mournfully at their empty cups.

'Could you? Excuse me . . . er . . . Could you . . . ?' she tried a few times, but went unheeded by the stockade of rounded backs.

Reuben appeared at her elbow. 'You'll have to shout,' he said. 'They won't mind.'

'I can't'

'Coward.' He faced into the room and called out, 'Ladies. Ladies.' The din in both rooms dissolved at once into mildly indignant question mark noises. A score of puffy faces turned and stared. He was quite unabashed. 'It's rather hard for us to get to you, so if you'd like some more coffee – and there is plenty – would you like to step out into the hall?'

They stepped out with a vengeance. Reuben set up a pouring station at the hall table, as a queue formed, thrusting the second jug onto Bee. She toured the drawing room, seeing to the less mobile. These sat on sofas and chairs, sticks at their sides, offending wrists or legs laid, ostentatious, before them. Miss Coley. Barbie Sears. Miss Rossington and Miss Pidsley. They showed no sign of enjoying themselves or guilt at being waited on. The room was just large enough for each to stare without encountering the eyes of the others. Bee exchanged a few words with each in turn, asking after their health and less healthy friends, checking that each had secured a copy of the magazine, watchful for any anxiety about where they could *powder their noses*. Then she crossed the hall, with muttered thanks to Reuben *en route*, and endeavoured to teeter through the suffocating room to Dinah.

The latter was counting a wad of notes into a shortbread tin.

'Dinah, are you all right?'

'Fine.'

'You've taken loads.'

'Always the same. You do a roaring trade in the first ten minutes. Everyone brings a thing, buys a thing, dumps it, and there an end.'

'Yes.' Bee recognized a jar of rhubarb chutney she had made two years ago, which had evidently been doing the benevolent rounds ever since. All her original horrors had been sold, and replaced with not dissimilar fare. There were a dry-looking sponge with thin pink icing, two tins of lychees and some elderly paperbacks. There were also some quite passable lavender bags, which she would pocket if no one else did. 'How's Mrs de Vere?' she went on. 'I couldn't reach her.'

'Oh, she's okay. Ripping and rolling away. There was a lull after Reuben summoned them into the hall, and I managed to get over and have a chat. Someone had given her a collection of those heavenly biscuits, and she was quite cheerful for once.'

'But she's not allowed biscuits. She said so!'

'Well she was munching away. Said how good they were. Hang on. The cake, Mrs Friston? Oh, I dunno. What do you think for the cake, Bee? I haven't had time to price it.'

'How about fifty pence?'

'Fifty pence it is.'

'But is it fresh?' asked Mrs Friston, giving the article a sharp poke.

'Oh I should think so, wouldn't you?' Dinah used her school dinners tone, and took the customer's uncertainly proffered coin. 'Thanks. There we are. Have a good tea.' She dropped the takings into the tin with a clatter. 'Her Nibs won't be pleased.'

'Why not? They all went to her first.'

'But that's just it. You always go first to the thing you're going to leave. I think the old trouts are here to stay.'

'Now now. We'll be among them before long.'

'Don't,' said Dinah, who was several years her senior. She looked across the bobbing tussocks of grey hairs and blue much as she would survey the field at the boys' football matches. She addressed Bee in an undertone without turning. 'Is *he* coming, then?'

'Dick Greville? Yes, but he'll be late.'

'Not him, you ass. You know. *Him*. Is he?'

'Teddy?'

Bee smiled involuntarily as she spoke the name and Dinah

laughed aloud. 'Well,' Bee felt herself redden. 'He said he'd try. Now I must go and help Reuben.'

Teddy Gardiner had kissed her all over her sofa. Over six foot, with dark, leonine hair and eyes of unexpected blue, he had arrived on the teaching staff the year before she did. He was a lay clerk in the cathedral, singing bass, taught English and coached the first fifteen. His body might have devastated were it not for the sense that it was the unconscious creation of wholesome pleasure, not an effortless endowment of birth. She had noticed him at once, but had stilled her interest with the reflection that, while no great beauty, Tony was blessedly indolent. Dinah had taken an immediate shine to him, but had passed unnoticed and so recovered. Just three weeks into Bee's widowhood, he had come, grave of face, to express his sympathy. He had said how sorry he was to hear, she had said not at all, then they had sat side by side on the sofa talking about the Dean's latest sermon and the tummy bug epidemic. The talk had flagged and, after a finger-itching silence, they had slid into a wild embrace. Things would certainly have progressed had he not kicked over the sherry bottle. Jennifer had come home in the middle of the mopping-up and he had fled in confusion to supervise the boys' prep. Over the twenty-four months that ensued, his sporadic courtship had not gone unremarked.

Bee made her way back to the kitchen, pausing only long enough to be told that the rival do at the Deanery had been the usual dour affair and that most, if not all, of the guests had come on to hers. She found Reuben sitting on the draining board swinging his legs. He was not alone. He was nose to nose with the young Precentor.

'Hello, Dick.'
'Bee. How splendid.'
Did she fancy that guilty start?
'I had no idea you two knew each other,' she said. Dick

Greville, who sang like an angel, was teaching the choristers plainsong technique and was rumoured to be a favourite at Clarence House, coughed and said, 'Well . . . er . . . yes.'

'Mrs Hewlings just introduced us,' said Reuben sharply. 'But actually we'd met once before at the Brills'. How is everything?'

'Oh, fine. Fine. Nothing left to do now but chat. Reuben's been a wonder, Dick. He took over all the baking for me.'

'Oh really? How splendid.'

'Yes, well, I was just saying I'd show our Precentor the old wasps' nest in the summer house.' So saying, Reuben opened the kitchen door and stepped out into the back yard. Dick, who had a reputation for purity, hovered on the doormat, wrinkling his brow.

'Are you . . . er?' he asked Bee.

'No thanks. I'd better take the jug again.' She beamed.

'Oh. Right. Bye.'

He shut the door behind him. Bee leaned on the kitchen stool and heard Reuben's laugh around the corner. Then she watched the two of them cross the lawn and, after a hasty look round, vanish into the gloom of the summer house. She had found a dried-out wasps' nest in there, glued to the rafters. Reuben had never seemed particularly interested.

She made a fresh jug of cofee and set out to refill cups. Everyone said how much they were enjoying themselves. No one had left, although a few had deserted the main body to go upstairs on an *explore*. Sister Veronica's stout-booted form was trotting across the half-way landing as Bee crossed the hall. She saw Bee in a mirror and stopped, turning with a twitter, a smile and a sparrow flap of her hand. A deeper voice barked from further up, 'Come on, Knickers. You'll get left behind,' at which Veronica hesitated minutely before scampering round the corner, out of sight. Bee saw Dinah surreptitiously collecting cups and saucers from behind drinkers' backs. Her friend caught her eye and gave her a wink. She turned into the drawing room.

'More coffee, girls?' she called, feeling suddenly tired.

'Rather. White and two shugs. Isn't that naughty of me?'

'Oh but no, I think there comes a time when . . .'

'Black, please. Yes. That's lovely.'

'Whichever's easiest . . . Oh, well, darkish brown, then, please.'

She met the chorus with bland smiles. She reached Miss Rossington, whose leg was stretched out on a pile of cushions and a footstool and found that she was fast asleep. Slowly she lifted the cup and saucer from off the woman's lap and slid them onto her tray. She turned and saw Teddy. Everyone else saw her seeing Teddy, too, and carried on chatting with eyes and minds in suspension.

'Hello,' he said. 'I'm late, aren't I?'

'Yes, but it's sweet of you to come at all.'

'Oh nonsense. I mean . . . Borneo and things are . . . Well. Let me help you with that. Are you going to the kitchen with it?'

'Yes.'

He took the tray in his great hands and swung out the way she had come. She watched his shoulder blades beneath the Harris tweed and wished again that he were not quite so sporty. In the kitchen she took the tray from him and opened the basement door.

'In there. Quickly.'

He obeyed. She glanced into the hall to see that she was unobserved, then darted in behind him, closing the door. She shot the bolt and turned on the steps.

His thick arms grabbed her in the dark and pushed her back against the floor polisher and some pampas grass she was drying for the harvest festival. She sought his mouth and pulled his rugger thighs against her. He smelled faintly of Old Spice. She ran her fingers into his tough hair and pulled his head back so that she could take a series of rapid bites around his Adam's apple. With a moan he broke free and thrust himself hard against her, making the shoe-cleaning things rattle in their box.

'Now,' he said.

'No.'

'Yes.'

'I say *no*.'

'Mrs Martin? Mrs Martin, are you there?'

'Blast. Her Nibs. Get down there and count to a hundred and fifty before you come out.'

He lurched down the stairs, kicking over a fertilizer bag as he went. Bee flicked on the light, smoothed out her skirt and twin-set, then slid back the bolt without a sound.

The Dean's wife was standing on the kitchen doormat. She was a tall, ugly woman and strained her goldfish eyes to see over Bee's emerging shoulder. Bee shut the door behind her.

'Mrs Crewe. I'm so glad you could make it.'

'Well I'm not really making it, you know,' she snapped. 'I'm looking for Mr Gardiner. I gather he's here.'

'Yes. He is. Why do you need him?'

Bee set out firmly for the hall again, forcing Mrs Crewe to follow her. She glanced out of the window as they went, noting that the summer house door was still shut.

'I gave a coffee morning today as well, as you probably heard, and he promised he'd come and help move my trestle tables when it was all over, but it finished a little earlier than planned and the Dean wants the room free for his heraldry class tonight. Mrs Friston said Mr Gardiner was here, so I wonder . . .'

'Yes he is, as I say. I'm not sure where. He followed me out to the kitchen then said something about going around the garden to take a look at my leaning wall for me.'

'Oh really? Well, perhaps I can find him there.'

'Mrs Crewe?'

Teddy walked in through the open front door, his hands thrust deep in his pockets. Bee flashed her praise.

'Ah, Teddy, there you are.' Her Nibs threw a glance at her hostess. 'I'm afraid I'm going to kidnap you a little early.' Without a word of thanks she stalked him from the house. Once again Bee faced a ring of enquiring faces.

'Has anyone seen the Precentor?'

'I thought I saw him earlier on.'

'I wanted to ask him about that dreadful Series Three.'

'Oh yes. King James is so much more . . . well . . . it feels more *right* somehow, doesn't it?'

'Of course, poor Mrs Crewe does have an awful lot on her plate.'

'Sixty-two, isn't she now? I must say, it's lasting rather a long time.'

'Bee, quick.' Dinah's face was colourless. 'In the dining room. It's Mrs de Vere!'

'Mrs de *Vere*? Is she here?'

'Well, perhaps she's just joined. There was something about new members.'

'I thought perhaps the committee . . .'

Ignoring the chatter around her, Bee ran into the dining room. The grey-haired sea parted before her. In her chair by the fire, Mrs de Vere was writhing. One hand flailed before her, where it had dropped a coffee cup, the other plucked at her throat. Her vein-strung legs, bandaged at the ankles, twisted and kicked in their sensible, brown walking shoes, and her old wool skirt was riding up over a greyish petticoat.

'God, she's choking!' Bee exclaimed, rushing forward. 'Dinah, could you ring for an ambulance?'

With little or no idea what to do, Bee reached the old woman and unbuttoned the top of her blouse. The lapels of her cardigan were studded with crude costume jewellery. A gold chain hung around her neck, tinkling with good luck charms.

'Mrs de Vere! Mrs de Vere!' she shouted, and banged her furiously on the back.

'Yes, ambulance, and quickly please. We have an old woman choking on a biscuit here.' Dinah's voice rang out in the stunned near-silence of the hall. 'What? Oh yes. Number eight,

Chaplain's Walk. But it's one-way, so you'll have to approach it from Bridge Street, at the other end.'

Halfway onto the floor now, Mrs de Vere was turning grey-blue. Her glasses had fallen off and her milky eyes were wide with pain and terror. Her breath came in deep agonized sucks that made her teeth whistle. The other guests kept outside a neat four foot radius. Some stared blankly, others touched their mouths with listless fingers or picked unthinkingly at their clothes. Reverend Pyke was among them. His wife turned on him.

'Jack, darling. What did you do to Kathy Roach that time? Quickly. Try to remember.'

'Well I . . . I punched her. You always have to punch them hard on the solar plexus.'

'Well do it.'

Breathless from belabouring the gasping woman's back, Bee looked up in despair.

'Oh yes. Please. Try anything you know. She's going to pass out any second.' He dithered, finding a place to set down his cup and saucer and she felt her anger rise. 'Well come on, then! She's dying!'

He darted forward, rolling up a shirt sleeve.

'Hold her back so I can get at her,' he said. Getting behind the armchair, Bee took Mrs de Vere under the arms and hauled her upright. 'Steady. Steady.' His voice was quavering. Bee noticed how black the hair was on his fist. 'Now!'

With a grunt of effort, he punched hard at the top of her ribs. Mrs de Vere's hooting cry was hidden by the gasp from the onlookers. Her sucking whistles continued, only fainter.

'Upside down,' called Dinah. 'We'll have to get her upside down, as if it was a fish bone or something.'

'Yes. That's right.'

'Upside down.' There was a suggestion of hilarity in the rejoinders. Swing the old trout upside down.

'I'll take her legs,' announced Reverend Pyke.

He took her by the ankles and walked round, almost ponderously it seemed to Bee. With her feet over the back of the chair, the choking woman's skirt flopped down onto her waist.

'No. Jiggle her up and down a bit,' called Miss Coley, who, chronic disabilities notwithstanding, had found her way onto a dining chair at the back of the crowd.

'You'll have to be quite fierce, though, Jack, if we're to shake it loose.'

Urged on by the well-wishers, Jack Pyke jiggled her up and down quite fiercely. Her tongue lolled outside her bloodless lips and her straggly hair began to swing against the carpet. Somebody laughed.

Bee could stand it no longer. She bent down and cradled the woman's jerking shoulders in her arm.

'Stop. Stop. For God's sake, stop! I think she's dead.'

But Reverend Pyke appeared not to have heard. Sweat streaming down his scarlet face, indignant from the fire, he continued to jolt his patient.

'Just a few more. I think we're nearly there,' he gasped.

'No, Jack,' his wife called. 'Stop. Stop.'

She ran forward and laid a hand on his arm. He looked at her, then down to where Bee, near tears, was trying to lift Mrs de Vere back to dignity. He let go of the ankles and followed his wife from the room. With Dinah's help, Bee turned the old woman round so that her feet were on the ground once more. The crinkled head dangled to one side. Dinah listened to her heart.

'She's dead,' she said.

A sigh – half apology, half disgust – ran through the crowd. Behind Bee's back, they began to find their coats, telling each other that perhaps the most useful thing they could do was to get out of the way and let the ambulance men deal with it.

'Where's the Precentor?' asked Mrs Brill. 'I did so want to ask him . . .'

'Perhaps tomorrow,' hushed her daughter.

The ambulance men duly arrived. As the two of them rolled Mrs de Vere onto a stretcher and covered her in a royal blue blanket, a nurse who was with them assured Bee that there was nothing more she could have done.

'Looks as though she had a good run for her money, though, doesn't it? At least she went out enjoying herself,' she said. 'Better than for it to happen alone.'

'Yes,' agreed Dinah. 'There's always something worse. Look, Bee, I'll ride up to the hospital in the ambulance to see if they need any details or anything like that. She won't have any next of kin that we know of. I'll get back as soon as I can.'

'Bless you,' said Bee. 'I'll cope.'

She stood in the porch and watched the forlorn little procession wend its way down the drive. Dinah was chatting to the nurse in the stretcher's wake. The coats had all gone except for Mrs de Vere's. Bee walked with a tray around the drawing room gathering cups and saucers, then did the same in the dining room. She plumped out a few cushions, rearranged the armchairs and walked over to the Bring and Buy stall. The lavender bags were still there. She slipped them into her pocket, then took a half-eaten biscuit out of the shortbread tin and counted the money. They had taken twenty-five pounds. Without the float that was nineteen. The remaining issues of the quarterly magazine had been knocked onto the carpet in the excitement. She gathered them up, threw them on top of the glowing logs, watched them flare up, then carried the dirty cups and saucers through to the kitchen.

There was still no trace of Reuben or the Precentor. She assumed that they had discovered a shared interest in Kashmir or something, and had gone for a walk. She stood at the sink, squirted some washing-up liquid into the bowl and turned on the hot tap. As the foam rose, she picked up the rubber gloves and blew into them to turn the fingers the right way out. As she pulled them on, someone pressed up behind her. She jumped, then realized who it was.

'She let you go early,' she said, leaning her head back onto his shoulder as his hands ensnared her waist.

'I heard what had happened and thought you might need a hand.'

'Oh Teddy, Teddy,' she murmured as he licked one of her ears, somewhat clumsily. 'I want you to put me in your little red car and drive me fast, anywhere else, for several hours.'

'Actually the big end's gone,' he apologized. 'I've only got the bicycle at the moment.'

Over the browning leaves of the geranium on the windowsill, she watched the summer house door open. Reuben emerged with a delicate yawn.

'There's a drying-up cloth on the back of the door,' she said.

PAINT

❧

for Paul Luke

ANDREW WAS MOVING an overgrown shrub when he heard the telephone. It was a lavatera which had outstayed its welcome in what had only ever been intended as a temporary resting place. The roots were huge now, and deep. He had abandoned the fork and was having to scrabble in the earth with sore fingers, heaving at the obscene growths with all his weight to free them from the moist, unyielding clay. He was not altogether sure this was the time of year to be moving plants. The thing would probably die, traumatized by such rough handling. He ignored the ringing at first, then realized the answering machine was off and hurried, swearing, back to the house, rubbing earth off his hands and onto his jeans. The telephone fell silent just as he reached it, causing his head to spin briefly with sad possibilities of who he might have disappointed. Just as he was turning back to the door, it rang again, causing him to jump.

'Hello?'

'Don't sound so uncertain,' his mother was always teasing him. 'You answer it as if it wasn't your phone and you were taking some awful liberty.'

'Hello?' he said again, more forcefully.

There was a clatter at the other end, as if the caller were doing several things at once.

'Hello, Andy. It's Dad.'

'Dad. Hi. Is there some problem with tomorrow?'

'No. No. Unless you want to cancel or something.'

'Of course not. No.'

The brief exchange was so typical of their relations; hesitant, uncommunicative, fraught with embarrassment at the very possibility of complications.

'You see,' his father went on, 'it's just that I wondered if you'd made any plans for our evening together.'

'Er . . . No. Not really.' Andrew wondered again whether he should have invited people, thrown his father a supper party. But he knew no people. Or no one he could comfortably seat at the same table as his father.

'Because I thought we might drop in on some friends. For tea or something. I don't think you know them. They're doing a job on a house down there. Somewhere called Saint Vaisey.'

'That's not far from here.'

'I know. We . . . er . . . I looked it up. They're nice people. You'd like them. But I don't want to mess up your plans.'

'I don't have any plans, Dad. I already said.'

'Fine then. You can pick me up at Truro okay? I could always cab it.'

'Course I can. Two-ten.'

'Want a word with your mother? She's hitting something on the kitchen table but I can get her.'

'Better not,' Andrew said, thinking of the lavatera roots drying above ground. 'It's an expensive time to be calling. Give her my love.'

'Will do.'

As he hung up he felt a stab of irritation that his father, who was coming West to visit Andrew's home for the first time in the ten years he had lived there, should already be diluting the bare twenty-four hours they would have together with an addition of strangers. Then, as he returned to do battle with the lavatera, irritation was joined by the apprehension he always felt at having to meet new people. There was a shaft of relief too. After thirty years of having nothing to say to his father, the sudden prospect of having the man to stay on his own had been daunting. Andrew had bravely determined that this was a heaven-sent opportunity, a chance to meet as independent adults, to view one another without the deflecting mist of his mother's nervous chatter. It was only twenty-four hours, after all. An afternoon, a night and a morning. As the days passed, however, those twenty-four hours had begun to loom over his pleasingly unsociable routine like an inescapable thundercloud. Having extra people to involve would relieve the tension. They might even have the makings of friends. Andrew lived alone and would not have had it any other way but he liked the idea, at least, of friendship.

Looked at with apprehensive eyes, the little house seemed too basic, under furnished, poorly decorated. The few antiques he had inherited from his grandmother – a longcase clock, a rocking chair, a uselessly delicate chaise longue and a dingy oil painting of a woodland cottage – clustered in a corner of the sitting room. There they seemed to form an unintentional shrine to his parents' effortless good taste, and sat awkwardly alongside the shabby but serviceable armchairs and once-amusing junk he had found in village jumble sales. His father had not noticed Andrew's small attacks of chronic depression, attacks which Andrew always felt never quite amounted to a respectably full-blown nervous breakdown, but he had disapproved strongly of their immediate effect – a decision to abandon a legal training to *run away* to Cornwall.

'It's not the sixties any more, you know,' his father jeered. 'Only idiots drop out now. Idiots and ignorant, ungrateful fools.'

Ironically, however, the spirit of the sixties, or at least selected highlights of the era, seemed to be creeping back into the nation's consciousness. After six years Andrew found that his untroubled existence, living in a small village, working as a National Trust warden on the county's beaches and coastal paths, was more in vogue than any city solicitor's could ever be. In her occasional, faintly surreptitious letters, his mother claimed that his father had discovered he could now speak of Andrew's *mad decision* with a note of pride and was describing him, absurdly, as *living on the land*.

'He couldn't help being a bit disappointed, darling,' she explained. 'You must see that. I suppose it's my fault really, for not having had more children. Big families leave more room for lovely eccentricity but only children like you have to play the be-all and end-all. I could have had more and I should have. But I didn't. So there it is. Now, about those bulbs you said you'd find me . . .'

The following morning he rose early as always and drove over to a large local supermarket he rarely visited. He laid in stocks of the sort of things he remembered his father liked to eat and drink – whisky, steak, potatoes, chocolate-ripple ice cream, Stilton, claret. It was an expensive basketful – on his own he tended to live off vegetables, brown bread and tea – but the expenditure calmed him, lending him a kind of irreproachability in the face of anticipated criticism. On the way home he stopped at a garage to give the Land Rover a rare wash and take an industrial-power hoover to its filthy interior. Then he cleaned the house from top to bottom – an habitual Saturday chore performed with fresh vigour in his father's honour. He made up the spare room bed and even arranged a jam jar of spring flowers on the bedside table before he decided this was somehow too soft and diligent a welcome and relegated the posy to the kitchen windowsill.

He arrived at the station far too early and was forced to sit in the car park, poring over the road atlas, needlessly checking on the route to Saint Vaisey. When the train, which was late, of course, pulled in, a bewildering crowd of passengers disembarked from doors all along its length. For a few minutes Andrew had to stand on tiptoe and crane his head this way and that for fear of missing him. And then there he was, jauntily swinging a small overnight bag and clutching, in his other hand, an herbaceous geranium from Andrew's mother. Andrew tried to relieve his father of both or either and, after the fuss, it was suddenly too late to shake hands naturally, so they did not touch at all. Claiming to be ravenous despite his sandwiches, his father insisted on stopping to buy some chocolate from a machine. He munched his way swiftly through two bars as they drove away, eyes bright with satisfied greed, snapping off pieces between his teeth rather than using his fingers.

'Sure you don't want any?' he asked, offering the last inch of the second bar.

'No thanks,' Andrew said and could not help smiling.

'What's so funny?' his father asked, munching.

'I'd forgotten how hungry you get.'

'Bloody sandwiches were an absolute rip-off. I'd have made some decent thick ones before I set off, but you know how late your mother leaves things and we ended up in a god awful rush. You look well.'

'So do you.'

He did. Andrew was surprised how young his father looked, even vigorous. He was fifty-three but could have passed for a prematurely greying forty-two. His hands, clutching the battered leather case on his lap, were thick but sinewy – not at all the soft, pink things one would expect on a barrister.

He asked Andrew questions on the way home. He asked about his work, about problems with pollution, footpath maintenance, erosion. He asked about the local population, unemployment and politics. To a stranger it might have sounded like genuine fatherly interest but to Andrew, it was like polite questioning from a visiting dignitary, benefiting from advance briefing at the hands of diplomats. Still, the impersonal questions and answers smoothed their way. He retorted in kind, with questions about his father's work and was surprised to hear him paying lip service, at least, to the importance of encouraging racial and sexual equality at the Bar and of introducing certain radical reforms in the Law. Like his father's youthful appearance, it made Andrew realize the extent to which he had coped with their unspoken estrangement by distorting his remembered image of the man into something older, more ogreishly hidebound.

Back at the house, his father continued to make appropriate noises, asking with surprising tact about any plans Andrew might have to redecorate. And yet, behind all the diplomacy, a restless energy seemed to be simmering that had nothing whatever to do with his son's life. He was keyed up, and not with any tension about meeting Andrew again. Andrew wondered whether he had some grim announcement to make. His father plainly was not ill. Perhaps his mother was? Returning to the kitchen after the necessarily brief tour of a small domain, his father seized the telephone and was already tapping out a number before he remembered to ask permission to use the thing.

'Just thought I'd –' he began to explain then was cut short when someone answered. 'Hi,' he told them. 'It's Kenneth . . . Hmm. Not bad . . . Soon I should think.' He turned to Andrew. 'We could drive over there pretty soon, couldn't we?' Andrew nodded and watched his father turn eagerly back to the mouthpiece. 'Yup. We'll be over in a bit . . . Yes. He knows the way . . . See you.'

They set out immediately. Andrew did not even bother to offer coffee. The hospitable gesture would have been entirely redundant and coffee was never hotter than when unwanted. Before they left, however, his father dug in his bag and retrieved an envelope which he handed over.

'I would have brought wine or something but I thought you might prefer these. It's two tickets to San Francisco.' He gave some complicated explanation about business traveller's perks.

'But don't you and Mum want to use them?'

'Not really. She hates America and I haven't got time. You can change the date quite easily if that doesn't suit. Just ring the number in the corner. Do you good to get away.'

As Andrew tucked the two tickets carefully behind a vase on the dresser, it struck him that they were probably now the most valuable objects in the house, after the longcase clock, inappropriate to the place as a whirlpool bath or sophisticated dishwasher.

'Well, thank you,' he said, and laughed. 'Thanks, Dad.'

Locking the door behind them, he wondered who he could take. He had a brief, heady fantasy of approaching the exceedingly pretty girl who always gave him a kind smile in the fruit shop but sensed, even as the fantasy evaporated, that he would

probably give both tickets away and see his own surprise repro-
duced on another's face.

In the car, it struck him as strange that his father offered no
information about the people they were visiting but had to be
asked.

'They're friends of your mother's as well,' he was told.
'They're decorators. Muralists. Things like that. Holly and Clif-
ford. Dreadful names, really; like a couple of hairdressers. Still.
I'm sure you'll like them.'

'How did you come to know them?' Andrew laughed at the
implausibility of the connection.

'They worked next door – for the Nicholsons. Cheered up
that gloomy dining room of theirs by turning it into a sort of,
well, I dunno, sort of Pompeian pavilion. But all with paint.
Very clever. If you like that sort of thing. Actually, I reckon she
could survive on her own as a proper painter but she supports
him. I mean, he's clever, and a pretty interesting bloke once you
get him talking – especially about Africa – but not really gifted
like her. Or *I* don't think so. Now, she said to turn left after the
church and keep on going straight towards the sea.'

And he channelled a now sporadic conversation into a series
of non sequential exchanges about signposts, wild flowers and
the extraordinarily good condition of Cornish roads after the
potholed stretches of the London borough *where your mother still
insists on living*.

The house was a sprawling Edwardian one, tucked deep in a
thickly wooded valley running down to an inhospitably rocky
cove. If there were any other houses in the area, they were
hidden entirely in greenery. Even half a mile away, Andrew
could hear the furious booming of spring tide waves and he
climbed down from the Land Rover. A beautiful lurcher, its
shaggy grey fur streaming in the wind, bounded frantically from
its nest in the long grass beneath a tree, circled the two of them,
panting as it went, then raced into the house announcing their

arrival with no sound beyond the swift clattering of its feet on the weedy gravel path. As they drew near the front door, it emerged again, leading a slight, boyish man with very short, black hair. He wore paint-spattered dungarees over bare skin and no shoes on his small, dusty feet. He reassured the dog then greeted Andrew's father like an old friend, with no hint of respect, as though they were of an age. Then he held his hand out to Andrew with a sweet smile.

'And you must be Andrew. I'm Clifford. Come in. Holly's got to finish what she's started as the paint's mixed, but she hasn't got long to go. I'll get us all some tea. She's through there, at the end of the corridor.' He turned to the dog and pointed. 'Show the way, Fingal. Show the way.'

The lurcher did indeed show the way, pacing gracefully before them down the high, sunny corridor towards a half-open door and the sound of piano music. The building was filled with a strong smell of paint and solvents. Everywhere windows had been tugged open in an effort to drive the smells away and the air was lively with sudden gusts of sea breeze which fluttered papers and banged doors. The lurcher pushed into the room, barging the door wide open to reveal a small, blonde woman perched on the top of a ladder to decorate a high, windowless wall. She had covered most of the wall with thickly painted foliage and the branches of laden fruit trees but the focal point of the 'illusion' was a man and a woman bathing and embracing in an ornamental fountain.

'Coming,' she said, not turning. 'Any second. This wretched colour's a bugger to mix right.'

'Hi,' said Andrew's father. 'Take your time.'

'Just one more peach. There!'

She picked her way daintily down the ladder – she too was in bare feet – dropped her brush into a jam jar of white spirit, flicked off the radio with a big toe, then came across an expanse of rumpled dustsheet to shake hands.

'Kenneth!'

They kissed one another's cheeks – again like old friends. And again it was a fresh shock to hear his father called by his Christian name – his mother always called him 'darling'. His father's hand lingered for a moment on the shoulder of her rugger shirt as she turned to Andrew. She flicked a strand of ash blonde hair off her face and examined her other visitor with humorous, grey eyes. She could not have been more than thirty. Her handshake was firm as a man's, her small, heart-shaped face so lovely, so hand-cuppable, that the fruit shop girl was eclipsed in a callous instant.

'Hello,' he told her. 'I'm Andrew.'

'I know,' she said, and gave him a conspiratorial smile. Just then Clifford appeared with a tray and she exclaimed, 'Tea! I'm parched. Let's go out on the terrace. I know it's a bit windy but the air's *poisonous* in here. Down, Fingal! Yes. I love you too.'

Sensing she was briefly released from the constraints of work, the lurcher had jumped up to flex his paws against her breasts. She hugged him affectionately and kissed his nose before pushing him gently from her. As they walked out through some French windows, the dog stayed close beside her, constantly glancing up at her face, plainly an abject slave.

She handed round tea, Clifford lavishly buttered scones, while Andrew drove from his mind a seductive image of her in Golden Gate Park, reflecting how unfair it was that two such attractive people should have found each other. They exuded cheerful self-sufficiency. He felt they enjoyed this temporary interruption of their exclusivity, were amused by it, but that it was precisely that: a *temporary* interruption.

Perhaps to compensate for his comments in the car, his father gave most of his attention to Clifford, asking about the house and its absent owners. Just occasionally his eyes were drawn back to Holly. Feet tucked up onto the bench beneath her, she drew Andrew out on his Cornish life and her wide-eyed fascination and frequent little pouts of concern imbued his account of his solitary tasks with a windswept romance. Suddenly she seemed struck with an idea and laughed, running a paint–spotted hand through her hair.

'Would you mind? Clifford do you think he'd mind? Kenneth?'

'Mind what?' Andrew asked her, quite sure that he wouldn't.

'Posing. I've suddenly realized you'd be perfect. I need a shepherd to peer through the undergrowth at my couple in the fountain in there.'

'Well I'm not sure I'd be very good at sitting still.'

'You wouldn't have to. You don't even have to take off your clothes. Not unless you wanted to.' She laughed. 'Go on. It would be fun.'

'Go on, Andy,' his father urged.

'All right,' said Andrew.

'Brilliant,' Holly enthused and winked at him. 'We were going to invent someone or use a photograph but real people are so much better. And Kenneth, I want you to come and see the beach. You're looking all grey and Londonish and in need of fresh air. You can manage, can't you Clifford?'

'I can manage,' said Clifford, stroking her arm as she passed his chair.

The tea things were abandoned where they lay as Holly led his father off beneath the trees and Andrew followed Clifford back into the house. He was peeved that it was not Holly he would pose for, but Clifford seemed to read his thoughts.

'I'll just do some sketches,' he explained, seating Andrew halfway up the ladder and setting to work with charcoal and a pad. 'The artist will do her stuff later.'

The sky was clouding over rapidly. Shadows hurtled across the lawn. A gust of wind billowed the thin curtains away from the French windows. Fingal trotted in.

'Got bored, did you?' Clifford muttered under his breath. 'Settle down, then.'

The lovely dog performed a quick, enquiring circuit of the

room, turned a few, nest-making circles on the spot then settled with a low grumble on a heap of dirty overalls, watching his master at work.

'Could you just pull a bit of your hair down?' Clifford asked. 'No. Like this. Hang on.' He stepped forward and, reaching up, pushed Andrew's hair back off his forehead with thin fingers before teasing down a single lock. Andrew must have stiffened unconsciously at the contact. 'It's okay,' Clifford assured him. 'I don't bite. None of us does.'

Andrew tried to relax but the cool draught had chilled him.

'Amazing place,' he said, for something to say.

'Yes. It's surprisingly noisy at night. There are owls and a fox and the house is full of creaks and bangs. Like a ship. We've tried sleeping in different rooms too. It's fun waking to new views. There! Look at yourself!' He held up a startlingly truthful sketch then almost immediately started on another one. 'Here,' he said, 'let's try you with this on,' and he crowned Andrew with a wreath of plastic leaves sprayed gold. 'Ah. *That*'s better! Holly wore that to a fancy dress party once. She said men kept reaching out to touch it then blushing. Did Kenneth let you have a dressing-up box when you were small?'

'Er . . . no,' Andrew confessed, thinking back. All he could remember was a train set with a realistic steam effect. And a neglected stamp collection. 'I was an only child,' he added, for some reason.

'We dressed up all the time. Even when it wasn't a fancy dress party we'd go as pirates or witches.'

'Did you have many brothers and sisters.'

'No. Just Holly.'

'Oh,' said Andrew. '*Oh*.'

Clifford laughed.

'You didn't . . . ?'

'Fraid so. Dad didn't explain anything.'

'She's my twin.'

'Oh yes.' Andrew saw it. 'You've got the same eyebrows.'

'Yes. Among other things.'

'But you share a room?'

Clifford frowned momentarily, glancing up at Andrew then back at the paper.

'Holly hates to sleep alone,' he said at last. 'One more sketch, then we're done and you're immortal. Let's have you the other way this time. Ah yes. That's much your strongest profile but you always show the other. I wonder why that is. Head up. That's it. Hold that for a bit if you can. So. Tell me. When you're out on your warden duty do you have to wear a uniform?'

'Yes. It's sort of khaki and brown. Not very interesting,' Andrew told him then wished he had kept quiet as he saw Clifford's interest quicken. Various facts about this rootless ménage were slipping into place. He was not entirely innocent, having had some embarrassing encounters when collecting litter in the more remote sand dunes by the military zone at Perranporth. A certain kind of male sunbather, he had discovered, became excited at the very idea of a coastal warden.

'Holly's extraordinarily attractive,' he said, in clumsy self-defence.

'Hmm,' said her brother, 'and sometimes fatally unaware of the effect she has.'

The sketches finished, Clifford took Andrew on a tour of the building. The owner was the grandchild of a famous artistic hostess and the place was littered with paintings and memorabilia. Ordinarily it might have interested Andrew but his thoughts were half a mile away, under the trees, on the beach. After the tour, he retreated into a bathroom and stole some poison-green mouthwash in case he had a chance to stand near Holly before he left. Fingal was waiting outside the door when he emerged and shepherded him along another, darker corridor cooled by a floor of great slate slabs, to the kitchen, where Clifford was absorbed in rapidly filling a cryptic crossword. Andrew peered through an overgrown window, straining to see across the daisied lawn.

'They're taking a long time,' he said at last. 'The weather's turning with a vengeance. I hope everything's all right.'

'She's probably making him go for a *proper* walk along the cliff path. They'll be fine. Anyway, you'll stay for supper, won't you?'

'Oh I think Dad's quite tired after his journey. And I hate to stop you both working. We ought to get back,' Andrew said hastily, thinking of the steak he would never eat on his own.

'Holly wouldn't like that.' Clifford tossed aside the finished crossword. 'Can you cook?'

'Not much. I can chop.'

'Come on, then. You can chop veggies while I'm creative. Have some wine.' Clifford pulled open the fridge and splashed the contents of a half-drunk bottle into two mugs. Pushing one across the kitchen worktop, he looked assessingly over Andrew's face and laughed at him again. 'You're really worried about your dad, aren't you?'

'No, I . . . No,' Andrew assured him and gulped some wine, but the mere denial brought nightmare scenarios to mind. How could he explain to his mother that Dad had broken his neck while exploring cliff tops alone with some absentmindedly seductive, shoeless blonde?

Holly brought his father back after another twenty minutes, by which time Andrew was thoroughly involved in preparing supper. The clouds had burst minutes before and the two of them were soaked. Clifford poured them brandies while Holly towelled her hair and then Andrew's father's. Andrew watched her pick pieces of fern off his father's back.

'How was the beach, Dad?' he asked.

'Wonderful,' his father enthused, shivering over his brandy but contriving to look even less fifty-three than he had on leaving the train. 'All my cobwebs thoroughly blown.' He raised his glass in a toast. 'Don't know how you ever get any work done, Clifford.'

'Easy.' Clifford slid a tray into the oven. 'We work with our backs to the windows.'

'Are we staying for dinner, Andy?' his father asked.

'Of course you are,' said Holly.

His father raised his eyebrows enquiringly.

'Andy?'

Andrew was torn. A part of him, a tight, celibate part, wanted everything to go ahead as he had originally planned, wanted his father to eat steak and ice cream, wanted to take him away from these dangerous people. Another part, frightened yet eager for carelessness, was glad that his stuffy father had not been afraid to cultivate these sexy friends so much younger than himself.

'Well I did buy us food,' he admitted, 'but it can keep. And look at the time! It's half past seven already.'

'That's settled then,' said Holly.

'It already was,' her brother murmured.

Andrew's father only replied by offering Andrew a strangely crestfallen smile. Or perhaps he imagined the crestfallen bit and his father was merely pleased to be promised a better meal than he knew his son could cook him.

'This shirt's soaked,' Holly said. 'I'm going to change.'

Before Andrew had time to control his expression or at least pretend to look elsewhere, she had tugged her rugger shirt over her head and walked, pertly topless, to the door, tossing the shirt onto a heap by the washing machine on her way. In her absence, Clifford asked after 'Margery', Andrew's mother. This conversation, in Holly's absence, made the evening feel slightly more ordinary and yet even now, something in the way the men discussed his mother made her sound perturbingly not herself. She was a dry-humoured chatterbox, a frustrated writer, yet on Clifford's tongue she became someone slightly wild and unpredictable, a creature dignified by strong emotion, a character in an unwritten novel. This new evocation was so strong that,

when Holly returned, in dark blue leggings and a teal—blue man's
jersey that hung just below her bum, it was briefly as though
there were two women in the room.

'Put this on, Kenneth. You're still soaked,' she said and held
out a dry shirt. This time Clifford as well as Andrew seemed
momentarily abstracted from bibulous chatter as Andrew's father
stood to pull off his wet things, revealing an expanse of hairy
chest that was broader and more muscular than in Andrew's
seaside holiday recollections.

The meal – chicken roast in a crust of herbs, salt and garlic, then
salad, cheese and fruit – was one of the best Andrew had eaten
in months. Holly sat at one end of the table, between him and
his father. She smelled faintly of turpentine and white spirit and
sometimes, when she leaned forward to laugh, he could feel her
breath warm on his cheek. She had slipped on long earrings
which ended in large balls of some dark wood which kept boun-
cing softly against her neck. Once or twice, emphasizing a point,
she laid a hand on his forearm but then she did the same to his
father, so he knew it signified nothing. Slightly giddy with the
insinuating comfort of it all, Andrew drank more glasses of wine
than he could count. When Holly produced dope from a small
Elastoplast tin and rolled an expertly tidy joint, he waited, astonished, to see his father take three deep lungfuls of it then felt
honour-bound to do the same. The drug, as always, made
Andrew talk, recounting minutely various strands of village gossip which seemed to amuse the others, who encouraged him.
He chattered all the more wildly when his father laid one of his
huge hands over Holly's and squeezed it and he was plunged
into sudden, stunned silence when, on the way to make coffee,
she no less unmistakably caressed the back of his father's neck.

If these were unguarded indiscretions, his father showed no
panic, flashed no warning message across the table. All was easy.
All was warm. His father's smiles to him were warm. Clifford's
passing touch to his shoulder was warm. At one point, Holly

actually picked up Andrew's hand and gave it a warm kiss; he forgot exactly why. Candles were produced when the electric light grew too hard to bear. Coffee was drunk, another joint smoked. Clifford lit a candelabra and drifted into a room across the way where he began to play Chopin preludes rather well. For the crazy symmetry of the evening to be complete, Andrew should have followed him; he was so stoned, he would have been putty in anyone's hands, man or woman. He stayed obstinately put, however, fiddling with candle wax and singeing pieces of orange peel.

'Do you want us to go?' his father asked at last.

Andrew could not believe his ears. The night had been allowed to progress this far and now his father seemed to be asking his permission to let it continue.

'Would you mind?' Andrew asked Holly and she merely smiled. 'I'm not sure I'm in any state to drive,' he added.

His father asked the same question three times in the woozy, elastic hours which followed. Nothing had been clearly spoken. His father and Holly were, by now, sitting on opposite sides of a fireplace, yards apart, and yet with each reiteration of Andrew's consent, he felt himself implicated more deeply in whatever was afoot. One moment they made him feel an innocent child, the next, a paterfamilias, whose permission must be sought at every stage.

At last, driven by a mounting tension between the two of them and dimly aware that Clifford had stopped playing the piano and slipped upstairs, Andrew rose uncertainly to his feet and asked where he should sleep.

'Well if, like me, you hate to sleep alone, Clifford's in the blue room – third on the left.' Holly came forward from the fireplace and stood on tiptoe to kiss his forehead.

'I . . . er . . . I don't think so,' he stammered.

'Then I should go right to the end of the upstairs corridor. That one's got a nice bathroom and a heavenly view when you wake up.'

'Night, Dad.'

'Sleep well, Andy.'

As he mounted the long stairs, Fingal skittering protectively upwards ahead of him, he could hear their low voices and his father's chuckle. He used the loo, splashed water on his face then found his bed in the darkness. The sheets were chilly and slightly damp, which sobered him briefly. For a few minutes he lay, the bed seeming to float beneath him, trying to make sense of the evening, but found that the sentences of his logic crumbled at their beginnings before he succeeded in forming their ends. Then a quilt of sleep enveloped him.

He dreamed he was alone on a huge, palm-fringed beach with Holly. He dreamed she was utterly available to him. She held him firmly by the wrists and rubbed a cut lemon over each of his arms in turn then encouraged him to taste his own, freshly citric skin. For some reason this was intensely exciting, like discovering one had a spectacular hidden talent. Then she held out the other half of the lemon to him and threw back her head while he squeezed the fruit's juice over her deeply tanned breasts. He lowered his mouth to lick then suckle at one of her sun-warmed nipples. It was slightly crunchy with sand and tasted, not of lemon, but sea water. Once he had tasted her nipple he was afraid to meet her gaze. He dreamed she sensed this and, lying back on the baking sand, pushed his face further down, so that his nose nestled by her belly button, where a lemon pip had stuck. She stroked his hair and encouraged him to sleep. Which he dreamed that he did.

He woke when Fingal, whom he had unwittingly shut in the room with him, pushed his muzzle across the pillows, eager to be let out. The sun was up and dazzled his sleep-sore eyes. He was momentarily disorientated by the huge, unfamiliar room with its ornate, canopied bed and (indeed astonishing) view across treetops to the sea. Moving slowly, because he found that as well as having a furry mouth, his head was beginning to throb, he let the dog out, wandered into the bathroom to pee copiously then pulled on the rest of his clothes. (He appeared to have fallen into bed while still half-dressed.) He walked to the bay window. Fingal had evidently found an open door or window downstairs for Andrew saw him racing away across the garden like a thin, black shadow, a long, pink tongue trailing back from the corner of his jaws. Overcome with a wave of exhaustion, he sank onto the window seat and closed his eyes.

Now the night before began to make perfect sense. With a spasm of remorse, he saw that his nocturnal suspicions were foolish paranoia. Swayed by dope, wine, his attraction to his hostess and the pathetic sexual envy of an overgrown adolescent, he had imagined the unimaginable. Evidently he had been single too long.

He pulled open the window and, closing his eyes once more, took deep breaths of cool morning air. The threat of a headache receded a fraction. He wished that his mortification might follow it. Suppressing the ignoble impulse to slip down to the Land Rover and beat a shy retreat, leaving his father to cadge a lift, he forced himself to retrace the events of the night in humiliating search of any behaviour on his part, any words, that might have betrayed the teenage imaginings that had so tormented him. He remembered pieces of gaucherie, bumpkin cack-handedness, but nothing worse than his perfectly innocent blunder in assuming brother and sister to be husband and wife. Perhaps, after all, he could face them without alarm. Fantasy followed hard on the heels of this comforting discovery. He reminded himself that Holly and Clifford would be working down here long after his father's departure. Andrew would invite them over for supper. Perhaps Holly might even visit on her own. He might even, in the subtlest way possible, and only on a third or fourth encounter, trail beneath her prettily uptilted nose the possibility of her using his second ticket to San Francisco. Just to see what she said, of course; it was most unlikely that she would accept.

He shivered, closed the window and went to find his shoes.

Halfway through tying the second lace, he heard a strange thumping noise. Thinking it might be Fingal, returned and pushing at the door, he stood and walked out onto the landing. There was no dog and the noise stopped before he could trace it. A delicious smell of fresh coffee and toast was curling up from below. He remembered it was a Sunday. Perhaps there would be papers, a rare luxury in which he could lose himself. He started along the corridor for the stairs then froze. The thumping had begun again and with it, voices, coming from behind a door to his right. The door had been left open a little and the few inches of darkness it revealed were dense at once with privacy and suggestion. The thumping, as was clear from the faint squeaking of springs which provided its rhythmical underlay, was the headboard of a bed knocking against the other side of the wall. Someone was gasping, sucking in thin breaths after each thump of oak on plaster. Louder than them, his voice distorted with painful urgency, his father was keeping up a stream of forbidden words.

Unable to walk on, unable to return to his room, Andrew sank slowly to the top step, one hand fingering the banisters beside him. Long ago, as a boy, he had learned to listen for the sound of his parents making love – usually on a Sunday morning – learned to associate its rare occurrences with the ensuing twenty-four hours of unusual, secretive smiles on his mother's face and uncharacteristic generosities practised by his father. His parents had made love in silence, however – doubtless unaware of the sympathetic squeaking their muffled exertions produced in the neighbouring bathroom. This new, graphic voicing of his father's deepest appetite, which now pinned Andrew to the spot, laid waste whole decades of boyish certainty. For a few seconds Andrew entertained the repellently hopeful possibility that sweet, beguiling Holly was downstairs brewing coffee and that it was Clifford who was so efficiently lancing his father's festered desire. Then the sighs swelled in volume and became unmistakably female and Andrew found himself watching tears splash off his cheeks onto the dusty step below his knees. He remained rooted to the spot until the yelps in the bedroom turned to laughter, then he wiped his eyes and carried on downstairs, heedless of whether the couple heard him blow his nose so close to its door.

Clifford had begun work in another room. He had washed a wall with a watery, terracotta paint and was rubbing it around with a rag, so that a paler colour below showed through here and there. Sensing that Andrew needed occupation, he brought him strong coffee then tied an apron round his waist, placed a brush in his hand and set him to washing colour over another section of wall. He was kind enough to sustain a pretence that nothing untoward had occurred overnight. At least, Andrew took it for kindness but on reflection it might have been a kind of moral delinquency in him. The work was calming, as, curiously, was Clifford's rich supply of scandalous erotic anecdotes. At last, when Holly called from the kitchen that she was frying bacon and eggs, Andrew felt able to face her and his father with equanimity, if not insouciance.

Predictably his father was all joviality, full of enthusiasm for the effects of the country and a good night's sleep. He gave even less sign than Clifford that anything out of the ordinary had happened, unless his cheerfully electing to wash up the remains of the previous night's meal was symptomatic of a need for expiation, which Andrew doubted. Holly kissed Andrew's cheek and earnestly asked him if he slept well.

'I hope I didn't wake you,' she went on before he could answer. 'I came up long after everyone – even poor old Kenneth. I suddenly felt this desperate need to get on and paint.'

She was interrupted by a sudden commotion. Pursued by Clifford's laughter, Fingal burst into the kitchen clutching a lifeless lamb in his jaws and evidently hugely pleased with himself. Andrew was horrified. He exclaimed that if a farmer caught him the dog would be shot. But Holly was utterly untroubled, as though this happened all the time.

'But he wasn't caught, was he?' she said, easing the lamb from Fingal's jaws and laying it on the *Observer* business section. 'How delicious. Get busy, Clifford, and we can have it for lunch.' She stooped to kiss Fingal. 'Clever boy. *Clever* boy!'

'Oh don't be such a prig, Andy!' his father exclaimed, seeing Andrew's expression at her rank encouragement of crime. 'Get her to show you the painting. She's caught you exactly. Even that expression. Go on, Holly. I'll watch the bacon.'

As Clifford began to sharpen a knife for skinning and butchering the lamb, Holly took Andrew's hand. He was sweating and might have slipped from her grasp but her fingers were relentless. She pulled him back to the big, dust-sheeted saloon, pulled aside the ladder and pointed.

Andrew stared and could not restrain a guffaw of recognition. There he was, wreathed in golden laurels, peering through the parted branches of a peach tree. It was not mere imagination which made him see Holly in the girlish figure in the fountain – she had Holly's hair and dark eyebrows. The broad-backed male figure, so keen to enjoy her, had his face turned away into the painting but his identity now seemed immaterial. It was Andrew she had recorded on plaster, pinned down, fingered, as the police would say.

They ate the lamb for lunch, with rosemary and new potatoes purloined from the owner's garden. It was quite delicious. Andrew's father was forced to catch a slightly later train than planned because they did not start eating until mid afternoon.

'Come again,' Holly called, waving as Andrew drove back up the drive. 'Now that you've found us, come again.'

He wound down the window but did not know what to say so merely smiled and pressed on the accelerator. While they drove to the station, his father's one-sided conversation began to assume a London gravity as his thoughts returned to the heavy load of long-winded commercial briefs and the tedious day of interviewing candidates for pupillage which awaited him.

Having made no mention of the strangeness of arranging to make a long-postponed visit to one's son, only to use him as a pretext for receiving the hospitality of another, his parting words were a casual request that Andrew ring his mother to warn of his later arrival.

'Andrew?' Her voice was rich with the evening's first drink. 'How lovely. How did it go?'

'Fine,' he told her. 'Thanks for the geranium. Dad seems very well.'

'He is.'

'And we visited some friends of yours. Those decorators.'

'Holly and Clifford? What fun. They're *so* nice.'

'Yes. Er. Mum?' Dialling her number, Andrew had steeled himself to risk sounding prudish. She ought to know. He was sure of it. But first he found himself picturing the needless pain he might cause her, then he felt obscurely guilty for the passive role he had just played in his father's off-hand infidelity. Mouthing silently into the mouthpiece, aware afresh of the tickets to California winking at him from their hiding place on the dresser, he found he could go no further. 'How was *your* weekend?' he asked instead.

'Fine. You know I'd have loved to have come too – Cornwall's such heaven at this time of year – but I did think it was important for Dad to spend a little time alone with you for once. Anyway, I had a friend of my own visiting. James Bedford.'

'Who?'

'Oh you *know*. That nice academic I met when poor Kate and I went to Florence last year. He's *so* nice. He's still here in fact, so I better let you go. I promised to let him cast an eye over some of my silly bits and pieces before he goes.' She giggled. 'Bye darling. Don't work too hard. Bye.'

As he soaked in the bath, preparing for an early night, it struck him that his mother's nice academic might be her lover. She might be well aware of his father's involvement, or whatever one called it, with Holly. It was his mother, after all, who had first so unexpectedly posited the idea of his father's coming to stay. If the business of his coming were no more than an elaborate charade for the adulterer, forcing his son to play alibi, then might it not also have proved an erotic convenience for the adulterer's wife?

Andrew reached out a soapy arm to turn up the volume on the radio, resolving to push the matter from his mind by an effort to focus on a laconic discussion of the Islamic Question. He must learn to avoid fantasizing. That way, as his mother was always saying, lay madness. He wiped away a tear and returned to scrubbing at the terracotta paint which clung so persistently to his fingernails.

OTHER MEN'S SWEETNESS

౨

for Tom Wakefield

'SARAH-JANE? Sarah-Jane? Wake up. We're nearly there!'

Jane opened her small, green eyes, yawned and focused on her mother from the back of the overloaded car. From as early as she could remember, she had loathed the name Sarah and the hyphen that accompanied it. People who really loved her, like her dolls and the sweetshop lady, called her Jane. Her mother smiled and turned back to face the road. Jane shifted and winced crossly. The rear of the car was hot and stuffy and she had outgrown her safety seat.

'I'm too big for it now,' she had complained as her father strapped her in.

'Nonsense,' he said. 'It's meant for ages three to five. You can have a new one on your birthday.'

She looked down at Jones, the only doll she had been allowed to bring. ('Quickly, Sarah-Jane! Choose one quickly! We don't have all day.') Jones's eyes clicked open to reveal a baby-blue stare. Jane tugged Jones's red nylon hair and felt a little more cheerful. Then she looked out of the window. They were in the flattest place she had ever seen. On either side of the slightly raised road, fields flat as carpets stretched out as far as the eye could see. Here and there was a line of sickly trees or a sinister stream straight as a ruler. The road was straight too and seemed to stretch as far as the horizon.

'Where are we?' she asked.

'Cambridgeshire,' her father said.

'We're about to cross the border into Norfolk,' her mother added.

'Where?'

'Any . . . minute . . . *now*! Here! Now we're in Norfolk.'

They passed a sign. The road looked just the same, as did the countryside. Flat. Flat. Flat.

'Where's Norfolk?'

'East Anglia. On the East coast.'

'And why did we have to get a cottage *here*?'

'You mum liked the idea.'

'And your dad found the perfect place.'

'And we got it at a bargain price,' her father went on. 'Can't think why no one else has discovered this bit. I mean, it was a bit grim having to drive out through the East End, but I suppose, if one were to keep clear of the rush hours and so forth, it wouldn't be so bad . . .'

Her parents lapsed back into one of their usual, incredibly tedious conversations, cobwebbed with adult impenetrables like *Hangar Lane Gyratory System* and *Miles Per Gallon* and *Post War Architecture*. They were not nearly there. Her mother had lied again. Sometimes she seemed to resent Jane's falling asleep in the car and wake her for the hell of it. Jane fell to pulling Jones's hair again then tried to push out one of the doll's eyes with its own, miniature thumb.

She had twenty-nine other dolls at home and a hammock and an exercise bicycle and her own fridge for cold drinks and her own colour television and a child size portable video camera and her own stereo system with compact disc player and remote control facility. She had her own bathroom, with a bidet and an extensive menagerie of clockwork bathroom toys and a whole wall of fitted cupboards to house the dress collection she planned to amass over the years to come. She had piano lessons and ballet classes and went to the cinema often and had only been refused a pet because her mother said she was too young to look after one. They had a lovely house in Islington, with two garages and a gym and both her parents seemed happy with their jobs. Why then had they seen fit to buy – another adult impenetrable – *a Little Place in the Country*?

'Sarah-Jane? Sarah-Jane? Look! We're here! There it is!'

Jane looked up from her ponderings. They were pulling up

on the outskirts of a village. There was a farmhouse in a cluster of outbuildings overgrown with creepers and long grass. To their left crouched a small, red-brick building not unlike a rather cheap doll's house, set near the road in a patch of windswept garden.

'Oh,' said Jane.

'Well you could show a little more enthusiasm,' her mother snapped.

'Don't bully her,' her father said. 'She'll like it when she looks around. Come on. We can unpack later.'

He unstrapped Jane's harness and lifted her down to the grass verge. She followed as he walked arm in arm with her mother up the garden path. A dead rat glistened with flies under a rose bush but Jane said nothing. She would save it to come back to later.

The house was quite nice inside. It smelled of wet paint and there was only one bathroom, but her bedroom under the eaves was so tiny and had such a small window that it reminded her of the houses she liked to build under her mother's dressing table or inside the airing cupboard. She began to understand her parents' enthusiasm. It was all a game.

'Do you like it, then?' her father asked her.

Jane bounced on her bed to make it squeak.

'When are we having lunch?' she asked.

'She likes it,' her mother said. 'Thank Christ for that.'

And Jane had to watch while her parents kissed exaggeratedly like a couple in a cartoon.

They were busy with suitcases and spice racks after lunch and Jane found herself repeatedly in their way. So, responding to their impatient suggestions, she slipped out to play by herself in the garden. At the back of the house was a cluster of tired fruit trees. An old tyre hung from one and she amused herself for a while by swinging on it until she felt dizzy. She tried an apple or two but they were hard and their sour juice made her tongue curl. Then she found a congregation of slugs glistening in the rhubarb patch and had fun squashing it with a stone. She needed to pee suddenly and felt pangs of hunger (lunch had been olives and salad) so she started back towards the house. Her parents were shouting at each other however, and she was frightened to go in. Instead, she relieved herself in some bushes below one of the windows. Crouching on the dry earth she gradually became aware of a delicious smell; warm, sweet, spicy. It was coming from the shabby farmhouse next door. She followed it across the garden as far as a broken part of the fence and stopped there to sniff again. The smell curled around in her head and made her stomach gurgle. The gap in the fence was not wide and she had to squeeze and shove to force her belly through.

Once she was on the other side it seemed impossible to go back the way she had come. So she went on. She was enchanted to find a small zoo at large in the yard. A cat was dozing on a bale of hay. Another was draped across a sack of fertilizer, swishing its tabby tail. An old sheepdog rose from his place by the back door to sniff and lick her face. There were ducks on a greenish pond and hens scratching in the earth. A donkey brayed and wheezed in a paddock where a huge black horse watched her from the shadow of a tree. A goat, safely tethered, paused in its munching to fix her with reptile eyes and she counted three cows grazing in the field beyond the paddock. She stopped to pat the dog and pet the cats, then she followed the delicious scent – which was making her quite ravenous now – to the open back door.

A batch of sugary Chelsea buns and two seed-dusted loaves were steaming on a wire rack below the window. Further into the room, in the shadows, a woman and a man were seated, one behind the other. She was gently combing out his black hair, which was nearly as long as hers. They were both beautiful. Not like her mother and father, who were beautiful and handsome respectively of course, but beautiful in a new, unsettling way. They didn't look altogether clean and the woman wore no make-up, but they had a kind of glow. It brought Jane to a sudden, hurtful realization that her parents might not be the most attractive people she would ever meet. The man had been working on the farm. He had no shirt on and there were streaks of mud among the black hairs which formed whorls on his chest where her father's was pink and smooth. His eyes were shut with pleasure but the woman saw Jane and smiled without stopping her combing.

'Hello,' she said, in a faintly mocking, low voice. 'Who are you?'

The man opened his eyes briefly but did not move.

'"I'm Jane," said Jane. "We live next door now. Can I take a bun?"

'Sure,' the woman said and, as Jane carefully picked the bun nearest her and sank her teeth into its sticky crust, she twisted the man's hair into a glossy braid and kissed the nape of his neck. The dough was still warm and one or two currants tumbled from its torn surface to the floor, where the sheepdog licked them up and sat, with a barely discernible whine, to wait for more. The man opened his eyes again then pushed back his chair and stood. He winked at Jane and walked out across the yard to the barn, where he started using a noisy machine.

'Like your bun?' asked the woman, grinning now.

Jane nodded vigorously. She would have liked another but knew this was best left for a sort of going-home present.

'I'm Jeanette,' the woman said. 'And that was Dougal. Do your parents know you're here?'

'No,' Jane told her. 'They're busy.'

'Well,' Jeanette winced, 'so am I, in a way. But you can watch if you like.'

'Yes please.'

'Come and sit on a chair, then, instead of standing there like a pudding.'

Jane came forward and clambered onto a kitchen chair. The woman, Jeanette, in whose honour she had already resolved to rechristen one of her better-favoured dolls, had switched on a light in a corner of the big, low-ceilinged room, and was turning her attention to a chest of drawers. It was painted dusky blue all over and someone had started to decorate it further with little clumps of painted leaves.

'Are you a farmer's wife?' Jane asked.

Jeanette chuckled.

'No. The animals are just pets and the field and paddock are all the land we've got really. This is how we make our living. Well. Our sort-of living. We buy old bits of bashed up wooden furniture at auctions. Dougal mends them and does the base coat and I paint on the twiddly pretty bits.' She shook her yard of blonde hair away from her face and tied it impatiently in a handkerchief, then she reached for a saucer of paint and a brush.

'What are you doing now?'

'Pull that chair closer and I'll show you.'

Jane moved closer and watched Jeanette paint leaves and buds and tendrils. She had a smell that was almost as good as the buns – Jane's mother never wore scent and stopped Jane's father wearing it either because it made her sneeze. There were other good smells in the room besides Jeanette and the buns. Bunches of pungent leaves were hanging from the beams to dry and there was a fragrant mound of orange peel and a pot of cooling coffee on the table. Jane watched, fascinated, as Jeanette's long, dirty fingers made deft twists this way and that with the brush. Dougal stopped using the machine and began to make gentle taps with a hammer. He sang to himself as he worked. Jane pulled her feet up onto the chair beside her. The good smells, the bun and the pleasing sense of doing nothing while adults laboured, conspired to bring a delicious drowsiness over her. For a few lucid seconds before she nodded off, she wondered why her life was not always like this, why this sense of well-fed contentment was so unfamiliar.

When she awoke, the cupboard was all painted and her parents were in the room making clucking, apologetic noises to Jeanette.

'She's been no trouble, honestly,' Jeanette was saying.

'We had no idea. I'm so *sorry*!' Jane's mother exclaimed.

'No bother at all,' Dougal added. He winked again as her father swung her up against his shoulder and followed her mother outside. He winked privately, so that no one else noticed.

'Come again,' Jeanette murmured, with her discreet smile. 'Pop round.'

Her parents rarely came again however. In the weekends that followed, they were preoccupied with adult impenetrables – *Hand Blocked Paper, Damp Course*, the demise of a *Feature Fireplace* and some lengthy and bad-tempered dealings with someone called *Artex Removal*. But Jane came. She could barely wait for each weekend to begin in order to squeeze through the gap in the fence and visit her new friends. Dougal let her stir paint and showed her how to milk the cows and goat. Jeanette taught her to plait her own hair (which seemed to make her mother cross). She gave her handfuls of bread dough to knead into shapes and bake and she used to stretch a sheet of yellowed lining paper across the kitchen table for Jane to paint on while she worked at her grown-up painting alongside her.

Jane's parents were perturbed at first, in case Jane were proving an embarrassment, then they seemed to accept the idea that Jane had adopted a second family. They chuckled, in her hearing, about the *Hippies* and pounced on any small infelicities that crept from their neighbours' speech into their daughter's. (Jane, uncomprehending, told Jeanette that her mother said that Jeanette had a *terrible Norfolk burr* and Jeanette laughed and fed her some cooking chocolate.) That Jeanette could be handy as a child-minder was swiftly appreciated. Jane's mother was often unable to come to the cottage for more than two weekends in a row. On these occasions, Jane's father would bring work with him and closet himself with the portable computer in the dining room while Jane went to play with the animals she now thought of as hers. It was not unheard of for Jeanette to invite him to come over with Jane for long, boozy meals in the farmhouse but

Jane preferred it when he stayed on his side of the fence. She was not above keeping a proffered invitation to herself and passing back some fabricated apology so as to keep her friends to herself.

When her nursery school began its holidays she was even left behind one weekend to spend seven glorious days as Jeanette and Dougal's guest. She fitted quite easily into their routines, rising and retiring when she felt like it, washing as little as they did and eating whatever pleasantly meatless meals Jeanette placed before her. Two things set the seal on the week's pleasure for her: lying awake listening to the loud sighs and open laughter that came from their bedroom – a far cry from the embarrassed coughs and inexplicable creaks that came from her parents' well-appointed own – and being woken by Dougal at the dead of night to watch one of the cats giving birth.

Her parents joined her for a fortnight's holiday after that and brought with them bad weather, bitterness and altercation. While Jane sheltered, bored, from the rain, they argued. Jeanette's name was raised as was that of a young Frenchman who lived with their neighbours in London. Adult impenetrables to do with *Planning Permission*, *Fraud*, *Silk Purses* and *Sows' Ears* crackled on the air over Jane's head and when she tried to slope off to Jeanette and Dougal, as had become her habit, she was faced with an inexplicable edict.

'You are *not* to go round there any more, Sarah-Jane,' her father commanded. 'You are not to see them. Do you understand?'

Stunned, Jane retreated both to her room and to the temporarily abandoned solace of her dolls and their unstinting fidelity. She sat them in elegant half-circles around her on the bedroom floor, trying not to listen too closely to the angry phrases that followed her up the stairs.

'I've a good mind to go round there and have it out with him.'

'*Him*? You think *he*'s behind it? Oh no. It was her. Her name was on that form. It was her application for planning permission that had so carefully been allowed to lapse until we'd had the searches done. She's the one that took you for a ride. Simple, unworldly hippies my arse. She saw you coming a mile off and if you hadn't been blinded by lust –'

'Well if we're talking lust, I hardly think last week's sordid little revelation leaves you in *any* position to –'

Jane quietly shut the door to keep out the sounds of their anger and climbed on the bed with a pad of paper and some crayons. She drew the perfect house where she and the more attractive of her dolls would live. They had a gym and a swimming pool and a bathroom apiece and there were dogs and kittens and a cow and a donkey and a place for Jeanette and Dougal to make her buns. Her parents, perhaps, might live next door. In a slightly smaller house because their needs were simpler and their natures undeserving.

Her mother came upstairs after a while, her hair newly tidy and lips newly red, to announce that the three of them were going to drive to the seaside for tea. For the rest of the week an unnatural parade of normality was mounted. Where they would formerly have amused themselves, they now did everything as a closely bound trio, or, rather, as a pair with Jane a necessary buffer zone. They had picnics and a boat trip. They made apple chutney and visited *historic* buildings where Jane was rewarded for her boredom with cake or ice cream. There were no more arguments apart from quickly stifled bickering about road directions and timetables. Jane saw nothing of Jeanette and Dougal – there was no time and the ceaseless activities left her whimpering only for sleep.

On the last evening of the holiday, Jane's mother delivered a startling piece of news. Jane's father had returned in high excitement from taking a phone call and a bottle of champagne had been opened. Jane could smell it on her mother's breath as she bathed her.

'Sarah-Jane, you do realize, don't you, that we're going back to London tomorrow and we won't be coming back here?'

'No.'

'Well we won't, you see. We've just managed to sell the cottage.'

'But why?'

'We had to. It turns out the naughty woman who sold it to your dad kept lots of bad things secret.'

'What bad things?'

'Oh. Well. That there are going to be a lot of horrid new houses on all the land around here. Things like that.'

'Oh.'

'So it was very important to sell quickly and get a good price before anyone else found out. Daddy's found a buyer today and we've accepted the offer. It's a shame but there it is. Now. Let's wash your hair so it's as shiny as a little doll's. You *are* getting plump, darling! We'll have to put you back on salads for a while. Whatever can that Jeanette have been feeding you?'

Jane started to ask why her father had kept bad things secret too but her mother had turned the shower on and her eyes and mouth threatened to fill with water. She cried while her hair was washed and grizzled as her mother rubbed her dry. But she quietened down when allowed a dusting of Chanel talcum powder and by the time she was tucked up in bed in her tiny room for the last time, she was utterly calm. She had forged a plan.

'Do you want me to read you a story?' asked her mother, who had unthinkingly ascribed her tears to a surfeit of tiring pleasures during the day.

'No,' Jane told her and enjoyed her mother's *moue* of disappointment at the small rejection. Left alone with the eerie reflection of her night-light in her dolls' eyes, Jane dwelt on her simple plan. She had tried for a while to share herself with two households. Now thoughtless decisions from adults left her no option but to choose. She had already transferred her loyalties from the household and parents she was born with to those she coveted. Now she had merely to follow through with a bodily transfer. She would swap families. Like any nicely brought-up girl faced with a plate of cakes, she would reach for the sweetness that lay closest to her.

In such familiar territory, the defection was easily performed. As Jane had suspected, the next day was taken up with frantic preparations for removal men. Many boxes of books had remained packed all summer for want of shelves but there were china and glass to wrap and linen to sort and pictures to protect. When she slipped out of the house after a perfunctory late lunch and squeezed through the gap in the fence, she was not missed therefore. She hid at the side of the barn and watched until she was certain that both Jeanette and Dougal were in the house, then she darted around the corner and through the barn door. Jules, the dog, stood and wagged his tail to see her but he was still tethered by the back door to keep him from bothering the kittens so he could not give away her whereabouts.

On one side of the barn, bales of fresh straw were stacked up high over Jane's head. She had played for hours on these, drunk with their heady smell, until Dougal frightened her off with a warning that children could easily slip out of reach, deep between the bales, and die for lack of air. Against the other walls clustered a collection of wooden wardrobes, chests of drawers, looking glasses and trunks in various stages of restoration and dismemberment. Jane walked over to a dusty looking glass to stare at her reflection nose to nose. Then she heard Dougal talking as he left the house. She knew he would be happy to learn she was adopting him, but sensed that it was wisest not to confront him until her former parents had safely given her up for lost. She glanced around and chose a huge wardrobe to the back of the barn. She slithered over the chest of drawers in front, tugged open the door and slid inside. She scrabbled the door almost shut again with her fingernails, put an eye to the crack and waited. Suddenly her mother's voice rang out, crystal clear, from the garden.

'Sarah-Jane? Sarah-Jane?' There was a muttered curse and she called back to the cottage. 'She's nowhere in sight, Brian. Are you sure she wasn't upstairs? . . . Well look again, could you?'

Dougal appeared, walking towards the barn entrance with a painted bathroom cabinet under one arm.

'Oh, er, Dougal?' her mother called out. He stopped, then walked out of view, towards the fence.

'Hello?'

'You, er, you haven't seen Sarah-Jane, have you?'

'Jane? Have you lost her?'

'Well. Not exactly. I just wondered if she'd come over.'

'Sorry.'

'Send her back if you see her, would you? We're meant to be leaving soon.'

'No problem.'

'Thanks.'

Dougal came on into the barn, set down the cabinet and gathered up some electric cable which he tidied lazily into loops over his arm. As he left again, Jane suppressed an urge to jump out shouting boo as she had done several times before. She leaned against the back of the wardrobe and listened to her mother's fretful, now slightly irritated cries.

'Sarah-Jane? Sarah-Jane? Where *are* you?'

Jane smiled to herself. She would miss her dolls and her party frocks but at least, after today, she would never again be called Sarah or given a hyphen. Her mother's cries stopped and for a while there was silence except for the clucking of two hens which had appeared to scratch at the earth and wood shavings in the doorway. Jane's stomach gurgled and she rubbed it reassuringly. Then she heard her mother's voice again and her father's, followed by a knock at the back door of the farmhouse. Jeanette answered. Jane couldn't make out the words but she heard the one woman's anxiety being passed on to the other and soon her parents and Jeanette were walking towards the barn. Her mother's face looked tight and cold, despite the warm remains of the day. Her father strode on ahead.

As he walked in he seemed momentarily subdued by the barn's looming shadows.

'Sarah-Jane?' he asked quietly. 'Sarah-Jane?'

Jane bit her lip and stared out at him, her fingertips holding the door in place before her. Her mother appeared in the doorway with Jeanette.

'Sarah-Jane?' she called out. 'Don't be silly, darling. Game's over now.'

She came forward and opened a large chest then let the lid shut with a bang. Suddenly both Jane's parents were galvanized into action. They hurried here and there, in and out of Jane's narrow range of vision, tugging open drawers and wardrobes and shifting things to peer into the shadows. Jeanette stood, hands on hips, and watched them.

'The hay!' Jane's mother shouted. 'She might have slipped down inside the hay!' The air filled with straw dust as, grunting, she had Jane's father set about tugging down bales.

'She isn't here,' Jeanette said softly. Jane's father came into view again. He started clambering over the chest of drawers to reach the wardrobe where she was hiding. Jane slid into the farthest corner and held her breath as he stretched out a hand towards the doorknob. Then Jeanette shouted, causing him to turn around. 'Look, I said she isn't here! Now would you both please get out?'

'Listen, you,' Jane's mother began then seemed to run out of words. Jane heard her panting.

'Come on, Christine. She isn't here,' Jeanette said, reaching out an arm. Jane's mother gave a little whimper and ran forward in tears. Jeanette led her gently out into the fading light. Jane's father lingered a moment. He had picked up a small carved box and turned it over in his hands, evidently admiring it. He glanced around, saw no one was looking and, to Jane's astonishment, slipped it into the deep poacher's pocket of his waxed jacket. Aimlessly he then opened a few more doors and slammed them shut again. Dougal walked across the yard.

'Come on, Brian,' he called. 'It's no use. We've called the police for you.'

In a sudden burst of anger, Jane's father turned and shoved hard on the chest of drawers in front of her hiding place. It slid back with a complaint of old wood and banged hard into the wardrobe, slamming the door firmly shut in his daughter's face. Jane waited a moment, rubbing her forehead where the wood had struck it and wondering whether to cry, then she pushed and found the door stuck fast. She couldn't shout out to Dougal yet. Not with her father still there. She looked frantically about her in the increasingly musty space and saw light coming through a tiny crack by the hinges. She shifted her position as quietly as she could and thrust an eye to the space. Squinting, she just made out her father's silhouette as he walked into the yard. Dougal was still there, looking around at the furniture. She would wait just long enough for her parents to get clear then she would call. Or perhaps she would wait until after the police had been? Perhaps she should call out now? She wanted to pee and she was getting hungry, but if the police caught her they might punish her. She might be punished anyway.

She hesitated a moment too long. Dougal turned on his heel, strode out into the yard and swung the barn doors shut with a terrific bang then shot the bolts on the outside. Cars and voices came and went in the hour that followed but through two great thicknesses of wood they might have been two fields away. Jane shouted herself hoarse, then slumped, exhausted and tearful, to the cramped wardrobe floor. She had no coat on and the evening was turning cold. A hen emerged from its roosting place in the straw. Losing consciousness, Jane heard its clucking as it scratched for beetles.

࿓

As Brian drove out through Hackney and Stratford, his mood gradually lightened. He had been angry at Chrissie's refusal to join him on the house-hunting trip since it had been her idea in the first place and he had taken a day off valuable work to make it. Her refusal had been of the kind that, left unheeded, would have poisoned the entire day, however, and there was nothing he disliked more than driving anywhere with her being monosyllabic and hurt in the passenger seat. It might have been fun to have brought Sarah-Jane along at least – they so rarely spent time alone together – but she was coming increasingly to mimic her mother's every gesture and mood and would only have been monosyllabic and hurt and squeaky.

A trio of Bengali women passed chattering over a zebra cross-ing before him, the sun catching on flecks of synthetic gold in their swirling, rainbow drapes and Brian reiterated his vow to spend one Sunday soon exploring rather more of the East End than the Whitechapel Gallery and Blooms. Chrissie had bought him a glossy book on Hawksmoor churches but it had gone unread. He drove on towards the motorway, accelerating as the traffic thinned out, and his irritation evaporated. He pressed a button and the car's roof folded away. It was the latest German convertible, with an engine so quiet one was said to be able to balance a fifty pence piece on it while driving at fifty miles an hour. Brian would have felt absurd testing this claim under his family's critical eye. It was a pleasure to have the car, as well as an excursion, to himself for once. He was on holiday. He would take his pleasure where he found it. He might try the fifty pence piece test on a quiet side road. He slipped on to the motorway and smiled to himself as the speedometer registered ninety with no discernible increase in noise level.

He stopped at Wisbech to pick up details from estate agents. He admired the prettiness of Georgian houses and enjoyed the bustle in the market square – such a far cry from the anger and desolation of shopping in London. Whenever he came to places like Wisbech or Salisbury he bemoaned the fact that he was not a GP or a solicitor or even a dentist – someone who could work equally profitably in a quiet provincial backwater where there was less tension, less overt competition and more time for the good things in life. Chrissie tended to be sharp with him when he mentioned this.

'You'd be bored,' she would say. 'You know you would. You're a very competitive man. You always have been. You'd wither without the cut and thrust. And there wouldn't be any good schools for Sarah-Jane. And anyway, what about me?'

Chrissie had a good job too. She travelled so much for it that there was no reason why she should not live in the country, provided she was within easy driving distance of an international airport. All she would need would be a telephone and a fax machine. But when he suggested this, she sighed, impatient but longsuffering.

'Brian,' she said, 'you *know* what I mean.'

'What? You mean parties and things?'

'And things. Yes.'

Brian looked at five cottages recommended by the agents. They were all fairly pretty, certainly, although the austere fenland landscape did not lend itself to a snug village atmosphere in the manner of rolling Cotswold hillsides or burbling Hampshire water meadows. But Hampshire and Gloucestershire were fast becoming part of the retirement belt boom whereas prices in East Anglia could only go up. There was something wrong with each of the cottages he saw, however. They were all close to the road, but that, the agents, had explained, was a fenland phenomenon dictated by the very gradual process by which the need for land had triumphed over the usefulness of water. They had gardens, they were in good condition, they were clearly loved and they were within his price range. The trouble was that too much money had been lavished on them, some of it tastelessly so. *Feature* fireplaces had been installed, an owner's pride and joy, as were neo-Victorian garage doors, obtrusively modern fitted kitchens and driveways of pulsatingly orange gravel. Even this would not have been a problem usually. In London, where comfortable convenience was of paramount importance in their hectic lives, he and Chrissie had been grateful to buy a modern house with every efficient luxury already installed, a house needing only the addition of a couple, a child, and their groaning pantechnicon of possessions. Yet Brian sensed that his needs – their needs – in a weekend cottage would be different. They did not want convenience – for that, all his friends would agree, one kept a single house in London and spent one's surplus on country hotels. They wanted distraction and difficulty. Brian wanted a challenge. He wanted somewhere he could make his own, a place where he could mark out individual territory. (In his weekly work, all-powerful market forces had him exploiting originality in others, and scarcely fostered it in himself.)

He fell to perusing a copy of the *Wisbech and District Chronicle*. There, amid ragged columns of classified advertisements for land auctions and lawnmower sales, he found what he was looking for.

Fenland cottage in need of loving care, he read. *Brick-built, pantiled roof, c.1850. 1 acre. Mature fruit trees. Suit young couple with small child and vision. 35,000 ono.*

He called the owners on the car phone and drew up outside their ramshackle farmstead twenty minutes later. He had spoken to a man but it was a woman who emerged as he shut the car door. She had long, straight, blonde hair and was, he guessed, about his age and height. She wore a loose, scarlet dress of rough cotton that clung about her full and braless breasts and swished about her long thighs as she advanced. When she took his hand in hers and said, 'Hi. I'm Jeanette. I assume you're the intrepid house-hunter,' a twinge of lust stirred his loins. 'Sorry,' she went on, brushing her palms together, 'I've probably got flour on you. It's baking day.'

Brian smiled and assured her it was quite all right. There was a streak of flour on her forehead, running into her hair like grey.

'Normally I get Dougal to show people round,' she said, leading him across the grass at the roadside. 'He knows more about building and joists and so on than I do. But he's getting ready for an auction in Cambridge so you'll just have to make do with me.'

'Oh. Well. I'm sure you'll do very nicely,' Brian said automatically, then coughed to cover his embarrassment. She merely smiled to herself and passed on.

The cottage for sale was immediately next door, set a short garden's distance from the road, with a gnarled, flower-strewn orchard behind it. Jeanette explained that she had inherited it from her mother but could not afford to keep it on. She drew his attention to the interesting brickwork then led him around the inside. Their proximity in the tiny rooms was intoxicating. She gave off a heavy scent, composed of baking spices, yeast and another, sweeter odour he could not place. He was vaguely aware of peeling paintwork and the sour taint of damp but found that he was concentrating on her lips more than on what she was showing him. Her eyes were grey and the kohl pressed thickly round their edges and the slight wateriness it had induced, summoned louche memories of earlier, freer days, before Sarah-Jane, before Chrissie. She showed him a stained bath with chipped enamel then followed him into a minute bedroom under the eaves.

'Now this would do for . . . Do you have kids?'

'Yes,' he told her. 'One. Sarah-Jane.'

'Ah. Sweet.'

'Yes. She'd love it up here.' Brian crouched to peer out of the small, low window at the dyke that lay, a still, dark mirror, along the other side of the road. 'Do you have children?' he asked, turning back to her. 'You and . . . ?'

'Dougal. No. We've tried, but no. Sometimes I catch myself peering into pushchairs at the supermarket and just, well, lusting. I catch myself planning how I could just reach in and take one.' She had to pass close by him to reach the landing again. She paused looked deep into his eyes and pressed his erection frankly with her wrist and fingertips. 'Believe me,' she said, 'I'm tempted.'

Brian felt himself blush hotly. She released him and moved on just before he made a move so that he lunged at nothing. He followed downstairs, watching the swishing of her skirt and wondering how it would be if he seized a handful of her hair and bit into her lips. Was it other people's babies who tempted her or his all too visible lust? She had blurred the distinctions. His head was full of her scent and the cottage suddenly felt as though it had been designed for smaller, surer-footed creatures.

She stopped in the hall and swung her hair behind her shoulders as she waited for him to come down.

'Well?' she asked. 'What do you think?' Her Norfolk accent would have been comical had it not been so intensely erotic.

'I like it,' he stammered. 'I like it very much. I think it's a good idea.'

'Are you making an offer, then?'

'I'll give you twenty-eight for it.'

'Thirty-two.'

'Thirty.'

'Done.' She held out her hand. As he shook it, a sly corner of his brain, unimpeded by lust, told him he had done her out of a bargain. 'I'll put you in touch with my solicitors,' she said. Then, rather than let go, she lifted his hand and rubbed its palm across her breasts then down to where, he could tell at a touch, she was knickerless.

'Oh God,' he groaned.

'Yes?' she teased, smiling.

'Your husband . . .'

'Dougal's off to Cambridge,' she sighed. 'Don't mind Dougal.'

The red dress came off over her head in one liquid movement. He forgot, in his haste, to take his shoes off first, so he was caught with his jeans locked around his ankles and had difficulty keeping his balance. Surprisingly strong, she lowered him to the foot of the stairs and sat astride him but he became fearful of splinters and they tried leaning in the doorway then moved to the kitchen table.

'Yes,' she cried. 'Yes! Yes!' and she struck him hard on the buttocks with her boot heels.

At that moment, Brian looked up to see an extremely handsome, pigtailed man swing over the farmstead fence and stride through the orchard towards the cottage. Seeing what they were at, the man stopped, raised a hand and threw them a dazzling smile.

'Er,' Brian said.

'Don't stop,' Jeanette ordered.

'Your husband.'

'Yes.'

'Oh God.'

'Yes!' Letting her head hang back off the table's end, she returned her husband's smile and, laughing, scaled a peak of pleasure on her own as Brian withered inside her.

༉

'Why don't *we* get a little place in the country?'

Chrissie, who had shortened her name when she first perceived it to be a feminization for Jesus's, had always been driven by things. As a child, she learnt to charm toys from hateful relatives. She had worked hard at school because she liked prizes. Love of things dictated her career, on the sales team of a firm of clothing chain stores. It dictated her choice of husband; Brian earned far more at his record company than her other candidates did in the city. He was also more generous. He would buy her more things. The danger of materialism, as her credit card statements reminded her with cruel regularity, was its infinitude. Love of things was a black hole, a ravenous virus, a galloping soul-cancer. Since to acquire was a compulsive pleasure in itself, quite unrelated to the individual attraction of the things acquired, each acquisition could only leave her hungry for more. A friend of hers, Nicci, had a similar compulsion where the telephone was concerned. Nicci used to spend hours, literally, ringing up friends, acquaintance, even near strangers on expensive services like *Dial-a-Pal*, *Chat-a-Lot* and the infamous *Hunk Junkie*. Eventually, when Nicci's bank refused to extend her overdraft any further, her mother had declined to bail her out unless she visited a hypnotist. The latter successfully induced an acute jabbing sensation in her ear whenever she held a receiver to it unnecessarily. He also offered a red-hot credit card service, but Chrissie scorned to approach him. She recognized her habit for what it was and made sure she earned enough to stop it turning ugly. She gained an ironic distance on it and, thereby, a measure of control. At a conference in Houston, she bought a Barbara Kruger tee-shirt which proclaimed with witty frankness: *I Shop Therefore I Am*.

In her youth, she had despised her parent's suburban rivalry with their neighbours; the race to the first Flymo, the first double garage, the first conservatory, the first retirement, the first brush with death. When she became pregnant, however, several years into her marriage to Brian, and the two of them decided it was time to exchange their sexy flat in Soho for something larger, cheaper and further out, she was brought to a fuller understanding. She and Brian had neighbours on either side in Islington; the Kilmers and the Pengs. The Pengs were Chinese and industrious and their house was council-owned. Not that Chrissie had anything against people in council housing – far from it – but the Pengs were somehow unapproachable. She always said hello and stopped to admire their (really very sweet) children, but she found it hard to understand why they continued to throw money away on rent when they could be investing it in an endowment mortgage. The Kilmers on the other hand became firm friends soon after the delivery of Brian's first BMW convertible.

Everything Chrissie wanted, Jade and Ian bought. Or maybe it was the other way around. They took midwinter holidays in Phuket, booked boxes at the opera, sent a son to Hill House and *had him down for a place* at Westminster. Ian played expensive, perilous sports while Jade belonged to a chic women-only health club and probably wore hand-sewn underwear beneath her kaleidoscopic array of designer clothing. These blessings of existence scarcely needed parading when the two couples got together; their abundance made them unmissable. As the younger, less wealthy pair, Chrissie and Brian could only fawn and coo. And envy. That Jade was *old* enough to have a son at prep school was small consolation to her masochistically observant neighbour and that her figure failed to justify so much expenditure was, if anything, a goad.

Then, after five cosy, neighbourly years, three things happened to change the course of Chrissie's life. She was promoted to marketing manager for her company's expansion into Europe, Brian came to fit less and less with her image of the life she felt she should be living and the Kilmers took delivery of an *au pair* boy from a *good* Bordelais family.

'Laurent has beautiful manners, he cooks like a dream and actually likes it *and* he's doing wonders for Sebastian's French,' Jade had exclaimed as Laurent, tall, tanned and twenty-three, set warm duck salad before them and went to open another bottle of wine. 'Besides, what would I want with some sulky girl around the house? I mean, Chrissie, can you picture it? Lisa had that Marie-Paulette all last summer. She almost had a breakdown, she and Vaughan barely speak now and Sharon still managed to fail her GCSE. Ask anyone. *Au pair* girls are torture, but *au pair* boys . . . well!'

'What do you do all day?' Chrissie asked Laurent, once he was seated before her and had pouted becomingly in response to the compliments on his *salade tiède*.

'Oh. Not much. I take the little ones to school, I tidy the house, I do some shopping and then perhaps I go swimming or play tennis.'

'The answer to every maiden's prayer,' laughed Ian and returned to some lecture he was giving Brian on market research and demographics.

'Quite,' said Chrissie. 'Actually, if you get bored, and if Jade can spare you, of course, I'm going to need to draw up five or six French documents for some presentations in Paris and Toulouse next month and you could be a huge help. The company would pay you, naturally.'

'Of course I can spare him,' Jade laughed. 'So long as you promise not to cook for her too, Laurent.'

'*Mais bien sûr*,' Laurent said, with a smile that revealed his dimples. 'I'd be delighted,' and Chrissie, who had the figure if not the clothing account, was not surprised to feel his shoeless foot unmistakably caressing her calf.

In the fortnight that followed, it caressed her again, as adventurously as an inquisitive typist and the glass partition walls of an open plan office would allow. Chrissie found herself stirred up to an uncharacteristic fever pitch of desire and frustration. She ached for a bed, for any discreetly situated horizontal even, but Jade could only spare Laurent on weekday mornings, times when Chrissie's employers could rarely spare her.

As usual, her love of things or, more properly, her love of other people's, brought her a solution. Jade and Ian owned a farmhouse a little north of Banbury, where they retreated most weekends and where they had often invited Chrissie, Brian and Sarah-Jane. Whenever he was there, Brian became soft and sentimental about his country childhood (spent in a red-brick suburb of Reading) and exerted pressure on Chrissie.

'It would be a good place to bring up children,' was a typical opening. 'Sarah-Jane loves animals.'

'What about schools?' she would retort. 'She'd have to board. She wouldn't love that. And if you think I'm commuting, you've another thing coming, Brian Warner.'

But later she noticed that Ian occasionally let Jade take the children to the farmhouse while he stayed behind to work, which seemed to involve his dressing in his smartest casuals and leaving the house on Saturday afternoon, reeking of aftershave (a waft of it blew through the trellis as he slammed the car door) to return in the early hours of Sunday afternoon. Brian typically failed to notice this dereliction. Chrissie, a childhood subscriber to *Look and Learn*, was extra kind to Jade and kept her observations to herself.

Another weekend was spent in Oxfordshire with their neighbours and Laurent's unbearably stimulating foot. Chrissie made a big effort. She cajoled them all to a nearby church fête. She taught Sarah-Jane to make daisy-chains and Laurent how to make scones. ('No, rub the butter in like this.' 'Like this?' 'Oh. Laurent. Yes. *Exactement*.') Leaning her head on Brian's shoulder as he drove them home, she asked, with just a hint of a knowing smile, 'Why don't *we* get a little place in the country?'

'So you want one now?'

'Why not? I mean, nothing large. Not like Jade and Ian's. That's too much hard work and, well, frankly I think they've made it rather common.'

'Mmm. All those paint effects.'

'And those fussy curtains. No. I was thinking of a cottage. A real cottage. A contrast to London.'

'Somewhere quite run down that we could do up?'

'Exactly. Everyone's going on exotic holidays nowadays. I think it might be rather smart to spend some time in England for a change. A cottage would be the perfect excuse.'

'When shall we start looking?'

'Oh God. Brian, you *know* how I hate house-hunting.'

'Do you?'

'You remember what I was like over Islington. I can never picture how things will look. I just see squalor and naff things that people have done everywhere. And I get so tired. Couldn't you go on your own. I trust your judgement implicitly.'

'Well that wouldn't be so much fun. Why don't you take a Friday off and we can make a weekend of it?'

'Not a weekend. Sarah-Jane's got her ballet classes on Saturdays until the twenty-fourth. Let's take off a day midweek. The roads will be clearer then. We could get a babysitter for Sarah-Jane after school and come home late. How about Wednesday? There was going to be a sales briefing but Janine had to cancel.'

'Okay.'

Their Wednesdays were taken off accordingly, a babysitter arranged and Laurent was informed by a message slipped across Chrissie's desk on the previous Friday: *'Jettes-toi les chausettes – mercredi on aura un lit!'* Then, on Tuesday night, she returned just in time for supper and announced, with a passable show of irritation, that Janine was now available again and the sales briefing was back on for the next day.

'But you've taken tomorrow off. They can't make you go in.'

'They can't *make* me, Brian,' she agreed, 'but I can hardly stay away. Now can I? You wouldn't in my position.'

They argued the question from every angle. Then, for several awful minutes, Brian threatened to spend his day off working at his accounts instead. Chrissie found herself, watched across the dining table by Sarah-Jane's pinched and questioning gaze, protesting that of course he should go ahead. He knew so much better than she what houses would suit them and which would not.

'It was your idea after all,' she added.

'It was yours!'

'Hardly. You've been suggesting we get a place in the country ever since Ian and Jade had us to the farmhouse for the first time.

You know how envious you were of them. Besides, it would be fun to have a day off. The weather's going to be great.'

'More fun with two.'

'Now don't start.'

Suddenly Sarah-Jane interrupted them with the unfamiliar sound of weeping. She hardly ever cried. She was a sensible, well-ordered little girl; her mother's child. Tears coursed down her sweet, fat cheeks at an alarming rate and she screwed her fists back and forth on her eyelids.

'Don't,' she sobbed, 'Don't don't don't!'

Brian lifted her into his arms and walked up and down, rubbing her back and stilling her cries.

The subject was dropped until the next morning, when he made one last abortive effort to dissuade Chrissie from work. She had put on her smartest blue linen suit with a deep purple blouse and jet black accessories. Sarah-Jane complimented her enchantingly as they left the house together. It was a pity she was getting so fat. Even her ballet teacher had commented on it. The Fultons' little girl was so lithe and pretty.

Laurent was loading his charges into Jade's other car for the school run. As he pulled out alongside Chrissie and the children waved and called frantically to each other, he smiled at her through the racket and showed his dimples.

'*A bientôt*,' she mouthed through the glass and smiled.

'What did you tell him?' Sarah-Jane piped up as they waited at the junction with Caledonian Road.

'I've a hard day ahead of me this morning,' Chrissie told her crisply. 'Try to be good.'

WHEEE!

✃

for Anna Gale

IT WAS NOT, she reflected, the way one imagined one's mother going. Elderly mothers were meant to slide peacefully to their death in a snoreless doze in lemon-yellow rooms scented with barley sugars and fresh lavender with wheeling seagulls beyond an open window and a distant sound of waves dragging through shingle. At best, they died in their own beds after a brief and painless illness, at worst, in hospital, after a harsh but still seemly medical crisis. They did not wantonly make spectacles of themselves. They did not leap to their deaths from cliff tops in bald daylight and high season. If they did commit suicide – and Matilda still saw no reason why *her* mother should have done so – they contained the urge until the wetter, greyer months, so as to do the deed unobserved. It was a wonder, she considered, that no holiday makers had been wounded or even killed by the body flying so suddenly onto the rocks in their midst. Retaining a shamingly sweet tooth to the bitter end, her mother had not been a small woman. No unworldly old bird she.

In her brief interview with the police, foul play was immediately ruled out. Not only was there no discernible motive – the old woman had little to leave her only heir and, however irritating, could hardly be believed to have goaded anyone into murdering her out of pure malice – but it was accepted that a person pushed from so great a height would let out a scream, or at least an audible gasp. The sound widely reported to have emerged from Matilda's plummeting mother was a full-bodied laugh. Either from tact or apathy, the old woman was allowed to have lost her footing.

'The grass can be slippery up there,' the policeman explained, 'even in summer. And there's a deceptive overhang. Could happen to anybody.'

The possibility of self-murder dangled between them

unacknowledged. Matilda had been brought up to trust in policemen and was happy not to question their wisdom now.

The funeral had been excruciatingly embarrassing. The sole surviving relative, she had assumed she could slip quietly down for the day and see the whole business conducted swiftly and with no fuss. The matron of the home had greeted her tearfully, of course, but one expected some of that; a good show of solicitude was one of the things one paid her for. But then the wretched woman announced that so many *friends* had been telephoning and calling round since the *unhappy event* that she had felt obliged to lay on a small spread of sandwiches, cakes and tea. Matilda's mother, it appeared, had actually made herself popular. Very popular. In her discussion with the recommended local undertaker, Matilda had booked the smaller of the two crematorium chapels, not wishing to have a grim event made grimmer by having to preside over the coffin as sole mourner in a grotesquely large space. There were already some thirty people waiting eagerly in their pews when she drew up behind the hearse, however. By the time the priest was intoning the opening sentences – again she had requested the smallest possible rite, with no fuss and no hymns – so many mourners had arrived that a crowd of them was forced to remain outside the open doors, craning their necks and discreetly jockeying for a better view. Young, aged, men, women, smart and down-at-heel, white, brown, swarthy and even Oriental; they were so heterogenous a crowd, so entirely not the kind of friends she might have expected a woman of her mother's age and background to have acquired, that she actually wondered if she had followed the wrong hearse and attended the wrong funeral. They all pressed around to wring her by the hand afterwards, however, and pursued her back across the town to the rest home for a funeral tea that was little short of riotous. Few of them were wearing black so she felt herself conspicuous in their colourful midst as a raven caught up in a chattering flock of budgerigars. This, like the ruling out of suicide, was some consolation in such a crisis; her status as chief mourner and sole next of kin was apparent for all to see.

The token servings of milky tea were soon superseded by alcohol as bottles of wine, and even stronger stuff, were smilingly presented and thirstily splashed into disposable cups. In her anxiety to have the ordeal done with as soon as possible, Matilda had fondly assumed that, once the small rafts of sandwiches, Battenburg and Jaffa Cake mis-shapes had been swept away, the guests would show some sense of decorum and take their leave. Rather, bags of crisps and small boxes of sausage rolls began to materialize. One ridiculous woman even broke merrily into what appeared to be her week's supply of grocery shopping, brought along to the funeral in several plastic bags.

'Plenty more where this came from,' she said and gaily offered Matilda a selection of lurid fondant fancies. Matilda flinched but found herself taking the nearest one, in a kind of desperation. It was pink. It tasted pink. Impulsively she snatched a second before a man in a turban and medals could whisk them out of reach. Someone took away her teacup and thrust a beaker of warm Chardonnay into her unwary hand. She glanced at her watch, saw with alarm that it was nearly six, and drank.

She had not once felt tempted to tears during the funeral. Ritual and the iron laws of good behaviour had saved her from that. As this unstructured, seemingly endless celebration continued, however, she repeatedly felt her nose-tip tingle and her tear ducts burn. Guest after guest came to pay their respects. Several, deeply moved, did so more than once. Some described themselves as friends of her mother's – women who played her at gin rummy, who knew her from her watercolour class – but many freely confessed to only a slight acquaintance but a strong impression of her character. There was a man from the library she had regularly dealt with, who recalled her taste for the most challenging modern fiction. A Hindu couple who often met her walking on the cliff paths cherished vivid recollections of a long conversation she had begun on the subject of the afterlife.

'We don't understand it,' she was told repeatedly. 'She seemed so happy-go-lucky', 'So bursting with vim', 'So audacious', 'So funny'.

She told the first few that the police had diagnosed an accident but she felt crushed by their sad, understanding little smiles of reply and, refusing to give them further opportunity to humour her with simpers, made no further allusion to suicide and let them infer what they pleased.

The picture they built up of her mother could not have been further from the woman she knew. Her mother was independent certainly – it had been she who insisted on entering a rest home after her second hip replacement, waving aside Matilda's (admittedly half-hearted) offer of a new base in her spare room – but she was hardly merry. She had always struck her daughter as the quietly humourless sort, the kind of woman who works years in the corner of an office only to be distinguished by her eventual absence. They saw each other rarely. Matilda had followed her husband to the other side of the country and remained there alone on his death. They rarely spoke – each hated the telephone – but Matilda had been a dutiful correspondent, firing off a tidy three-and-a-half sides on blue Basildon Bond once a month. Her mother's replies were erratic, which Matilda put down to a lack of news in her life, and largely composed of dry comment on the gossip Matilda had passed on. She wondered if, were she to read them again, she would detect a note of vigorous, even cruel merriment in them.

The possibility that she had misjudged or underestimated her mother's character did not occur to her. Instead she felt wounded to the quick that her mother had felt the need to mute her natural exuberance when Matilda was around. Matilda was not partial to excessive display of any kind, even as a child, but she appreciated vivacity in its place. The thought that her mother had suppressed such a side to herself, had been on dully good behaviour in her daughter's presence, awakened at once a sensation of profound regret at losing a companion whose company she might, after all, have enjoyed and of shock at the bitter possibility that here was an older woman who had not *liked* her.

'Don't be silly', she was fond of telling her more yielding friends when family matters were discussed. 'Like or not like doesn't come into it. They're your family. They're what you're born to. They're the only people in your life you don't get to choose.'

But she had always spoken, however bracingly, from the secure belief that her mother had loved her with unquestioning loyalty, however vague or erratic its expression. Admittedly her feelings towards her mother had long since cooled to the merely dutiful, but she allowed herself the odd crisis of sentimental warmth at birthdays and Christmas, and soothed any pangs of conscience with the thought that the love of the young for the old was, by its very nature, a less vigorous growth than the helpless bond between mother and child.

At last she could bear it no longer. The matron was tearfully recounting the happy evenings she and Matilda's mother – 'more like a pal than a resident really' – had spent at the cinema on the sea front and how very up-to-date her mother's taste in films had become, when Matilda felt a great surge of childish envy pass over her, a wave of bilious heat. How *dared* this woman, any of these people, lay such tender claim to her mother? *Hers!*

Leaning against the hostess trolley in which the matron had seen fit, in view of the hour and the lingering guests, to warm up some individual meat pies, she cried tears of outrage, hot on cheeks tired from smiling. The matron was kindness itself, quite prepared to break up *the little party* but Matilda, who hated scenes, seized the opportunity of escape and, with a quick moan about the sudden need for solitude and fresh air, hurried out through the gathering crowd to the front door. Her first thought was only of peace, which was swiftly found in such a quiet neighbourhood, but a natural momentum seemed to drive her down the garden path, out of the gate and along the road towards the sea.

The house was on the genteel side of town, in a district of large, outmoded Victorian mansions on streets named after long forgotten Bavarian resorts. The sea was clearly visible at intervals between cedars or over shrubberies, and the air was bracing, but the houses nestled a safe distance from the palmy turmoil of the esplanade. Golf links lay close to hand (inexplicably her mother had refused to take up the sport despite the benefit the exercise would have done her figure) and helped preserve the area's tranquillity. Rosenheim Avenue ended abruptly with the golf course club house beside which lay the beginning of a cliff top footpath.

The grass was mown, there was a sign enforcing a pooper-scoop bylaw and, here and there, wooden benches had been constructed a little higher than usual to make them easier for less flexible citizens to vacate. Thus tempted, Matilda walked on for some ten minutes, recovering her composure and admiring the first hints of a sunset. A few last golfers were striding about the links in pastels but apart from a young man with an old dog she met no one on the path. Relishing the sense of being quite alone again, she sat on a bench with a fine view out to sea and back towards the esplanade. Seagulls wheeled and dropped, cackling, into their colonies on the cliff face below her. Occasionally she heard a shout or a burst of laughter from the beach. As a girl she had loved heights. She used to stand right on the edge, whooping into the wind, until her mother called her back. At some stage, puberty probably, she acquired a fear of them, however. She grew taller and wiser and learned geological dread and social embarrassment as if by the same hormonal process. Her husband could not understand this. He made her ride lifts to the top of towers to teeter out on pigeon-haunted platforms. He convinced her that if she lay on her belly to peer over a cliff edge it was less dizzying but she found it all the more so, like some film effect where an actor was meant to be hanging from a window ledge and one knew they were lying on their belly in front of a back projection. Once she was doing this, at his insistence, when he lifted her feet off the ground *for a joke*. It was the cause of their first major argument and caused her to fall out of love with him.

Matilda closed her eyes and basked. There was still some heat in the sun. This was where her mother had walked. This, or somewhere near it, was where she had brought her watercolours and talked with the young Asian couple. This was where she had jumped.

She opened her eyes again abruptly. Had her mother walked calmly to the edge or made her way gingerly? Had she perhaps sat on the precipice first then bounced off as one might from a low wall? Had she made herself drunk beforehand? That would, at least, explain her reported laughter. The bench was some forty feet from where the grass began its gentle slope down to the void but Matilda shuddered and glanced instinctively over her shoulder and grasped tight on the bench wood as though some malevolent stranger were about to give her a murderous shove from behind. There was no one there of course. The sunset was beginning in earnest, dyeing some clouds an unpleasant shade of salmon pink not unlike the curtains in her late mother's room.

'I should be getting back,' she said aloud, surprising herself with the sound of her own voice. Mutely she wondered if a single plastic cup of wine could have been enough to inebriate her.

In the distance she made out a small boy running along the path towards her. He could not have been more than eight, although, childless, she considered herself a poor judge of age in the young. He was solidly built, his little legs pounding like pistons. His head was down, his small arms pumping. She sat back to watch him, remembering the childish pleasure of following a narrow path with the blind obedience of a train. If anyone were to meet him walking in the other direction, she had no doubt that they would have to stand aside to let him pass. As he drew closer, she saw that he was in school uniform: grey shorts, a short-sleeved grey shirt and a purple tie. At least, she assumed they must be uniform. No modern mother would dress her child so formally. One saw so few children in uniform now. It was something she missed. Children now seemed barely to touch upon a childish phase before they were hanging around on buses and street corners like so many vengeful unemployed. Children had become insolent, even intimidating. She was glad she had not become a teacher. Her youthful ambition had been based on recent memories of a school where girls wore elegant brown gymslips over cream blouses and where teachers called Miss This or Mrs That were regarded with a respect approaching adoration.

She rose to go but as she returned to the path she glanced back along it. The boy's face was red with the effort of running and as he drew closer she saw that he was crying. She avoided addressing children as a rule but something in his uniform and pitiful state inspired confidence. She stood until he approached her, his run slowing to a panting walk. He was rather chubby. There was a deep cut on his knee which needed a mother's attention; a dab of iodine and perhaps a bandage to make him feel a hero. She mustered her kindest smile.

'Hello? Is something the matter?'

He glanced around him, at the sea, at the grass, bashful in his tears.

'I . . . I've lost my mother.'

So few children called their mother's that anymore. He was nicely spoken too. Like a child from an old film.

'Oh. Oh dear. Where did you see her last?'

'I . . . I'm not sure. Here somewhere. I've been looking for simply ages.' As a slightly cross note entered his voice, he looked at her, his small, black eyes searching her face as if only just noticing her.

'Well why don't you blow your nose, first, then you can tell me all about it and I'll see what I can do. Have you got a handkerchief?'

He searched his pockets, producing string, some shells and a quantity of what looked like seaweed.

'Lost it,' he said and seemed about to cry again.

'Here,' she told him and passed him hers. 'It's quite clean.'

'Thank you,' he said. He gave his nose and eyes a perfunctory wipe before handing it back to her. He looked calmer now, almost distinguished. She thought back to her girlhood, to the panic of losing her mother while shopping, to the constant, trustless fear of being wilfully left behind at the swings and slides, in a hospital, on a beach . . . Mothers nowadays were so slatternly.

'Where do you live?' she asked.

'I . . . I can't remember.'

'Oh. Well. What's your name?'

'Tom.'

'I'm Matilda.'

'Hello.'

'Well it's going to get dark in about an hour so I suggest I take you to a telephone and we call a nice policeman to help us out.'

'Thank you.'

Entirely trusting, he put his hand in hers. Despite the run he had just taken, it felt cool. She wondered if he was in shock. She glanced at his knee. Blood was trickling down to the rim of his sock and soaking in. Perhaps there had been an accident. Perhaps the poor thing's mother had slipped and fallen and he was too traumatized to recall anything. Welcoming the diversion from her own, sad affairs as she did any opportunity to take responsible charge of a situation, she began to lead him back towards the town. There was nobody else in sight. The club house was further than she remembered.

'Are you on holiday?' she asked.

'No,' he said. 'Are you?'

'No I was . . . visiting a friend.'

As she said this the weight of her mother's death and that afternoon's grim rituals seemed to slip away from her and she received a fleeting intuition that her mother was a good age and had spared herself the indignity of senility. She had also, in a curious way, set Matilda free from an implicit burden of guilt and frustrated duty. Matilda had no ties. No husband. No mother. She was free as air. She could emigrate. She could dye her hair. She could run a little wild. She had been at liberty to do all these things for some time, of course, ever since her widowing, but the knowledge that she still had a mother, albeit a fiercely independent one, had placed a check on her.

They were reaching an upward slope in the path. Strangely elated, almost gay, she squeezed the boy's hand and began to sing to cheer him up.

'*The grand old Duke of York,*
He had ten thousand men . . .'

She stamped in time to the tune.

'*He marched them up to the top of the hill* . . . Do you know this?' she asked him, breaking off.

By way of answer the boy swung her hand in his and sang back,

'*And he marched them down again.*
The grand old Duke of . . .'

Together they marched and sang to the top of the gentle incline. The club house seemed so far away still she could almost believe they had been walking in circles, or on the spot, were that not patently absurd. She sighed to herself, foreseeing a visit to a police station, time-consuming giving of statements, a reunion with some unsuitable, probably unmarried mother and a delayed journey home to her London friends, perhaps even an enforced night in some bleak hotel full of pensioners and friendless sales reps.

'Can you skip?' the boy asked cheerfully.

'Of course,' she said.

He began to skip, tugging her along so that she was obliged to skip too to keep in step.

'*He marched them up to the top of the hill*
And he marched them down . . .'

What did it matter? What did anything matter? There was no

one to see her behaving so inanely and what if there were? She had no plans to return. She had forgotten what fun skipping was; the lilting step, its surprising, elegant swiftness. And the view was delightful from this point. Small boats on the water, a row of palms on the promenade, a grand hotel, creamy pink in the setting sun. She laughed as she sang, growing quite breathless, and glanced down at the boy, happy that she should have raised his spirits so effortlessly and her own in the process. He glanced back at her, black eyes shining like a small bird's, sharp little teeth clenched in a grin.

Quite suddenly they swerved off the path and were skipping across the grass towards the dangerous slope. Taking this for youthful high spirits, she tried to tug him back towards safety, but he yanked her along with him.

'Stop,' she cried, imperious now. 'Tom, stop it. This is silly. Tom!'

He ignored her. His fingers had imperceptibly changed their position so that instead of enlacing with hers they were now grasping her by the wrist. His grasp, like the force in his fat little arm, seemed steely as a grown man's.

'Stop it! You'll make me fall. Stop!'

She swung her hand out at a last passing bench but missed her grip on it, succeeding only in grazing her wrist painfully as she flew by.

He had stopped the ridiculous song and stopped skipping. Now he was running, with that same pistoning movement she had seen him use in the distance, pulling her with him towards the brink. As he ran he let out a piercing, incongruous whoop of delight, as though he were merely about to jump a ha-ha or vault a fallen tree. One of her shoes came off and, hobbling, she cried out as she stamped on a thistle mat. Then her stockinged foot slipped into a rabbit hole bringing her flat on her face mere inches from the cliff. To her horror, the dreadful, crazed child seemed to fly onwards, still whooping. His hand wrenched from her, sending a spasm of agony through her wrist. Perhaps it was the Chardonnay taking effect on her imagination but she fancied his triumphant cry was tinged with fury in the seconds before it stopped.

For a full minute she lay face downwards, winded, snatching pained breaths, assuring herself that she was still safe and that her ankle and wrist were unbroken, then she clumsily hauled herself to her knees and lurched abruptly backwards, sickened at the dazzling void before her. Impelled, dreading what she was about to see, she inched forward on her hands and knees to the very edge. Perhaps there was a grassy ledge only feet below. Perhaps the little wretch knew about it and played this trick regularly by way of tasteless sport. She steeled herself for his hideous 'boo' of surprise.

There was no ledge. She saw, quite clearly, that there was no trace of him. The seagulls were crowding over a dawdling beach refuse cart, not the freshly pulped corpse of a stout little boy. He must have tricked her, jumped sideways and sprinted back across the grass as she fell. Doubtless he was watching her indignity and fear from behind a bush and giggling.

To her horror a middle-aged couple out walking had spotted her and hurried with their dog across the grass.

'Are you all right?' the man asked.

'The grass gets so slippery. You should be careful,' his wife added accusingly.

'I'm fine, thank you,' Matilda told them gruffly as they helped her up. 'I wanted to look over the edge, at the nesting birds, and my foot went in a rabbit hole.'

'Your other shoe.' The man returned it with a ridiculous, caring expression on his insipid face.

'Thanks,' she told him. 'I'll be fine. Honestly. Thank you.'

She dismissed them. They were treating her like some old thing escaped from a residential hotel.

As they continued their walk, talking, she slipped her shoe back on and made her own way back to the path, shaking the grass and mud from her clothes as best she could and determined to appear as untroubled as possible. She glowered at the nearest clumps of gorse and thornbush. She would not give the little bastard the satisfaction of seeing her upset.

Pausing to blow her nose and make a few repairs to her appearance on the corner before the rest home, she reached into her pocket for her handkerchief and was revolted to find it quite wet. She drew it from her pocket. He had scarcely dabbed his eyes and nose with it yet it was soaked, almost dripping. With a spasm of revulsion, she thrust it into a neatly clipped hedge and walked on. Dabbing at her nose with the back of her hand, she frowned to discover that even a brief contact with the wet linen had left her fingers as pungently briny as a fishmonger's.

OLD BOYS

for Susanna Martelli

THE LAST VERSE of the school hymn was stirring stuff about strapping on breastplates, guarding imperilled shores and standing shoulder to shoulder against some unidentified foe. Foreigners presumably, or Sin. Boys in the gallery, spared the embarrassment of sitting with family, bellowed the familiar words with the clannish fervour of a rugby crowd. Below them, the fourteen diminutive choristers piped a descant, barely audible above the efforts of the heartier element. Wives, fragrant and carefully dressed for a long, summer day, faces raised over hymnals, delighted in the relative fragility of their own voices.

'But of course it's sexy. It's *desperately* sexy,' Elsa had insisted as they were dressing that morning. 'You can't imagine. Standing there surrounded by all that young masculinity. The odour of testosterone is quite overpowering. I'd *love* to be a headmaster's wife. I'd be a tremendous tease, wearing lots of scent and rustly silk things.'

The chaplain commanded them to prayer and the chapel filled briefly with the sounds of thumping knees, dropped hymn books and skittering leather cushions. Colin glanced across at Elsa, her lovely face partly shaded by a hat brim, subtly painted lips barely parted, eyes obediently closed. He could imagine her here, as a master's wife, jet black hair shaken out over a tumbled silk headscarf, hugging herself against the cold on a playing field touchline, calling out, 'Come on House!' with a fine show of loyalty then catching the eye of a nearby prefect and making him blush. She would be bewitching and shameless and boys would jostle to sit by her at lunch so as to admire her cleavage. On the whole, he decided, she was safer cloistered in her cubby hole at the World Service; left too long in an environment like this one, she would become more than ever like the young

Elizabeth Taylor and prove the catalyst for some drama of horrific erotic violence.

Between them Harry clasped his hands tightly together and recited the Lord's Prayer slightly too loud. He had a summer cold and had just started confirmation classes. Elsa looked first at him then at Colin, smiling mischievously over their son's head.

This, of course, had been her idea. She had often said that she thought Harry should follow in his father's footsteps and he had only recently seen that she meant it seriously. He had promised himself that no child of his would be sent away to boarding school but already Elsa had persuaded him to parcel Harry off to an eminently respectable prep school in the South Downs where, apparently, the small boy thrived on pre-breakfast Latin. Enjoying lazy Saturday mornings in bed at an age when most of his contemporaries were woken at nine o'clock sharp and dragged off to fly kites and throw rugger balls, Colin was coming to understand the terms of the similar betrayal his parents had practised on him at the same age. Public school, however, was different. He had always sworn he would draw the line there, that Harry would attend an excellent day school, with girls in every year, not just the sixth form. Somewhere he could drop Latin for Spanish or Italian. And yet here he was attending an old boys' day for the first time since leaving the place eighteen years ago with a view to *casing the joint*, as Elsa put it, for Harry.

'If he doesn't like it, mind you,' he had stipulated, 'if he has the slightest reservation –'

'Then he doesn't have to go,' Elsa broke in, reassuring him with a soft touch on the back of his fist.

And Harry adored her. Colin remembered loathing his mother at that age, never forgiving her for sending him away. Yet Harry still seemed to drink Elsa in with his eyes. She handled him so well, Colin reflected. She knew when to be sweet, when to be boyishly joshing, when to be sexy. And she *was* sexy with him. Colin had watched the care with which she chose clothes for the boy's Sundays out of school. She tended to wear firmer bras for him and clinging cashmere.

'Little boys like tits, silly,' she explained. 'Haven't you noticed? All the popular boys have mums who are a bit, well . . .' and she smoothed down her jersey in explanation, smiling to herself.

'Well?' she asked as they left the chapel and headed out into a flagstoned quadrangle where swallows swooped through the sunshine in search of flies. 'Are the happy memories flooding back?'

'Not really,' he said. 'Thank God most of my teachers seem to have left.'

'Probably dead,' Harry piped up.

'Thank you, Harry,' Colin told him.

'What about friends? Surely you recognize somebody?'

'No,' Colin said, faintly relieved. 'Not yet. Let's go and find some lunch.'

'Sherry with the housemaster first,' she reminded him.

'Oh fuck.'

'Harry!' Elsa seemed genuinely surprised but could not help smile at the evident pride on Harry's face at having produced an adult expletive in adult company. 'Darling!' she added and chuckled, patting his shoulder.

They drifted with the noisy crowd out of the quadrangle and Harry expressed a wish to piss.

'I'll wait here,' Elsa said, arranging herself on a bench below a towering horse chestnut. 'Don't be long. I'm thirsty.'

Following a line of instinctive memory, Colin led his son along a corridor, across another quadrangle and into a dingy, green-tiled lavatory where they peed side by side at a urinal and then, only because each had the other with them, laboriously washed their hands.

The old swathes of graffiti had been painted over and the roller towels had been replaced with hot air hand driers but the room retained an inexpungable dankness and a threatening quality. For the first time that day, Colin was assailed by memories, none of them sunny ones. He flinched instinctively when three tall boys burst noisily in through the swing door. He panicked that Harry was taking so long over drying his hands, then remembered that he was forty-one and these hulking bullies had become children. The boys fell respectfully silent and went seriously about their business as he shepherded Harry back into the sunlight.

'How do people know if it's a ladies or a gents?' Harry asked. 'There's no sign on the door.'

'There aren't any ladies,' Colin told him. 'And when there are I suppose they just hold on until they find somewhere safe.'

Elsa came smiling from beneath the tree to meet them.

'I just met Keith Bedford,' she said.

'Who?'

'He's a newscaster,' Harry explained patiently.

'You never told me he was here with you,' she went on.

'He wasn't.'

'Well he said he was.'

'Must be younger than me, then. You never remember the younger ones because they were so unimportant. They didn't count.'

'You boys are so hard and peculiar.'

Elsa took his arm as they cut back across the first quadrangle and headed out onto a broad stone path that lay along one side of a huge lawn studded with old plane trees and bounded by a high flint wall. Colin was surprised that Harry forsook his habitual place on Elsa's other side and came to walk beside his father, touched perhaps by the exclusive maleness of the place. Again she caught Colin's eye and gave him a discreet smile. At such times, when some parents would be saddened at their impotence in the face of nature, she seemed soothed, taking little reminders of biological determination as signs of a covenant that, having produced a perfectly adjusted male, she could soon relinquish all responsibility for him. Colin sighed.

'What is it?' she asked.

'I'd forgotten it was so beautiful. It's idyllic, really. Do you like it, Harry?'

'It's okay,' said Harry. 'It's very big. Isn't there a playground?'

'All this,' Colin said gesturing at the trees tall as cathedrals, the old wrought iron benches, the distant cloisters. 'This is the playground.'

With perfect timing, a troop of boys in military uniform jogged out from behind the rifle range and went puffing pinkly by, in tight formation. Harry turned to stare openly.

'Would I have to do that?' he asked.

'Only if you wanted to. Well, actually, everyone has to do it for a year then you can give it up and do social work instead if you prefer.'

'Social work?'

'Doing gardening for old ladies, clearing weeds from the river, helping out at a school for the handicapped, that sort of thing. There was even a group that helped build houses on a sort of estate for the unfortunate somewhere.'

'You're joking, of course,' Elsa said.

'God's own truth.'

They walked on past the art gallery, the theatre workshop, the music school, the serried tablets to the loyal fallen in the War, Cloisters and the house famous for having produced a prominent fascist, two trade union leaders and at least three Russian spies amongst its boys.

'Those were just the ones that got caught,' chuckled Elsa. 'Perhaps Harry could be a spy? His languages are getting so good.'

'There it is,' said Colin and pointed.

They were out on a public street now, but every plot of land and building in sight was still school property. Up ahead loomed Colin's old house. It was a towering red brick affair with turrets, curious flint teeth around each window and such a mess of fire

escapes and extensions added on that it was hard to tell which
was the front and which the back. A bevy of well-upholstered
female servants, fraudulently got up in black and white for the
occasion instead of their usual nylon housecoats, were variously
directing guests to the cloakrooms, handing them sherry or waving them on out to join the crowd in the garden where their
sisters circulated with trays of canapés.

'Look, darling. That was Daddy's house. You could go there.'

'Why?' asked Harry, singularly unimpressed.

'It's no beauty,' Colin confessed. 'If you want to live in the
really old bit by the chapel as well as having your lessons there,
you'll have to go in for the scholarship exam.'

'You must be joking,' said Harry and Colin abandoned the
briefly dangled possibility of annual holidays somewhere hot
which a scholarship would have afforded them. Elsa demonstrated her frightening ability to read his mind.

'We can start borrowing mummy's cottage in Devon,' she
said with a quick smile into the air before her. 'Oh look, Harry,
they've put out a trampoline in the garden. Do you want to
have a go?'

At last, just when he was congratulating himself on their
absence, Colin began to meet contemporaries from his days at
the school. They were none of them friends – sex, geography,
money and, in one case, death, had dismantled all his schoolboy
friendships. The thickening silhouettes before him were merely
those of old acquaintance. In every case he found himself remembering not only a name but a nickname and at least one cruel fact
to which they would be vulnerable; an armoury of psychological
stings – flat feet, ginger pubic hair, a tendency to stutter, dead
fathers, alcoholic mothers – which he reached for out of a long
dormant instinct to wound before he was wounded. They stood
around on the lawn holding their careers against each other's
to compare them for size, inspecting one another's wives and
mustering a chortling *bonhomie* which in seven out of eight cases
Colin estimated to be entirely phoney. Acute discomfort drove

them all to assume the speech patterns of men twenty years their senior, of their fathers, in fact.

'You called that man *old chap*,' Elsa said, appalled, as they were herded in through an entrance hall as drab as Colin remembered, to the sludge green dining room where a *fork luncheon* awaited them. 'You never talk like that.'

'I know,' he said. 'I'm sorry. It just slipped out. I think it's infectious.'

'The housemaster's a darling.'

'Really? We haven't spoken.'

'Oh really, Colin, that's what we're here for. Go and introduce yourself. He's the one by the fireplace with the toddler on his hip and the smile.'

'But he looks about twenty-five.'

'He is. Much healthier than the crusty types you had in your day. And the wife's no battleaxe either.'

Colin did as he was told and spoke with the housemaster who was, indeed, a darling. There was something of Peter Pan about him and Colin realized that this was why he was good at his job. A part of his development seemed to have been arrested. He had failed to acquire the calloused outer layer that marked every other man in the room. He spoke to boys with the authority of a gentle older brother and to fathers with the cheerful respect-fulness of their ideal son. He was enthusiastic about everything from crab vol-au-vents to the school viol consort. His irony was confected from natural wit rather than harsh experience. He was entirely unsuited to life in an adult community. Colin was surprised, after introducing Harry then having a chat that seemed to be about nothing of any consequence, to hear the man say, 'Well we'd be delighted to have him in the house, provided he passes the exams, of course . . .'

'Oh,' Colin said. 'Well, then. Thanks very much. I'll tell Elsa the good news.'

They shook hands and Harry's small fate was sealed. Colin glanced out of the window and saw his son sitting on a low wall

crumbily munching a meringue and watching some comparatively huge boys kick a football about a caged-in yard. He was
disturbed at how the boy was finding his place as swiftly and
naturally as a newly weaned addition to some fiercely hierarchical
animal society.

Elsa was one of those rare women with a genuine interest in
cricket. She came from a long line of cricketers and, being an
only child, had received the full benefit of her father's instruction.
She liked knowledge, particularly when it had so little practical
application. It pleased Colin to watch her sweep aside the patron-
age of cricketing men with the breadth of her understanding,
not least because he had not a sporting bone in his body. When
he took her a cup of coffee, he found her arguing a fine point
of test match history with a tall, mop-headed youth who wore
the kind of cricketing jersey only permitted to members of the
school's first team; a deity, in schoolboy terms, yet she was
winning the argument.

'But then,' she sighed, gently tapping the youth's broad chest
with one long finger, having pressed home her triumphant point,
'I can see you're an expert. What do *I* know? I've never even
played the game.'

The youth flushed as Elsa turned to Colin. 'Coffee. How
lovely. Darling, this is Hargraves.'

Hargraves offered Colin a hand. 'How do you do, sir.'

'Marvellous to be called sir,' Elsa said. 'Madam always sounds
supercilious and shopkeepery.'

'He's offered Harry a place,' Colin told her. 'Subject to exams,
of course.'

'But of course he did.'

'I thought I'd take a look round. See how things have changed.
Want to come?'

Elsa wrinkled her nose.

'Changing rooms and things? Do we have to? I was going to
catch the start of the match. Hargraves can show me the way.'

'Of course I can,' said Hargraves.

Glad to have a chance to explore on his own, Colin took a second coffee and wandered off. The house was on its best behaviour, the presence of parents neutering its habitual rowdiness but here and there its true nature pierced the skin of decorum with a reassuringly rude noise. Colin inspected the changing room, rank with sweat and sweet shampoo, the pitifully stocked library, the day room, and a new study block, where, from the momentarily hostile glances, he sensed he had interrupted something and retreated. Here and there, boys unhampered by family were engaged in small acts of vandalism or self-improvement. One little older than Harry pored over a surprisingly undistinguished newspaper, frowning at a pouting model's breasts as though checking through a page of algebraic calculations. Uncertain of what he was looking for – some confirmation perhaps that these familiar scenes were not so irrelevant as they now felt – Colin walked back to the staircase and made for the dormitories. Here, too, little had changed. There were still no radiators or curtains but the old, thin mattresses which dipped in the middle had been replaced. He sat on a bed and was happy to find that it still betrayed the slightest movement with a creak. He walked to one of the big windows, merciless in cold weather, and saw a crowd of visitors trailing over the athletics track below towards the cricket fields nearer the river. A woman turned and called out. It was Elsa. He saw Harry sprinting to catch up with her. The boy looked up to chatter to her as they walked. If he liked the place, did Colin have the right to deprive him of the experience?

Thinking he should join them, he left his coffee cup on a chest of drawers and started back along the dormitory corridor. He passed an open door and looked in just long enough to recognize the face of a large man peering up at the beams. He moved swiftly on, halted when he heard people on the stairs and doubled back to dart into the linen room. He sat on a bench where he would not be visible from the door. He needed to recover. His heart pounded as though he had just run up the stairs. Sweat beaded on his forehead and he swept it away with a handkerchief. It was him, unmistakably him. The black hair had grown grizzled, the rangy frame become slightly leaner but the thick eyebrows and large, once-broken nose had been instantly recognizable. Colin touched the handkerchief to his upper lip recalling how the man's eyes dropped to meet his for a fraction of a second before Colin hurried on.

❦

The day room was where all but the eldest boys spent their free time and evenings. It was high-ceilinged and L-shaped. Around the walls huddled wooden cubicles. Each boy had a cubicle. It comprised a desk, a cupboard, a bench and an electric light, all of them ancient. This cramped territory – sizes varied and the less cramped ones were highly sought after – was the only space in the entire school wherein one could be moderately private. The new boy had to make a mental adjustment in which the cluster of rooms, garden, pets and family he called home was compressed into a space a Victorian street urchin would have scorned. Here his individuality could be expressed in postcards, ornaments, toys, a choice of curtain and cushion cover, a store of food and even a corrugated plastic roof. Here, too, he would learn his first brutal lessons in the danger of expressing individuality of the wrong sort.

Colin and, crucially, Colin's mother, had been drilled in these matters by an older cousin. The cousin was still at the school but would be prevented, on his honour, from coming to Colin's assistance or in any way singling him out, once Colin joined him there. Colin had been scrupulous. His curtain and cushion were of a wholly unremarkable green fabric. He had no photographs of his parents but, at his sudden insistence, had brought along one of his older sister looking sulky in a bathing costume. This he pinned up alongside a calendar with a different dog breed pictured every month. He brought no toys, nothing whatever of especial monetary or sentimental value beyond a tinny transistor radio. Yet somehow, obscurely, he was found wanting.

At first insignificant violence was offered him, daring him to react and so give an excuse for fiercer reprisals. Boys would trip him from behind – *ankle-walking* it was called – as he passed along the corridor from the dining room. He was flicked with wet towel-corners when queuing for a washbasin. They made small verbal attacks, too, mocking, relying on the support of those around them.

'Hey!' they would call. 'Hey, you!'

'Yes?' he would ask, turning.

'Nothing,' came the smirking reply. 'Nothing.'

And by common consent, Nothing, then Nuts became his nickname, until long after anyone could remember the reason why.

'Above all you must learn not to react,' his cousin had insisted. Everyone, it seemed, went through a period of being picked upon but the brief spell of initiation could be prolonged into indefinite persecution if the would-be initiate gave the wrong sort of encouragement. So Colin met whips, trippings and mockery with polite equanimity, if not quite gratitude.

He wrote home saying how much he was enjoying himself, and there *were* things to enjoy. He enjoyed singing, with no great finesse, in the school choral society. He took up pottery and made an ashtray for his father. He won a small measure of popularity among his immediate peers as cox of the first year rowing team – even if this did mean being tossed into freezing river water whenever they lost a race. But as well as being designed to transfer all one's respect from the adults – who vanished from view and consequently power soon after six o'clock – to the prefects, the school's social system induced a tantalizing sense that there were unspeakably grown-up pleasures to be tasted, if only one could chance on some secret password.

He was kept from despair by the salutary spectacle of other boys, often well into their second year, who had been cast forever beyond acceptance and were fair game even for *new bugs* like himself to tease. There was one with grotesquely protuberant ears who appeared to have given up washing, one who could easily be provoked to spectacular tantrums in which he actually stamped his feet and cried and a third, called Bollocks, because his balls had still not dropped, who babbled in a high-pitched voice about the consolations of Christianity even as one tore his essays and scattered his textbooks into muddy puddles. The one with the ears and sour smell was later diagnosed as a schizo-phrenic, but only once exposed to a society with marginally less appetite for aberration, in his first year at university.

Colin's initiation came six weeks into his first term, on a Sunday night. Sundays were always a dangerous time. Envy was in the air, because some boys had been whisked out to lunch by their parents and a bogus holiday mood tended to curdle without warning. A few boys were still trying to finish their Saturday night essays but most were idle, bored and fractious, their dissatis-faction fuelled by a thorough perusal of that other world of luxuries and freedom paraded so unfeelingly through the Sunday colour supplements. It was the housemaster's night off, which meant he was more thoroughly absent than usual, being interruptible only *in extremis*. A boy had once been blinded with a fencing foil on a Sunday night. Only last Sunday evening, the day room had taken on a nightmarish air when someone pro-duced a set of darts stolen from the pub and began throwing them at people's ankles for a laugh. Colin's cousin had warned him about Sunday nights. Colin was duly lying low in his cubicle behind his irreproachable curtain, reading Balzac and trying not to be noticed. A fight with cartons of gone-off milk had flared and died. A game of table tennis was threatening to turn nasty. Someone was playing *Dark Side of the Moon* yet again, with the usual cluster of boys gathered religiously to mouth the lyrics and strum imaginary guitars. Any minute the youngest *new bug* would be called on to ring the bell for evening prayers. Only minutes lay between Balzac and the relative safety of a frosty bed.

It was a rogue attack, begun by Bollocks in an extravagant bid for acceptance by the crowd. Colin was startled as the other boy whisked back the curtain and yelped, 'Do you accept Jesus as your personal saviour?'

A few boys jeered out of habit, mocking the squeaky voice and stutter but others simply gathered to watch.

'I'm not sure,' Colin admitted.

'Do you accept Jesus as your personal saviour?' Bollocks repeated and Colin decided to gamble on his superior status, as would-be initiate over pariah.

'Why should I?' he jeered. 'Sp-sp-spastic features!'

For a moment it was uncertain which way the scene would turn, as Bollocks groped in his sports jacket for something, then he produced a can of lighter fuel, liberally anointed the curtain and pronounced, 'Then, heretic, you fry.'

And he struck a match. Colin swore and shrank back into his cubicle as the air filled with the smoke and the irreproachable green was engulfed in flames. Then one of the third years, secure in his status as a useful football player and twenty-a-day smoker, decided that Bollocks was going too far. To loud cheers, he set off a fire extinguisher, dowsing the flames then turning the jet on the pariah. Seizing the moment, Colin dashed out to land a vigorous kick on Bollocks's backside but he had misjudged the feelings of the crowd.

He was grabbed. His trousers and underpants were gleefully tugged down around his ankles and he was bent over the ping-pong table while his arse was given a stinging *douche* from what remained in the fire extinguisher. When that was no longer deemed amusing, hot, bony hands hoisted him into one of the large plastic dustbins and a saucer of meatily rancid butter was pressed down on his hair. When he tried to clear it off it was followed by a faceful of long-forgotten milk and something wet and nameless down the back of his shirt. Blinded and fighting back the urge to retch, Colin flailed out wildly in his effort to keep his balance, as his tormentors lifted the dustbin into the air.

Once his eyes were sufficiently clear to see where they were carrying him, he froze and swore again. The walls above the cubicles were clad in handsome wooden panelling which reached twelve feet or more. The panelling was very thick – built like that, perhaps, to disguise pipe work – and it was possible to clamber around the room on the top of it. Colin and his dustbin were hoisted overhead and, with much cheering, balanced precariously where two sections of the panel pathway formed a corner. Then the bell rang for evening prayers and the room emptied as everyone raced up the corridor to kneel at their chairs in the dining room. Apathetic sixth-formers drifted through from their studies to follow them. Most ignored him. One blew a gobbet of chewing gum at him and another shouted some witticism in German which raised a knowing laugh.

Then he was alone. Gingerly he tried to stand but the dustbin rocked sickeningly and he dropped back to crouching in the garbage. If he fell he had no doubt he would break his neck, or at best crack his skull, on the grimy parquet floor. He pictured his funeral. There would be white lilies and the headmaster would speak damningly and at length, summoning his murderers by name and making them pray around the coffin. There would be mass expulsions, reported in the national press and a new, fiercely disciplinarian regime would be instituted. First-years would keep Colin's name alive with tears of gratitude.

For the first time since his father had left him sitting on a trunk in Waterloo station six weeks before, Colin lowered his guard and allowed himself the luxury of homesick tears.

'Oh for fuck's sake!'

He blinked and looked over the rim of the dustbin. It was Hardy, one of the prefects and a senior officer in the school army corps. Tall, dark, terrifying, Hardy rarely spoke to his juniors, keeping discipline by the sheer authority of his presence. When he did speak, it tended to be with withering sarcasm.

'Sorry, Hardy,' Colin stammered, expecting to be punished for the wrongs done to him, which was the usual way.

'Can't you get down?'

'I . . . I don't think so.'

'Well in Christ's name stay still then.'

Hardy tossed the novel he had been carrying onto the ping-pong table then clambered over the cubicles below Colin and steadied the dustbin for him. 'Go on. Get out.'

Hastily tugging up his underwear and trousers, Colin clambered out onto the ledge. Hardy dropped the dustbin to the floor, magnificently impervious to the mess he created. He jumped down after it. Colin followed more carefully. Hardy looked at him and wrinkled his nose.

'You stink. Christ!'

'Sorry, Hardy.'

'Not your fault. What's your name?'

'Cowper.'

'Well take a shower, Cowper. Now.'

'But what about evening prayers?'

'Oh sod those. Come on.'

Hardy led the way to the changing room and through it to the showers, where the air was still ripe with cigarette smoke. While Colin hastily undressed, Hardy set a shower running. As Colin slipped in past him, he shut the door behind them then he lent against the wall casually smoking while Colin washed himself in the blast of hot water. Rubbing his pale skin with soap, he became aware of bits of him that had been scraped or bruised in the attack. He looked around for a bottle of shampoo and began to wash the butter out of his hair.

'It'll need more than that,' Hardy told him, tossing his cigarette stub into a puddle where it fizzled. 'Here. Let me.' He came to stand so close that the shower splashed onto his jeans and linen jacket leaving dark stains. Colin wondered if he was drunk.

'Give,' Hardy said and Colin passed him the shampoo. Hardy

179

filled his palm with the dark green liquid and began to rub it into Colin's scalp, brow furrowed with concentration.

At prep school, the assistant matrons — bored daughters of good families, marking time — used to let themselves into the bathrooms to wash one's hair. They were breezily teasing about his coyness and it was all acutely embarrassing. This was quite different. Hardy had been at the pub and his breath was sour-sweet with beer and tobacco. Their hands had scratched busily at his scalp as though conquering an itch but Hardy's hands moved slowly. His touch was no less firm but he used his finger-tips instead of his nails. He reached round to the back of Colin's head, while working fiercely at his temples with his thumbs. He was getting soaked. Colin felt wet denim against one of his thighs. He felt an overwhelming urge to pee and found, to his horror, that he was getting an erection. Desperate that Hardy shouldn't see it, he tried his usual technique of taking deep breaths and imagining his hand being cut off with a breadknife.

Outside the bell rang again, calling first years to bed. There was a stampede of boys out in the corridor. Any minute someone might come in for a smoke. Smiling faintly, as at some private joke, Hardy pushed Colin's head back into the water and began to comb away the lather with his fingers. Nothing would get rid of the erection. Panic seemed to be making things worse. Colin felt his cock actually brush against Hardy's jeans. Hardy spotted it and chuckled.

'What's this, eh?' He tapped at it experimentally with a huge, wet hand. Colin was mortified. He shut his eyes.

'I . . . I'm sorry, Hardy.'

He tried to turn away but the older boy still had a hand on the back of his neck. Pummelling his back, the water seemed to be getting hotter.

'For fuck's sake, stop apologizing,' Hardy told him. 'Look at me.'

Colin opened his eyes just in time to find Hardy bending down to kiss him. He gave a little yelp then was silenced by a rough mouth against his and the extraordinary sensation of a tongue plunging between his lips to seek out his own. The hand that was on the back of his neck slipped down until an arm grasped him across the shoulder blades while another hand slipped between his legs and began to wank him, vigorously.

Colin had only learnt to toss himself off a few weeks before. The age at which such knowledge was acquired depended entirely on the company into which chance threw a boy. He had risen swiftly through his prep school hierarchy and so found himself, at the age when he might have learned, captain of a comparatively prepubescent dormitory and thus deprived of exemplary demonstrations. He was haunted by painful erections, and the occasional wet dream, and forced to join in the smutty bragging of his peers in the hope that many were as ignorant as he. It was inconceivable that one might ask even a close friend how to masturbate, so he suffered in silence. On graduating to public school, he was placed at last in a mixed-age dormitory and had to wait only weeks before being made a party to a guffawing discussion of comparative techniques. Left hand, right hand, underwater, upside down against a sheet — suddenly he had not only knowledge, but choice. His experience of induced orgasm was still novel, so experiencing it at the hands of another was, literally, staggering. After freezing with his hands at his sides for a few seconds, he found his knees buckling and flung his arms around Hardy as though teetering on a cliff edge. He wanted to piss. He wanted to come. He wanted to cry out and he wasn't entirely sure he had not done all three by the time Hardy had done with him. Hardy took one last, long kiss then turned off the shower and held Colin's sobbing face to his chest.

'Well!' he said softly, as though the whole thing had surprised him too. 'Well, well.'

There were footsteps and chatter suddenly in the changing room and the door to the showers was flung open. Two fifth formers stood in the doorway, laughter dying in their throats.

They stared for a moment. Colin tried to pull away but Hardy held him close.

'Fuck off,' he told them.

'Sorry, Hardy,' one of them said. 'The lights were off and we didn't –'

'Just fuck off.'

'Sorry, Hardy.' They turned to go. Hardy called after them. 'Gilks?'

'Yes?' One turned.

'Leave your cigarettes on the step and we'll say no more about it.'

'Of course. Sorry, Hardy.' Gilks left his cigarettes and closed the door quietly behind him.

'Ignorant, *nouveau-riche* wankers,' Hardy muttered and started to chuckle. Colin looked up at him uncertainly as his chuckle turned to full-chested laughter. How could he take this crisis so lightly? Surely they were doomed now? Hardy ruffled his hair.

'What did you say your name was?' he asked.

'Cowper, Hardy.'

'This isn't quite a death camp. I meant your *Christian* name.' He lent a sour emphasis to the epithet, as to an obscenity.

'Oh. Sorry. It's Colin.'

'Colin,' Hardy murmured to himself as though trying the name out. He tugged someone's towel down off the hot pipes. 'Colin Cowper.' He wrapped it around Colin's shoulders. 'Well mine's Lucas.' He held out a hand and Colin obediently shook it. In the gloom he saw Hardy smile.

'Um. Hello,' Colin said.

'Know how to cook scrambled eggs?'

'Yes.'

'Good. You can make me some tomorrow.'

So saying, Hardy sloped out of the shower room, his soaked clothes leaving a trail of water. He tugged another towel down in passing and walked out, rubbing roughly at his hair.

*

The next day there was no scandal. Although Gilks and his friend would certainly have told everyone about what they had seen there was no allusion either to the dustbin episode or to Colin having been found in Hardy's embrace. Far from finding his initiation into house society compromised, Colin found himself suddenly, cosily in the ranks of the accepted. He was never teased or bullied again and, if any outsider threatened him, his elders in the house drew ranks to protect him. An intellectual as well as a sportsman, extravagantly hip yet not so rebellious as to damage the system he knocked, Hardy was a house hero. As his implicitly acknowledged *little man*, Colin attained an unofficial official position overnight, not unlike the pretty convict singled out as his cell mate by a respected murderer serving life. Awed, Bollocks paid for a new cubicle curtain in suitably pagan red velvet.

Hardy called Colin regularly to his bedsit in the prefect's wing where, behind a locked door, their gasps and cries smothered by the guitars and serious lyrics of the latest concept albums, they had sex. Perhaps, even, made love. In retrospect, their bedplay was unadvanced, innocent even, consisting of no more than hour upon cheek-pinking hour of kissing culminating occasionally in rushed mutual masturbation. As the weeks progressed, however, the crude lovemaking was punctuated by moments of unbridled romance which, for Colin at least, would never be matched. Hardy acquired someone's car for the evening and drove him to London for dinner. He borrowed a punt and took him for picnics on the river. He summoned him to deliciously transgress-ive moonlit trysts in the cricket pavilion – during one of which they took great pleasure in defiling the sacred grass of the cricket square. He introduced him to port, read him Cavafy, and once, when they were both drunk with regret at it being the last night of term, stole a key and led Colin up a spiral staircase to the roof of the chapel tower where they lay shivering, gazing up at the stars.

Looking back, from the years when he began a painful

education in the difficult wooing of women, Colin realized that similar scenes could never be re-enacted with as much pleasure, however delicious his female partner, because with Lucas he had played the part of a girl; an old fashioned, politically incorrect, all-demanding girl. Within the ritualized, hermetic environment of the school, Lucas, too, had been able to play a role – that of the all-powerful hero – which would be ridiculously unsustainable in the world beyond the institution's venerable confines.

As it was, the relationship had no reality beyond the school terms. In the holidays, each returned to his family which, in Lucas's case, meant Iran, where his father worked for an oil company. Neither would have dreamed of corresponding. They saw each other for the last time a little over a year since their first encounter. Lucas won a scholarship to Cambridge and vanished into the glamour of a year off, honouring Colin with a brief succession of postcards from the Mediterranean, which petered out somewhere in the Peloponnese. After that, Colin's only sexual experiences at school were with his fist. He snubbed all approaches that were made. Lucas had lent him stature, protected him from the system. He had worried that, with Lucas gone, he would be vulnerable again but his fears were groundless. He remained safe, coloured by boys' respect for the one who had gone, protected *in absentia*.

෴

'Colin? It is Colin, isn't it?'

He had found him. Oh God, he had found him! Colin stood hurriedly, brushing his palms on his trousers before shaking hands.

'Lucas!'

He felt fourteen again. Lucas still towered over him. His grip was firm as ever. His forearms were now wreathed in black hairs. He wore a chunky gold watch. He smelled of money.

'What were you doing in *here* for fuck's sake?'

'I was just, er –'

Lucas grinned.

'You were hiding. That's okay. I was hiding too.'

They laughed. Lucas slapped him on the shoulder and held open the door to the corridor. His accent had acquired a touch of American, like a suntan. It suited him.

'The old boys are a pretty grim bunch, huh?'

'Yes,' Colin agreed as, by unspoken assent, they headed for the stairs and the sunlight. 'Ghastly.'

'So what are you doing here?'

'Casing the joint for Harry. My son. He's nearly thirteen. I wasn't sure. I'm still not, but Elsa's been on at me. My wife.'

Grinning, Lucas nodded, showing a wing of fine lines around each eye.

'I know.'

'You met her?'

'No. I mean I knew you'd got married. I saw it in the papers.'

'Ah.'

Lucas held open the door to the yard and Colin could not help but notice that he too wore a plain gold band.

'You're settled too?' he asked, unsure how he felt about this.

'And how. Ten years now. Funnily enough, we're sniffing around for a place to send Willy.'

'Could do worse.'

'Could do better. Christ, this place still has tin baths! I know America's spoiled me but even by English standards the plumbing here is medieval.'

'Ah but the academic standards . . .'

'Yes. I know I know. I've heard it. It's always the ones who didn't come to these places who fight to perpetuate the whole thing. Left to us it would turn co-ed and be handed over to the state, right? I tell you, Colin, night after night I've had nothing but *academic excellence, valuable networking, cultural heritage*. I had to agree to come just to get some peace. Where's – Elsa, did you say her name was?'

'Watching cricket. She's a fanatic.'

'That's where I left my lot too. We brought a picnic. Seeing the alma mater was one thing, but I baulked at sherry with the housemaster. So. It's been a long time.'

'It certainly has.'

Again Colin felt Lucas's great hand on his back only this time it moved up to his shoulder and rested there. What the hell? No one was staring. They were two married men now. Two very obviously married men. He fought back a disturbing desire to kiss him full on the lips then and there and forced himself to talk personal history. By the time the cricket match was in sight, and its dense band of brightly coloured spectators gathered around the drinks marquee, he had told Lucas everything. The year off teaching in the Sudan. Oxford. Law school. The Bar. His mother's death. Elsa. Harry.

'There they are,' he said, raising a manly hand in reply to Elsa's languorous wave from a deck chair. 'But what about you? You've been to America?'

'Ever since Cambridge. I studied film at UCLA and wasted some time directing budgetless art, then I got into scripts and hit lucky. Sucked into Hollywood. A living hell but obscenely well paid. But that's where Fran came along so it was worth every minute.'

'Your wife.'

'My *man*, Colin, my *man*.' Lucas laughed, giving Colin a playful punch in the ribs. 'Jesus. There he is now, the impossibly cute one chatting up your wife. He was married, of course, but she's a wild thing and very understanding, so she let us have custody of the kid. Fran had always spent more time with him in any case. Anyway, I've gotten into production now and Fran's company are transferring him to London so –' he shrugged and gestured around them with his spare hand, 'here we are sorting out Willy's future. Christ but I hope he can pass the exams. American schools are so *backward*, you have no idea.'

'Darling!' Elsa raised a hand, which she clearly intended Colin to kiss. He merely clutched it, masking his panic with a sort of benevolent leer. She was drinking Pimms. The questionably blond American at her side stood to introduce her.

'Elsa, this is Lucas.'

'How do you do?'

'Hello.'

They shook hands.

'And this is *my* one!' Elsa laughed. 'Darling, meet Fran. It's such fun. They're moving to England and I've promised to help them find a lovely house. I've been telling Fran about that nice one for sale near us. You know? With the pretty old conservatory? Lucas, do sit here. I don't think those old trouts will dare come back. Darling? Can you see if the boys are all right? I gave Harry his pocket money and I think he might be trying to buy them both Pimms.'

Colin walked into the mouth of the tent. The air inside was baking, heavy with alcohol, flowers and the smell of hot, damp grass. He spotted Harry buying innocuous enough ice cream for himself and a boy with snowy blond hair, jeans and a baseball cap. In his suit and tie, Harry looked like a bank manager beside him. Suddenly thirsty, Colin turned back to ask the others what they wanted. Mid-anecdote, Elsa was tapping a hand on one of Lucas's knees as he sprawled in his deck chair. His – Colin sought a usable word – friend was laughing uproariously. Contenting himself with a more elegant chuckle, Lucas flicked a glance over Elsa's head to meet Colin's gaze and Colin felt a huge, threatening alteration in the scene, as though the ground had changed its angle or all the trees had suddenly grown another yard. Perhaps it was just the heat.

THE LIST

for Suzy Eva

'Mother will have a fit,' I told her.

'Polly,' she said, taking my hand in hers beneath our discarded coats. 'Calm down. It'll be okay. It's not as though it will be any great surprise for her. She knows about us and everything.'

'Yes,' I said. 'At least she should do by now – she can be evasive. But I'm her baby. Her littlest.'

'Even littlests have to fly the nest some time. You're twenty-six for Christ's sake.'

'Twenty-five.'

'Is that *all*?'

'Twenty-six next birthday.' I smiled. The taxi pulled over. Mother's street. Holy Mary, Mother of God.

'You make me feel so old,' Claudia complained.

'Mother will think you're a cradle-snatcher.'

'She won't, will she?' A moment of panic from Claudia.

'Just teasing.'

Now it was her hand's turn to be pressed.

'Anyway,' she went on, 'with you having lived it up in Rome for the last year, she can scarcely accuse me of ripping you untimely from the maternal nest.'

'Mmm,' I said, thinking of Rome, of Claudia's enormous bed in Rome, of the old pewter plate of figs and nectarines on the bedside table and the buzz of afternoon scooters beneath the shuttered window. 'But that didn't count. Abroad doesn't count as long as your mother has a room full of your things.'

'What things?' She withdrew her hand to push some hair back, exposing a silver earring in the shape of a shell. She saw me look at it. Renaissance silver. I had the other one but was not wearing it today. Mother had superstitions about wearing odd earrings. Like so many younger habits, she found it spiritually unhygienic.

'Oh. Just things,' I said. 'Books. Boxes of letters. Clothes I never wear. Winter coats. My bears.'

'Bears?'

'Teddy bears. You know. Toys. I have several. They were my grandmother's. They get passed down.'

She smiled and looked out of the window.

'We must adopt a baby *subito*,' she said.

The cab driver was counting the numbers on the white-painted porticos. Forty-six. Forty-eight. Now and at the hour of our death.

'Just stop right here.' I tugged his little window open. Claudia had shut it earlier to give our conversation privacy.

'But I thought she lived at eighty-something,' she protested.

'Yup. Right here's just fine. Thanks,' I told the driver. 'I want to walk a little,' I told her. 'Fresh air will do us good.'

'Sorry we're in the dark,' Mother said. 'Mrs Sopwith's polishing silver.'

All the thick downstairs curtains were drawn. The dining room table had been opened out and covered with several old flannel sheets. The family silver, which was kept in a broken twin-tub in the basement, was spread out on it, its variety of impractical or impenetrable shapes glistening in the light of a single, low-wattage lamp. Mrs Sopwith was hunched over a coffee pot, scrubbing at it with the brush my late father had used on his false teeth.

'Come up, come up,' sang Mother, mounting the stairs, 'and let me have a good look at you. Both of you.'

Claudia slipped a hand between my legs as we followed. Mrs Sopwith saw. I know she did.

Mother led us into the morning room. It was full of things. Even without her silver knick-knacks (which Mrs Sopwith was polishing along with the bulkier stuff) its table tops were cluttered. Family photographs smiled equably over one another's shoulders. Potpourri mouldered in assorted Chinese containers.

African violets and small begonias thrived on several surfaces and a vase of lilies sent out scarves of scent from the mantel shelf. New, unread novels, freshly delivered on account, caught the autumn sunlight on her desk-top. A sheaf of well-thumbed magazines had been painstakingly fanned out on the low, rectangular table between the sofas. A coffee table in any other house, it had always remained nameless in ours, scorned by Mother for its blameless lack of antique charm. I wished myself in Rome, furled in Claudia's matchless bed linen.

'I do wish Mrs Sopwith wouldn't do that,' said Mother, sweeping the magazines back into a vertical pile. 'Makes the place look like a chiropodist's waiting room.' With a few soft pats to the sofa cushion, she gestured to Claudia to sit beside her. I sat on the sofa before them and saw with a shock that they looked almost the same age, although Mother was the older by at least ten years.

Mother was what I had always thought of as a Chelsea Blonde. I was blonde too, but to qualify for Chelsea Blondedom one's hair had to be dead straight, hanging just to the shoulder, and preferably with the subtlest hint of who-gives-a-damn silver. Seen at its best oiled sleek on a beach or revealed, *après ski* by the removal of an unflattering woolly hat, it was worn around town as occasion demanded. The severity of the look could be (and usually was) offset with all manner of frills and flounces down below and had the advantage over the dowdier Mayfair Perm of conveying an unerring purity and youthful vigour rather than mere respectability.

'So,' Mother said, fatuously, 'you must be Claudia.'

Thoughtlessly I corrected her pronunciation.

'Thank you, dear. Claudia. *Claudia.*' She turned to Claudia for confirmation, smiling girlishly. '*Claudia* to rhyme with *rowdier*?'

'That's right.' Claudia gave her a slow smile.

'*Claudia.*' Mother tried it again. 'But it sounds so much more attractive that way; quite fresh!' She laughed. I slipped off my shoes and drew my feet up onto the sofa, retreating. 'Polly's told me so much about you in her letters: Claudia this and Claudia that.'

'I hope she didn't bore you too much.'

'On the contrary. What an enchanting earring that is.'

'Thank you.'

'May I?'

'Of course.'

Mother was actually lifting Claudia's hair for a closer look. How *dared* she? Her liver-spotted digits on Claudia's silky darkness! She would never have shown such intimate interest in the few boys I had ever brought home. Smiling at the thought of her stooping to fondle Jeremy's belt buckle or Simon's latest loafer, I feigned interest in some new photographs of my cousins.

'I've given the other one to Polly,' said Claudia. 'They're pretty, aren't they? Mamma always swore they were seventeenth century, but fakes are so clever nowadays, it's almost impossible to tell.'

'Good Lord! Polly, have you got yours on now?'

'No. It's . . . It's back with my things.'

'Well I hope your things are somewhere safe.'

'Oh yes.'

'My brother's flat has more security than Fort Knox,' put in Claudia. 'Quite absurd because Enzo seems to spend his every daylight hour at the bank and has nothing to steal.'

'Is he married?'

'Enzo? No. Only to his bonds and his little screens. He does drive an absurdly powerful car, though, so I suspect he may yet surprise us all.'

'Like our Polly,' said Mother and giggled. 'But you won't be living at his place indefinitely, surely?'

'We're flat-hunting already,' I broke in.

'We?' Mother queried.

'Claudia and I.' I crossed my fingers. 'We're going to live together.'

'But surely you have to get back to Rome for your studies, darling?'

'The course is over. I must have told you several times in my letters. It finished in June. I was thinking of staying on for a bit but then Claudia's partner had this idea of opening a London office so we decided to come and set up house over here.'

In the space of a few, sunlit seconds, a miniature drama of reaction and snatched understanding was played out across Mother's greyhound features.

'Oh!' she said. '*Oh*,' (this with an undermining smile of self-mockery), 'I see.' She stood quickly and came to sit beside me. 'Darling, I hadn't realized. You must think me so stupid. It'll be so lovely having you back for good. It is for good, isn't it?'

'Fairly good,' I said. 'Yes.'

She kissed me then pushed back my hair to reveal where the other earring should have glistened. She was showing all manner of unfamiliar emotions and I was not sure I was altogether happy with any of them. She kissed me again.

'I'm so glad for you,' she said, then turned to Claudia. 'And Claudia, too,' she said, holding out her hand which Claudia, bemused but smiling, took. 'I'm so glad. We must have a party.'

'Why?' I asked.

She prodded me in the ribs and scoffed.

'You're so like your father, darling. *Why*? To celebrate. To welcome you back, to introduce everyone to Claudia and to *celebrate*! Have you found somewhere to live yet?'

'Well, as a matter of fact,' Claudia admitted, 'we looked over somewhere yesterday which was perfect. Right on the park, with a roof terrace and some good-sized rooms which would be convenient for showing off pieces to clients and a quite extraordinary bathroom . . .'

'But they were asking the earth for it,' I said. 'It was fairly huge.'

'. . . and I wasn't going to tell Polly until I'd had some

confirmation, but I rang them this morning and made an offer which they accepted.'

'Claudia!'

'Are you cross?'

'No. I'm thrilled. But . . . you didn't tell me.'

I was thrilled. I was very, very happy. The flat was indeed perfect for us. Somehow the whole treat had been spoilt, however, by being revealed in Mother's presence. Our new love-nest was twenty minutes' or more drive from where we sat but suddenly I felt as though its newly painted, spectacularly empty spaces were merely a previously undisclosed adjunct to Mother's overfurnished domain. No sooner was the precious territory offered me than it was annexed by the Kingdom of Knick-Knack.

Excited, Mother clapped her hands. 'Now you mustn't say no. As my only daughter you can't escape a proper send-off. Your father set aside a tidy sum for just such an eventuality – well, maybe this wasn't *quite* the eventuality he had in mind but still – so it won't cost you a thing. By rights I feel we should put an announcement in *The Times*.'

'Mother!'

She pointed at my face and laughed at its expression.

'*Just* like your father! Don't worry. No announcements. I'm not utterly grotesque. But I do insist on giving you both a proper reception with invitations and I'm damned if I see why all your dreary brothers should have got married and had lists and you shouldn't.'

'But I'm not getting married.'

'Well you're not going to marry anyone else are you?'

'No, but . . .' She was breaking every rule. She was quite mad. I looked to Claudia for help but she was sitting back, stroking her gentle smile with the back of a forefinger and looking to see what Mother would say next. She was charmed. I could tell.

'There we are then. Why don't we go round there now? It

would be such fun.' Mother uncurled herself from the sofa and stood, giving her Chelsea blondeness a quick flick as she glanced in the looking glass. 'Have you got much to do this morning?'

'No. Not really,' said Claudia, still smiling to herself. 'But tell me, Mrs Reith . . .'

'Prudie, please.'

'Prudie.' Claudia's pronunciation was right first time, although the pout it lent her lips was perhaps unnecessarily seductive. 'I don't quite understand. What is this *list*?'

'When you set up house together . . .'

'Get married,' I broke in.

'Same thing,' Mother snapped.

'But it's meant to be a reward,' I said, astonished. 'For doing the right thing.'

'Just like her father,' she told Claudia again, shaking her head in mock sorrow. 'Such a shame you never met him. Anyway, when you set up house together – or marry,' she added, with a bow in my direction, 'you run up a list at your favourite shop of all the things you need to make domestic bliss complete and your friends and well-wishers call in there and buy them for you. If you get your timing right and don't go living in sin for too long beforehand, you don't have to buy a thing. You'd be amazed at people's generosity. You shall be.'

We drank a quick, celebratory gin while Claudia met Mrs Sopwith and was asked to cast a charitably professional eye over some of the more outlandish family silver. The few excuses I could drum up were quickly quashed by both Mother and Claudia and soon the three of us were walking down the road to Sloane Square.

'It's an inexplicably dull shop,' Mother explained as I held open a swing door for them both, 'but utterly trustworthy. You could leave a child in its care. I quite often did.'

The *Bride's Book* was still appropriately close to the department selling prams and pushchairs. The only apparent concession to modern living was the computer on which its lists were now maintained. Twisted with mortification, I dawdled by a shelf of soft toys and succeeded in making Claudia drop back to find me.

'What's wrong, Polly?' she asked. 'You look quite grey. Do you want to go back into the fresh air?'

'Quite right I do. She's only doing this to embarrass us. She wants to punish me for not bringing home some dull man she can approve of and tease.' I snatched a donkey and pulled on its pink felt ears. 'She's going to make a huge scene, I warn you. And so will the shop. They only do lists for nice young girls with fiancés. Not . . .' I hesitated.

'Not what?'

'Not not-so-nice young girls with elegant, titled but undeniably female partners.'

'So?' Claudia purred, setting the donkey back on its shelf and taking my hands in hers. 'Let Prudie have her joke. Let her show her feelings. Maybe it's easier for her this way. After all, it's only a shop, not the *Castello* Windsor.'

The precision of her pronunciation of Windsor made me smile through my discomfort. I called to mind the beauty of the flat she was buying us. I let her lead me forward.

The woman behind the counter was old enough to have grand-daughters. Unable to meet her eye, I fell to examining her uniform, wondering how something so ill-tailored could convey such irreproachability in the wearer. She would be scandalized.

'Good morning,' she said.

'Hello,' said Mother.

'Have you come to choose something from a list?'

'Not exactly,' said Mother. That was my cue. She was smiling at me and the woman behind the counter was waiting with her head at a politely enquiring angle.

'We've come to make one of our own,' I confessed.

'Lovely,' said the woman, her face impassive the while. 'Congratulations. I'll just open a file for you.' She tapped away at the computer keyboard. 'Your name, please.' Now she smiled at me briefly.

'Polly Reith,' I told her. 'Miss Polly Reith.'

'And the gentleman's name?'

'Er . . .' I faltered and looked to Mother for help.

'Not a gentleman,' Mother told her. 'Not a male, that is. Is there a problem?'

I noticed that the woman wore an unusual jet ring. She turned it briefly on her finger.

'Not at all,' she assured us. 'The lady's name?'

'Claudia Carafontana,' said Claudia. 'Contessa.'

I saw Mother's eyes glitter with vulgar pride. The woman behind the counter tapped in Claudia's title.

'Contessa,' she repeated under her breath. 'And will you be wanting the gifts delivered as they are bought,' she asked, 'or would you rather arrange for collection at a later date?'

'Oh, delivery would be better, I think,' said Claudia, evidently entering into the spirit of the occasion. 'Don't you think so, darling? Of course, the address is not quite certain as yet.'

'That's not a problem. If I could just have a phone number in case of queries.'

'Of course,' I said, anxious not to be quite passed over, and I gave her Lorenzo's number and address.

'Fine,' we were told. 'Walk around the store at your leisure and when you see things you'd like, just write their details on this form. Here, I'll fix it on a clipboard to make writing easier.'

'Not a perambulator,' said Claudia as we headed towards the household appliances department. 'Not just yet.'

Claudia's solicitors and those of the property developers who sold her – who sold us – the flat, worked fast. We were able to take possession within a month of her offer being accepted. In the interim, I discovered Claudia to be far richer than I had imagined. In Rome she had existed within a *mise-en-scène* completed long before my arrival. Her chests, mirrors and portraits, her rugs, pewter plates, even her vast bed with its carved head-board, were so encrusted with Carafontana family history that they seemed an extension of her personality, barely material and certainly nothing one could buy. It was something of a shock, therefore, to see her cut adrift from her historical moorings. Free to create a new setting of her very own. Of our very own. She dedicated her mornings to setting up the new branch of her antique business. Claudia and her cousin Maurizio, did nothing so sordid as buy and sell. Rather, they found antiques for clients too busy to shop themselves, discreetly arranging purchase and well-insured delivery for a large commission. She swiftly found a clutch of London clients who were either eager to buy the kind of Italian antiques that rarely found their way into auction houses or keen to sell their English furniture for the inflated prices Claudia could easily persuade her Italian clients to pay. I spent my mornings sustaining the illusion that I was searching for gainful employment.

Claudia devoted her afternoons to Mammon and Mother in equal proportions. Trailing me, astonished, in her wake, she bought paintings, looking glasses, Bokhara carpets, candelabra and vases. We pored over whole epics of fabric samples and she ordered curtains and drapes of a luxury that rounded even Mother's bridge-table eyes. She was dissatisfied with much that the property developers had done and painstaking hours were spent planning the undoing of their costly work and choosing replacement doorknobs, window catches and taps. Until then I had no idea that taps could be so expensive. This booty was stored in what had once been my bedroom, which was, as Mother pointed out, only twenty minutes' drive from the new flat. Mother would admire each new purchase judiciously, rob-bing it, as she did so, of the charms that had briefly seemed to distinguish it from others of its kind. She would then invariably take Claudia on some social excursion.

'You don't mind my borrowing her, do you, darling?' she asked the first few times, making it plain that I was surplus to her requirements. 'Just silly old friends who bore you rigid, but they will insist on laying eyes, if not hands, on dear Claudia before the reception.'

Claudia's capacity for such socializing astounded me. In Rome she had only met people in the evenings and then only in strictly monitored doses. She regarded her own mother and her fustian social rounds with undisguised contempt, which made her unlooked-for charity towards Prudie and her no more interesting bridge cronies doubly curious.

Left to my own devices, I indulged in cinema matinées, enjoying the excuse some of the more far-flung repertory houses gave for lengthy taxi rides. A cinema in Hampstead was showing *Rosemary's Baby*. I had missed it first time around and found the plot oddly compelling. I saw it three times in one week. Like *Othello* (which Claudia claimed had one of the theatre's richest histories of audience interruption), the more one saw it the more maddening it became.

'Open your eyes!' I wanted to scream at Mia Farrow. 'Put down that milk shake, pack your bags and run!'

But I never did.

We moved into the flat only two days before the reception was to be held there but the process was remarkably unstressful. Claudia and Mother between them had scheduled the delivery of her larger purchases with the precision of a military campaign. Unfortunately, my half-hearted trail through the job market had proved successful and I found myself committed to a mornings-only post as a researcher.

'Never mind, *cara*,' Claudia told me. 'You can come for lunch and have a lovely surprise.'

So I set off to work from Enzo's flat as usual then came home to our own, for lunch.

Two men had been to remove taps, knobs and window catches and Claudia's choices were now in place, as were her rugs, the booty stored in my childhood bedroom and a Jacobean bed that was almost as big as the one we had shared in Rome. I stood in the doorway looking around me over the wall of cardboard boxes. Claudia shut the door, stooped to remove my shoes, kissed each of my stockinged feet then led me to the bed.

'And so,' she said, unbuttoning my suit, 'begins our new life together.' She made her habitually subtle love to me on new matchless bed linen after which she fed me champagne and, in memoriam, figs. 'Mmm,' she sighed contentedly, 'Prudie was right to have the bed delivered first. I was all for concentrating on the pictures.'

'This was *her* idea?!'

Claudia laughed nervously at my tone.

'Well, only the bed. I thought of the figs myself.'

'Glad to hear it.'

'Polly, don't sulk. It's childish.'

'Well maybe, but spending so much time with old women is unnatural.'

'Unnatural?'

'Yes.' I sat up and swung my legs off the side of the bed. 'Anyway, they're only interested because you're a countess.'

'Hardly,' Claudia snorted. 'Prudie's circle is a lot more sophis-ticated than you seem to realize. They haven't batted an eyelid about you and I living together and if the way that wedding list is being ticked off is any indication, they're giving us a substantial blessing.' She rubbed my shoulder. '*Cara.*' She hesitated. 'You really don't see it, do you?'

'See what?'

'When did your father die?'

'When I was about three.'

'And how many boyfriends has Prudie had since then?'

'I don't know. She's always been very discreet. Several, I should think.'

'None, Polly. She's had none. And she's still an attractive woman. Does she cherish his memory?'

'Not exactly. He was much older than her. There's a photograph of them somewhere.'

I turned at last. Claudia was leaning on one elbow, dark hair swept back to reveal her silver earring. She raised her glass to drink and her ivory bracelets slid with a clatter to her elbow. She smiled slowly.

'*No!*' I breathed.

I dressed fast, left the flat and caught a taxi to Sloane Square. My mind was filled, as in some Satanic slide show, with images of Mother and her *nearest and dearest* – Heidi Kleinstock, Tricia Rokeby, Daphne Wain, the Crane Sisters (about whom I had always had my suspicions) and even Mrs Sopwith, in a fast-changing line of sexual arrangements. The editrix of the *Bride's Book* greeted me with a knowing smile and twiddled her ring. I realized why it had first caught my eye. Daphne Wain had a jet ring too, though larger, of course, and so did Heidi Kleinstock and, when blowsy peasant fashions had held sway, even Mother had sported one, with large jet earrings to match.

'Good afternoon, Miss Reith,' said the woman. 'Come to make a progress check? I'll do you a print-out to take away with you.'

She pressed a button then, somewhere beneath her desk, a printer hummed into action. When it came to a rest, she handed me a sheet of paper. There were all the plates, bowls, cutlery, glasses, salad bowls and napkin sets chosen, as I had then supposed, merely to humour Mother's fantastic game the other day. And there, beside most of them, were women's names. Numerous women's names. Many of them were quite unfamiliar and all of those I recognized were single by death, solicitors or choice. Half in jest, Mother had suggested I set down the name of a highly-developed dishwasher. A chronic exhibitionist, Tricia Rokeby had bought it for us. I pictured it being delivered in a large, jet-black bow with a card attached, swirled over with her jet-black greetings and unwanted solidarity.

I drank a cup of strong tea, not because I wanted it but because the store's top floor café, The Coffee Bean, carried unfailing associations with the well-buttoned certainties of childhood. I drank a second cup because I had begun to realize that I was, perhaps, a little disorientated from drinking champagne with nothing more substantial than a few figs. Two walls of the café were taken up with windows onto the square and one of the bustling roads that fed it, a third, which I was facing, was panelled with mirrors. I stared at myself long and hard, stared at the long, un-Chelsea curls of my hair, at the unmade-up face which Mother had once called *quiet* in my hearing, at my small, ringless hands. I had bought my navy coat on a trip to Milan and it had done its best to look too big for me ever since, dissociating itself from my neck and shoulders at the least opportunity. I sat up straight and tugged slightly at the lapels. Obediently, it fitted me once more. I had taken shelter from a downpour – unprepared as usual – although Claudia was waiting for me in a restaurant on the other side of the piazza. It was the only important garment I had bought on my own since meeting her. Normally she was at my elbow, purring, 'Or this, perhaps?'

I paid for my teas and hurried down the stairs to street level. There was a hair salon a few doors away, far too fashion-conscious and young for Mother, whatever her proclivities. I let myself in. Its atmosphere was stridently chemical; bubble gum and bleach. The music was loud – Claudia tended to listen to Baroque productions performed *authentically* – and gave me back the strength the mirrors had sapped. I would have my hair cut to within an inch of my scalp and dyed red. Traffic light red. It was what my coat had always needed. Mother too, perhaps.

'Hello, there. What can we do for you, then,' asked a stylist, picking incuriously at my hair. The words sounded like a challenge but her mind was plainly on other things.

'Oh,' I said. 'Just a trim, please. And a wash.' I offered her my quietest smile.

CHOKING

***

for Barry Goodman

'I THOUGHT, perhaps, sardines,' Charlie said, after pecking her cheek, patting her shoulder and casting an automatically assessing eye over what she was wearing. 'I know they're a bit cheap and cheerful but we've discovered they're delicious barbecued with a bit of lettuce and some new potato salad and cooking them outside means you don't get that awful stink hanging around the house for days afterwards.'

'How lovely,' she said. 'I love sardines.'

'I remember.'

Now that he was no longer her husband, Charlie was Maud's best friend. Not that one excluded the other – he had been her best friend all along, which was one of the things that scuppered their marriage – but he was *still* her best friend despite now being her ex-husband. This was something other people found hard to understand. It was also, for her, a source of quiet pride.

His garden was a strenuous demonstration against what was expected behind a North London terraced cottage. There were no mundane flowers, no vegetables and no lawn. Instead Charlie had created a small jungle of big leaved foliage plants – gunnera, rhus, palms and other things too exotic for her to recognize. Water trickled over a pile of attractive rocks and striped pebbles into a square pool whose sides he had painted a nocturnal blue.

'It's a jungle!' she laughed. 'Your neighbours must think you're mad.' She could tell from the way their windows were dressed that his neighbours grew vegetables, dahlias and hideous Blue Moon and Cheerfulness roses.

'I don't speak to my neighbours,' he said quietly.

A small table and chairs stood in a kind of clearing beyond the first swath of glossy greenery. The fish were already sizzling on a small barbecue to one side, a mute reproach to Maud for her lateness. As she sat, slipping off her jacket to enjoy the early autumn sun, Charlie wiped the drips off a bottle that had been cooling in the pond and poured them both some wine.

'So,' he said, sitting too. 'How's LA?'

'I told you before,' she laughed. 'It's not *really* LA. We're so far down Sunset Boulevard, we can see the sunsets. Amazing sunsets. And if I stand on the balcony and lean out a bit, I can see the Pacific.'

'Nice.'

'You should come. Both of you.'

'Yes. Well . . .' he sighed, allowing the impossible optimism of her suggestion to settle on the table between them. 'The tan suits you,' he added.

'You call this a tan?' she exclaimed. 'I went this colour by staying *out* of the sun and wearing total block. There are people there with necks like old shoes but they persist in lying by their pools and *baking*. For a culture so founded on vanity, it's inexplicable. Mmm. Lovely wine.'

'It's nothing special,' Charlie shrugged. 'Something Portuguese Kobo picked up.'

'How is Kobo?'

'Fine. He's with a client in Moscow; one of his German property developers. He'll be sorry he's missed you.'

Their marriage had foundered when Charlie spent some time in therapy because he was worried that he kept losing his temper over insignificant things. Guided by the therapist, he came to see that he was not a cowardly bisexual, as he had always claimed, but a homosexual liar who should never have married. They did their best to adapt – they loved each other dearly, after all, and he had no desire to hurt her – but their attempt at an *open relationship* was doomed once his safaris into the realms of uncomplicated sex caused him to stumble into love with someone else. Maud had given him up with tears but little struggle, since he was still her best friend, and she knew when she was weaker than the competition. There had been a flurry of lovers since then, and more therapy, but then Charlie met Kobo, a Japanese lighting consultant, who brought him stability and a second marriage, longer and doubtless more fulfilling than his first. Kobo was handsome and clever and Maud had little difficulty in befriending him, but he made her nervous. She felt that her manner and appearance were too untidy for him, that he must be forever rearranging her in his mind. His poise, too, could madden her. Passing through his workroom during a drinks party she had once, in pure malice, unzipped his little black rubber pencil case and shaken the contents across his immaculate desktop.

'Why are you here for such a little while?' Charlie asked, helping her to two sardines, flakes of whose charred skin fell into her helping of potato salad.

'It's not a proper trip,' she explained. 'I hitched a ride with Alvaro. The company was sending him over for a couple of meetings and he'd clocked up enough miles on his frequent flier card to bring me along for nothing. He lives in airports. It was only an economy ticket but when the stewardess saw he was in club, she upgraded me to join him. He always flies with the same airline and I think they must have his name on their computer for extra nice treatment or something. Sorry, I'm gabbling. It's jet lag.'

'Lettuce?'

'Please. Thanks.' She could tell from Charlie's abrupt change of tack that he was not about to ask about her boyfriend, even after she had asked after Kobo. She decided to tell him anyway.

'He's fine, by the way. Only he works so hard it's quite scary,' she said. 'He went straight from the airport to a meeting in Wardour Street when the most I could do was brush my teeth and crawl into bed.'

Charlie merely snorted and lifted a tab of flesh off a sardine skeleton. 'Have you got a job out there?' he asked.

'Not really. I wanted to take time out and get some painting done again. The light is wonderful, even in a flat. There's a nice bit out at the back where the kitchen is, with a glass roof and I paint in there when I can. But I've been doing a lot of child-minding for Clara – that's his sister. She's so nice, and Enrique – that's the kid – is adorable. She pays me quite well. Cash in hand. But it does make it a bit hard to get on and paint sometimes because he keeps getting in the way or wanting me to play with him. Anyway for the moment it's strictly cash jobs or letting Alvaro pay for everything, because I haven't got a green card. I shouldn't even be living there. We're probably going to have trouble from immigration on the way back in.' She laughed at the memory. 'Alvaro's asked me to marry him,' she said. 'While we're over here. He proposed in the departure lounge.'

Charlie paused a moment then frowned so that she wondered if the news had hurt him.

'Just so you can get a permit?' he asked.

'I . . . er . . . I think there'd be more to it than that. He wants to make an honest woman of me.'

'And I suppose he wants you to have his babies too.'

'Yes, actually. I think he probably does. I should give it some thought. I'm not getting any younger.'

'Then you'll never get a job again. You know what your family are like; you'll be permanently pregnant or breast-feeding.'

'I'm not sure I want a job,' she said defiantly. 'I hate work. I'd quite like to lie back and have babies. I might write a book. I could write a book while they were sleeping.'

His pager bleeped, interrupting her. He apologized and went to call his surgery on a portable telephone. She ate on, watching him pace about in the far end of the garden as he talked. His voice was curt, slightly hectoring, the way she remembered it. It reminded her of disagreements they had suffered in the past and of the little things that made him that much easier to divorce. He used to correct her stories at dinner parties. He used to curb her drinking even when he was the one that was driving them home. When he returned, she was ready for a skirmish.

'You knew Alvaro was over here with me,' she said. 'Why didn't you ask him over too?'

'He was busy. You said he had meetings all day.'

'That's beside the point. You didn't ask him.'

'But I didn't want to see him,' he laughed, exasperated. 'I wanted to see you.'

'He noticed.'

'Good. Maybe next time we meet he'll be a bit more polite.'

'What do you mean?'

'Maud, we had you both to dinner last time, at very short notice. And he barely addressed three words to Kobo – and those were only questions. Then he dismissed my work on the NHS as a waste of resources and spent the rest of the evening banging on about market forces and the power of the almighty dollar. He's right wing.'

'No he's not. He's American. They have a different system to ours.'

Charlie dismissed this with a snort, adding, 'And he belittles you.'

'He does not.'

'He squired you around all evening. He always had a great hand clamped on your elbow or your arse. Treating you like a piece of property. It's so *Latin*.'

'Of course he's Latin. He's a Cuban. Anyway he loves me. He's very physical. He likes to touch me in public. I like to touch him. You never touched me.'

Charlie froze for a moment in passing her the last sardine. She didn't want it – the taste was turning acrid in her mouth – but she could not break in to say no in case her voice trembled.

'Yes. Well,' he said. 'If you say so, but that night I think there was more to it. He was using you as protection. You probably couldn't see it – why should you – but we both noticed it. Kobo's especially sensitive.'

'You're going to say he's uncomfortable around gays.'

'Homophobic. He's homophobic. His skin was crawling. He hardly ate a thing –'

'He was getting over food poisoning.'

'And his relief when he saw there was another straight couple – he practically congratulated them.'

'I don't see how you can say this. He works in an office surrounded by gay men. The place is *run* by Marys. He works for an entertainment corporation, for Christ's sake!'

'Precisely. And I bet not a day goes by when he doesn't wish it wasn't.'

'How can you judge him like this?' she exclaimed. 'You don't even know him. You've only met a few times. How do you know he wasn't just nervous? You're always underestimating how scary people can find you. You're a very intimidating man. And when Alvaro's nervous he can get kind of aggressive and give a bad impression.'

'So! His skin *was* crawling!'

'Oh *honestly*!' She gestured as though to brush his words off the air. 'There's no dealing with you when you're being like this. Let's just let it go and talk about something else. You don't like him. Fine. The two of you will hardly ever meet in any case. It was naive of me to expect you to get on. I mean, the only thing you have in common is me, which is hardly grounds for a beautiful friendship.'

Indignant, she took a last, large mouthful of fish and chewed it vigorously by way of a full stop. Charlie collected a forkful of potato, dipped it in a pool of dressing then left it on his plate. He topped up the wine instead, his eyes lowered, his mouth pinched in a way she knew of old to bode only ill.

This was not part of her plan. She was barely across his threshold and they were arguing already. She had woken, dressed and travelled up here from the hotel with such high expectations, longing to see Charlie again with a true fondness, innocent of an ex-lover's spite or insecurity. Since her spur-of-the-moment dash out to California the previous year, she had written to him regularly and he wrote back; they sent each other distillations of their mood and witty accounts of recent adventures. She noticed, however, that they avoided the less spontaneous intimacy of the telephone and judiciously edited their accounts of any material pertaining too closely to their respective lovers. Perhaps she was guilty of having sustained a fiction, withholding the whole business of Alvaro from his attention, the longer to sustain his old support.

The brutal truth was that Alvaro was the first lover since her divorce who had eclipsed Charlie, the first to have proved more than a divertissement, the first she loved more than she liked. She had met him while working briefly in the graphics department of his corporation's London office. Wooing her with single-minded charm, seducing her with a kind of boyish greed, he had proudly overstepped her broken marriage rather than be intimidated by it. Divorce, her enduring love of Charlie and the overly protective eye her ex-husband kept on her had left her in an unromantic limbo, locked in a glass tower whence it took Alvaro's forceful passion and, dare to whisper it, machismo to wrest her.

'What do you want?' she asked.

'How do you mean?' Charlie said, setting two small fruit brulées before them.

'Because I'm not going to give him up just because you want me to.'

'I never said I wanted you to give him up,' he protested.

'You didn't need to. I could tell it was what you were hoping.'

'I can't pretend he and I have much in common.'

'Evidently. But you can't let that be a reason for me to give him up, any more than I'd expect you to give up Kobo.'

'But you *like* Kobo.' Charlie's statement was half a plea for reassurance, allowing her anger to pass its peak.

'Only because I went out of my way to get in a position where liking him would be possible,' he said.

'You make it sound hard.'

'It wasn't. Not really. Kobo's easy to like. Kobo's a charmer. Alvaro isn't. Not with men. He's Latin, as you say, and he tends to view men – gay men included – as rivals until they prove themselves not to be. This is delicious.'

'You don't think I burnt the sugar too much?'

'No. It's perfect.'

'Kobo bought one of those little kitchen blow torches for me on a trip to Brussels.'

'As I say, he's a charmer. Is this sour cream?'

'Crème fraîche.'

'Heaven.'

'The beauty of it is the speed.'

The flawless puddings, caramel carapaces giving way to minia-ture marshes of raspberry, peach and ratafia, seemed to dispel the discord the smoking sardines had unconsciously unleashed. Obese for several years of her childhood before hormones taught her vanity, Maud had always laid herself open to the voodoo of food. The fizz of ripe mango on her tongue, the yeasty elasticity of warm white bread could improve her mood in seconds. Tell-ing juxtapositions of taste – tender anchovies *au vinaigrette* laid across a waxy new potato, tayberries bleeding rich juice over a bittersweet island of chocolate parfait – could arrest her thoughts in their tracks, leaving her staring in speechless wonder at her plate. Some people were at their most vulnerable behind the wheel of a car or dandling a child on their knee. Those who understood Maud well knew that favours were best asked while she was eating. She emptied her ramekin in contented concen-tration then looked up at Charlie with refreshed affection.

'I'm sorry,' she said at last. 'It's the younger child in me, always wanting everyone I love to love one another. My mother was just the same – always trying to maintain a sort of umbrella of men about her. I'm always pathetically bewildered when it doesn't happen, which is daft since there's no earthly reason why it ever should. I mean, if Alvaro lived in London, all this would be more of a problem. You'd *have* to get on because I'd be forever bringing you together. As it is, you need never meet till my funeral. And even then, one of you can send apologies. But it's sad if it means I see less of you. Do you mind? Can you face being kept in separate boxes?'

'All I mind is his taking you away from us.' Charlie muttered, lighting a cigarette from the barbecue. 'I miss you. Especially when Kobo's away. And he's away so much nowadays.'

'Darling.' She squeezed his free hand then poured them the last of the bottle. 'But I had to go. Even if you don't like him, you *must* see that. I couldn't have stayed here trailing after you two forever. It wouldn't have been fair on Kobo, and it certainly wouldn't have been fair on me. Fairies' godmother is a thankless role.'

'No one said anything about trailing. You could just have found yourself a bloke in London.'

'Someone you approved of.'

'Yes,' he said then shrugged, crossly exhaling smoke as he saw the futility of his wishes.

'I don't think,' she said carefully, 'you'd have approved of *anyone* I fell in love with.'

'I would,' he insisted. 'Michael Manners was all right. And I liked the one from that magazine. The one with the streak in his hair.'

'Terry. Hmm. Yes.' She smiled wistfully, recalling Michael's statuesque legs and the little, childish sun tattooed around one of Terry's nut brown nipples. Then she cleared her throat. 'But neither of those was love.'

'It looked like it at the time.'

'Well believe me, it wasn't. It was lust. Lust on the rebound. Great fun, very good for my morale but –'

'Not love.'

'No.'

She was not meeting Alvaro until early evening so Charlie disguised his medical bag in a rucksack and they took a walk. They headed up Highgate Hill to look in an antique shop then strolled around Waterlow Park admiring the warmth of the autumn colours and berating the dullness of the council's planting schemes. Something was tickling the back of her throat and she kept pausing to cough into a handkerchief. He patted her on the back in an effort to relieve her discomfort then left his hand comfortably across her shoulder as they moved on beneath the trees. They talked of other things as they walked, chiefly of old friends and distant enemies, of books they had read and films they had missed. They stopped for a cup of tea in the park refreshment rooms before she caught a train back into town.

He said, 'All right. We'll give him one more chance if you like. But let him know he's on parole.'

'We could meet in a restaurant,' she suggested, more relieved than she cared to show. 'Neutral territory.'

'Good idea.'

'Should we invite some camouflage along?'

'No point. He's the one I should be talking to.'

'Thanks,' she said. 'I *so* want you two to get on. Just a bit. You don't have to become best friends or anything but he's so clever and funny once he relaxes and he loves talking about films and exhibitions. He's a very keen gardener too –'

'Don't push it,' he warned her. 'I said he's on parole. We can dress down, go Dutch and steer clear of private medicine. But I'm only doing it for you, remember.'

'I know.'

'I know I should be happy you're happy and I *am* trying to be, believe me, but if I don't like him, I don't like him.'

'I know.'

Something – the staleness of the bun they were half-heartedly sharing, the long shadows on the grass outside or the too familiar sound of the waitresses squirting jets of scalding water into metal teapots – something began to cause her an ache of nostalgic regret. Possibly it was the unexpected sound of him backing down after taking a stand, touching in its way as the first time she noticed her father having to lever himself from an armchair or caught herself smiling encouragement as her mother unwittingly told her a piece of news for the second time. His pager bleeped again. He called his answering service on the pay phone then announced that he had an urgent house call to make and would have to leave her. He kissed her briskly on the lips and was gone, running off after a slowing taxi.

Gathering her things about her and walking out through the park and down to Archway tube station, she realized he had omitted to ask her response to Alvaro's proposal. Promptly she felt her nostalgia sharpen into homesickness. This was where she belonged. She had missed autumn leaves, missed the sensation of a coat furled about her, missed living in a city with regular rain, where walking for the sake of walking and taking public transport were not regarded as little short of social dereliction. Now that she was emerging from her jet lag, she felt a bizarre sense of dislocation at staying in an hotel in what still felt like her home town. She needed to hurry back to Alvaro, reground herself in reality after spending a day so pointlessly rubbing her nose in the now irrelevant past.

She had thought that the tea had driven away the tickle in her throat but, coughing again, she found the irritating sensation had returned. It was not painful, not sharp. She knew from experience the little jabs a trapped fish bone inflicted, and the instinctive panic they induced. This was less intrusive. It felt as though something were lightly resting just beyond the back of her tongue. She coughed once more, standing to one side of the pavement to let people pass by. She swallowed. She felt it there again. She bought a packet of toffees at the station entrance. She sucked them, one after another, on the train back to the hotel, thinking to induce a little rush of saliva that would wash whatever it was into her stomach and safely away from the mouth of her windpipe, but whenever she swallowed, she felt whatever it was still there and, try as she might to concentrate on her paperback, her thoughts twitched back to the irritation like fingers to an itch.

By the time she returned to the hotel, she felt petulantly in need of comfort. However luxurious, the hotel room was desolately impersonal, not a place to linger on one's own in a state of poignant indecision. Luckily Alvaro was already there, and he had missed her. His kisses tasted of coffee and beef. After Charlie, he seemed delightfully big and invasive; a great lunk of a man, her mother would have called him.

'I missed you too,' she said softly. 'Hold me.' He took her head in his hands and kissed her then she backed onto the bed and drew him about her like a human quilt. 'That's better,' she said. 'That's nice. How was your day?'

'Cruddy,' he said. 'Men in suits talking too much. It looked so great out. I wanted to be out sightseeing with you.'

'We had a nice walk around Highgate.'

'Yeah? And how was lunch?'

'Lunch was fine.'

She had promised herself there would be no more pretence now, no more dressing up the facts, no more telling them, 'He said to say hi,' or 'He was *really* sorry he missed you.' Some vestigial caution however prompted her to turn the carefully planned, too intimate sardine barbecue into something else. Barbecues, she had learnt, were the American equivalent of mowing the lawn. Barbecues, for American men, carried daddish, male, territory-marking, Labour Day connotations.

'Bread and cheese and some soup and salad,' she said and saw the corners of his mouth twitch downwards at the thought of so emasculate, meatless a meal.

He had made them a reservation for dinner and she had planned to lead him somewhere amusingly old fashioned for drinks first. It was time to shower and dress up but for one reason or another, because he was tense and she was cold and perhaps because they both needed some reassurance, they began to make love instead.

Alvaro was on the neanderthal side of hirsute. Charlie's skin was pale and marble smooth, unambiguously Saxon, so she had been surprised, amused indeed, that the contrast already so evident in their natures should be extended to the nature of their flesh. 'Oh. So my brother is a hairy man,' she had murmured when she first unbuttoned Alvaro's shirt; making the first of many literary references he failed to pick up.

While covertly regarding his hairiness as the mark of true manhood, just as he saw large breasts and fecundity as badges of womanly splendour, he treated it with a certain coyness. He liked Maud to shave the back of his neck to leave his nape boyishly naked and he habitually wore modest tee shirts beneath his unbuttoned shirt front, their whiteness enriching his golden skin. In bed, he was peculiarly sensitive to finding hairs in his mouth. Used to the vagaries of male taste, conditioned, in particular, by Charlie's squeamishness, she offered to shave herself. He was horrified at the suggestion. He often did not wait for her to undress before burying his face in her bush and claimed that picking her hairs from his teeth was one of the few free pleasures left him. Rather, it was his *own* hairs that caused him trouble, as though finding them in his mouth were deadly proof of narcissism or a species of autoerotic cannibalism. Tonight he abruptly broke off in the middle of making love to her, picked briefly at his tongue, tried to continue but broke off again with an angry sigh.

'Uh-oh,' she chuckled, familiar with the signs. 'Pube patrol.'

She watched him paw and scratch at his tongue. Aroused as she was, she was impatient for him to find the hair and get on with the matter in hand but then she realized, with a pang of relief that her own throat was no longer itchy.

'Shit,' he muttered. 'Sorry. If I can just – '

She watched guiltily as he climbed off the bed and padded through the shadows to the bathroom. She heard him curse, heard him try gargling, heard him curse again then heard the sound of a wash-bag being unzipped after which he made a series of unappetizing gagging and coughing sounds. Chafed to a pink of passion, her body was rapidly cooling in the breeze of conditioned air. She pulled the bedding up around her and stretched across the pillows to turn on her bedside light. She glanced at her little travelling alarm and saw that they were going to be late for their dinner reservation unless she started dressing now. Suddenly she felt a consuming thirst, brought on by wine at lunch and the undiluted succession of toffees.

'Look,' he was saying. 'Look at this! What the hell . . . ?' He emerged from the bathroom triumphantly parading a cotton wool bud. He thrust it into the pool of light.

'Come back to bed,' she said, not looking. 'I want you. Let's eat somewhere else. Let's order room service.'

'Look,' he said again.

She looked. There was a fish scale on the tip of the bud; a sardine scale, translucent, charred at one end.

'Did you have fish for lunch?' she asked. Alvaro rarely touched fish, certainly not if it had skin on it still.

'I had steak,' he said indignantly. He glowered at the scale more closely, as though it provided some crucial piece of circumstantial evidence whose significance would be revealed to him if only he stared at it long enough.

'These British restaurants,' she said. 'They probably gave you a dirty plate.'

'I could have choked,' he said. 'I should sue. You didn't have fish, did you?'

'I told you,' she sighed. 'Charlie gave me soup. Carrot soup. And bread and cheese and some salad.'

She pulled back out of the light because she could feel her cheeks warming at the lie. She took the cotton wool bud from him and laid it on the bedside table then coaxed him back into bed. After kissing and pawing her absentmindedly for a while, however, he fell to wondering about the fish scale again. He lost his erection entirely and, when they arrived at the restaurant too late for their table, lost his temper as well. Their evening was ruined.

Lying in bed beside him – Alvaro had fallen asleep abruptly after complaining of a headache – Maud felt increasingly stifled. His heavy arm pinioned her on her back; a position in which she could never sleep for fear of snoring. The hotel bedding was at once too heavy and too short. Worst of all, Alvaro was obsessed with the mechanics of air conditioning, insisting that the windows be left hermetically sealed while the unit below them sighed its chilled, second-hand exhalations into layers of motion-less net curtain. Maud could have coped if the machinery had gone about its business in silence but its constant, mournful whisper put her in mind of the sterile preservation of meat until she suffered a kind of panic attack and had to slip into her dressing gown and flee the room.

She wandered the corridors, growing close to tears in her frustrated search for a balcony or an opening window. She fell in, at last, with two Colombian chambermaids who laughed at her, ushered her onto a blissfully windy fire escape beyond their tiny kitchen then soothed her with sweet tea and biscuits. They had been admiring Alvaro from afar but laughed when Maud told them he was sound asleep.

'I love it when they sleep,' one told her. 'It's the only time they leave you free to *think*!'

There was no question but she must marry him, they said, divining the turmoil of indecision in which she found herself. He had the kind of good looks which would only improve with age, he would work hard to keep her in comfort and he would give her beautiful children. One of them read her palm and clicked her tongue at the happiness she saw there.

Reassured by their envious certainty, just as she was calmed by their tea, Maud returned to her room, switched off the air conditioning and wrapped Alvaro's sleeping arm about her like a valuable fur.

DANGEROUS PLEASURES

for Audrey Williams

THE BREATH was now coming so slowly from Shuna's mouth that Shirley found herself beginning to count in between each painful, creaking exhalation.

'Not long now,' she thought and found she had said it aloud. She shook out her hanky and pressed it gently to her daughter's sweating temples, first one, then the other. If there was any feeling left in the poor child's body, she thought she might enjoy the cool sensation of the well-ironed cotton on her fevered skin.

'Go on,' she added, as Shuna took another spasmodic breath. She might have been encouraging her to jump into a swimming pool or let go at the top of a playground slide. 'Go on. I'm here.'

And then she found she was counting past thirty, past fifty. She allowed herself a little cry. Shuna's eyes were already closed – Shirley had not seen them open in the four days since the phone call – but she reached out and gently closed Shuna's mouth. The lips were cracked and looked sore. She took the jar of Vaseline from the bedside cupboard and rubbed a little on them with her forefinger. Then she opened the window and walked back along the corridor to the visitors' room, the crepe soles of her light summer shoes squeaking on the vinyl floor.

Karl, the nice boy from the charity, with the earring, had finally persuaded Arthur to stop pacing, sit down and drink a cup of tea. He sprang up as Shirley came in. Arthur merely raised frightened eyes.

'It's over,' she told them. 'She's gone.'

'Christ,' said Arthur.

Karl came over and gave Shirley a hug, which was nice. She had not been hugged in years. He was a polite, clean boy and probably good to his mother.

'Arthur, do you want to go in for a bit? Say goodbye?' she asked. Arthur merely shook his head, swallowing the tears that had begun to mist his eyes.

'Need a fag,' he muttered and pushed out of the swing door and onto the balcony.

'Do you mind if I do?' Karl asked.

'Be my guest,' Shirley told him. 'She'd have liked that.'

'Have you told the staff yet?'

'No,' she told him. 'Would . . . Would you mind, Karl?'

'Course not,' he said.

As he padded sadly out, she admired again his leather boots with the funny little chains and rings round the heels. She sighed, made herself a cup of tea at the hospitality table and joined Arthur on the balcony. He too, she could tell, had indulged in a little cry. She was glad. Men could be so bottled up.

Shirley stood beside him in companionable silence for a while, admiring the view of Chelsea stretching away from them. She could see the pumping station in the distance and, beyond that, just before the view melted into summer haze, Westminster Cathedral.

'She picked a beautiful day to go,' she said. It was a thin, silly thing to say, she knew, but it was true and she felt it needed saying. The remark slipped into the silence between them which absorbed it like dark water about a stone. When Arthur finally turned to her, it was with a face like thunder.

'Why'd she have to get such a dirty disease? As if what she was wasn't bad enough.'

'Now Arthur, you remember what Karl told us: it's not dirty, it's just a –'

'What's a pansy like that know?'

'I think he knows rather a lot, actually. I think he's already lost several of his friends.'

But Arthur was not listening.

'Why'd she have to do it to us?'

'She didn't *do* anything to *us*, Arthur. She caught a virus and she died. If anything happened to us, we did it ourselves, as well you know.'

He rounded on her, his face suddenly tight with fury.

'Shut your fucking hole,' he hissed.

Shirley turned away, angry in turn. He knew how she disliked unnecessary language. He was not really angry. He was upset. Perhaps he had not had a little cry after all. Not a proper one. He would tell it all to Bonnie when they got home; he had always told his Jack Russell the things he could not tell his wife, mostly things to do with the mysterious workings of his heart and a few others besides. She would send the two of them out to the allotment, say she needed the house to herself while she organized funeral cakes and sandwiches and so on. Death always made people want to stuff their faces. And drink. Juno at the Conservative Club could probably find her way to slipping her a case of that nice sherry cut-price.

'When do you think we can go?' Arthur asked her in a softer tone – the nearest he would come to an apology.

'There'll be forms to sign, probably,' she told him. 'That's all. And she'll have some things for us to take away or throw out or whatever.'

'Well, let's get it over with then we can catch the three-thirty before the rush hour starts.'

'No, Arthur.'

'What?'

'We've got to sort out her flat.'

'Are you mad?'

'It's Shuna's flat.'

'She only rented it. Anyway, it sounds like more of a bed-sit.'

'Yes, but she lived there for eight years and I've never seen it and there'll be things to be sorted out there.'

'Leave it, Shirley. Leave it all. She didn't have anything valuable. You can be sure of that. And what there is the landlord can have in case she was behind with the rent.'

'Shuna was always meticulous about debts. That nice friend of hers said so that visited yesterday.'

'That mangy tart, you mean.'

'Arthur!'

He snorted, holding open the door for her into the visitors' room. Ordinarily Shirley would have sighed and acquiesced, but not today. Her mind was made up.

'Well you can do as you please,' she said. 'She's our daughter and I'm going to do right by her. Honour her.'

'Honour?'

'You catch the three-thirty. I'll come home when I'm ready. I might even have to spend the night.'

'You'll do no such thing.'

'I'll do what I have to do. There's food in the fridge. You know how to work the microwave. You'll survive. You're a cold bastard, Arthur, and one day it'll catch up with you.'

'Shirley!'

'You can sign all the forms for me and bring back her overnight bag and whatever. You've done nothing else of use these last few days.' Shirley was utterly calm in her rightful fury. Karl was waiting for them at the nurses' station. 'Shall we be off, Karl? I need some fresh air.'

'Of course, Mrs Gilbert.'

She turned as they waited for the lift and took a short, hard look at her husband. She would never leave him. They fitted together now like two old shoes and divorce was grotesque in a couple over fifty. There were times, however, when she blithely contemplated murder.

She had taken the keys earlier. They were lying in the bedside locker beside an unopened carton of long life fruit juice and a bottle of Chanel No. 5, which may have suited Shuna, but which Shirley had never greatly cared for. Keys were important, personal things, unlocking secrets, disclosing treasures. She had picked these ones up instinctively to distract her while Shuna was having a long needle pushed into her arm and had forgotten to replace them. They had an interesting fob – a big, silver hoop, like an outsize curtain ring – which felt pleasingly heavy and cool in the hand. Now, as they travelled down in the lift, Shirley's fingers clasped on the bunch of metal as on a talisman.

'Shall I give you both a lift to the station?' Karl asked when they reached the lobby.

'Mr Gilbert's going to the station,' she told him. 'I'm not. I want to see her flat. Would you take me?'

'Of course. But I haven't got keys.'

'I've got keys,' she said and he gave her a quiet but twinkly little smile and she knew at once how his young life was probably rooted in small, harmless deceits and acts of sly kindness. 'Thanks,' she added. 'You're a good boy, Karl. Are you going steady with someone?'

'Yes,' he said and blushed a bit. 'Three years, now, but he's in the army, so I haven't seen much of him lately. He's out in Bosnia.'

'Ah,' she said, adding, 'that's nice,' foolishly, because she was uncertain what to say.

Karl's car was a Mini, black as sin with zebra-striped fur covers on the seat.

'It's okay,' he assured her when he saw her hesitate at the open door. 'They're ironic.'

Shuna had run away from home after one flaming row too many with her father. It had been time for her to leave anyway – she was eighteen – but Shirley was not ready to be left alone with Arthur and the girl departed in anger with no plans and no future, so it *was* a kind of running away. For three weeks they heard nothing. Then a postcard came, pointedly addressed only to Shirley. It showed a guardsman in his busby (Karl's friend had a busby, apparently), and said she was alive and well and living in London now. She asked that they do what they liked with the things she had left in her room. Arthur threw most of them out and made a great, purgative bonfire at the bottom of the garden from the rest. Shirley had retained a few things, however, retrieved from the dustbin bags without his knowledge; Shuna's old school cap, purple with yellow piping, a photograph of her as a sheep in a nativity play and a Saint Christopher medallion. Finding the medallion casually abandoned along with all the ragbag litter of youth, Shirley had felt a momentary panic that her child should be braving the big city unprotected and she had put it on herself at once, shielding Shuna by proxy. She had worn it constantly ever after, hidden from her husband's incurious gaze under slip or nightdress. Glimpsing its cheap silver plate the previous night as she gave herself an unrefreshing top-and-tail in an overheated hospital bathroom, she reflected that she had picked quite the wrong patron saint for the girl, as redundant in Shuna's life as a cake slice at a witches' Sabbath.

More postcards followed the first, all addressed to Shirley, which pleased her hugely, though she said nothing. Shuna found a job as a waitress then as a secretary. She found a flat. She only paid one visit home, two Christmases after she left, and Shirley knew at once what her daughter had become. Shuna brought them champagne and absurdly generous presents and wore clothes she could never have afforded on a typist's income. This in itself would not have signified much – her daughter might simply have fallen in with a louche crowd or acquired a lover with criminal connections. There was no talk of boyfriends, only the constant if hazy implication of a *gang* of nameless, party-loving friends. What clinched it for Shirley was that something had died behind Shuna's eyes. The old, girlish desire to please men in general and her father in particular, had withered. Correspondingly, as if answering some age-old, unconscious stimulus, Arthur spent the festive season following Shuna around, looking at her with a new, indecently saucy brightness in his eye and he talked incessantly of how *well* she was turning out after all.

'Yes,' Shirley had thought, 'after all. After all your sarcasm, your slaps and put-downs, your relentless, stunting prohibitions, your liberty-pruning.' She had said nothing to him of what she had noticed. He, needless to say, was too dense to draw conclusions. She held her counsel, accepted the presents with embarrassment and forced herself to be glad, at least, that Shuna had found a way of making ends meet, was proving more resourceful than her father ever had. Subsequently, when Shuna refused to return home for either his fiftieth birthday or silver wedding parties, he turned against her memory again, calling her a whore, but it was only at her deathbed that he came to see the truth in his words.

They received a phone call from the lad, Karl. That was the first they knew of it.

'Hello,' he said. 'You don't know me and officially I shouldn't be contacting you, not without her permission, but she's too sick to talk now and I know she'd want to see you. And I think you've a right to see her too before it's over. She doesn't have long, you see.'

They could not stay at an hotel because neither of them liked being away from home and now, more than ever, they needed the comfort of a nightly return to the familiar, so they came in on the train every day at some expense. They had spent the night this last night, however, marking out the long vigil with cups of watery tea from a vending machine and mournful bars of chocolate. Karl had done all the talking. Arthur was struck dumb, first with grief at the sudden *fait accompli* of her terrible condition, her wasted skin hanging on her protruding bones, her death's head eyes, and then with his understanding of what she had become.

Karl was diplomacy itself. He spoke strictly in terms of the disease and how it was only a disease and not a moral judgement. He illustrated from the depressing scrapbook of his recent memories the deadly impartiality of its appetite. He encouraged Shirley to talk too, asking her about Shuna's youth.

'There's so much she never told me,' he said. 'So much I'd love to know.' He was skilful, well-trained at drawing people

231

out. He was a volunteer assigned months before to befriend Shuna. Shirley thought it strange and rather sad that her daughter had so few friends that new ones had to be trained and assigned to her.

The revelation for Arthur, confirmation of what Shirley had known all along, came on the second day at the hospital, when a woman called in on the ward to see Shuna. She was unnaturally tall, with an astonishingly unlifelike red wig and thigh-length, leopardette, high-heeled boots. And she wore a perfume which lingered, cutting through the hospital smells long after her brief, tearful appearance, and spoke to father and mother alike of moist, unspeakable things. After she left, Arthur, staggered, finally found his tongue.

'Who in Christ's name was *that*?' he asked Karl as she slunk away up the ward, for all the world like some pagan goddess bestowing dubious blessings. Karl had seemed utterly unfazed, kissing the woman tenderly on the cheek and leading her to the bedside with a kind of courtesy.

'Oh, that was Ange. Angela. She and Shuna work together. Used to, I mean.'

'But she's a . . . ! You mean *my* daughter was . . . ?' Arthur had a rich vocabulary of insulting terms, especially for women, but for once in his life he seemed unable to name names. Karl helped him out.

'Yes, Mr Gilbert. Shuna was a sex worker.'

And Arthur must have believed him because he was too crushed to pick a fight.

It was funny how names changed the way one looked at things. *Sex Worker* had an utter rightness in Shirley's mind. It was truthful, unadorned; a woman's description. Sex was work, hard work where Arthur was concerned, a strenuous matter of puffing and panting and getting hot and flushed and sticky and trying hard to concentrate and not let one's mind make that fatal drift onto wallpaper choice and obstinate claret stains. She had been not a little relieved when he granted her an early retirement about the same time he had his degrading little fling with Mary Dewhurst at the golf club. Shirley was sure that Arthur was more appalled at his late discovery of how his daughter had paid for her generous Christmas presents and fancy imitation fur coat than at her cruel and senseless early death. Sure of it. But she did not greatly care. As her mother used to say: it did not signify.

It took them a long while to drive the short distance across the park and even longer to find a parking space. London had been taken over by cars; smelly, useless things.

'It gets worse every week,' Karl told her as he failed a second time to snatch a parking space and Shirley imagined car upon car clogging the already scarcely mobile queues until a day was reached when no more cars could get in or out of the place. It would become known as the Great Standstill or Smoggy Tuesday. People would die from the poor air quality, children preferably, and finally something would be done, something sensible like persuading men it would not hurt their sexual prowess to ride a bus occasionally.

Shuna's flat was in an unexpectedly leafy square with big plane trees, a well-kept residents' garden and glossy front doors. As she clambered up out of Karl's Mini she realized she had expected something sordid; wailing children in rags, women drunk at noon, surly menfolk with too many rings. This amused her and she laughed softly.

'What?' Karl asked.

'Nothing,' she said. 'Just being silly. Is this hers?' She pointed down to a basement with a tub of flowers outside the door.

'Yes.'

'I should know the address,' she said, 'but she didn't like me to write. I rang sometimes, when Mr Gilbert was out, but I always seemed to get other people – that Angela probably – and I don't think they passed on my messages. Here.' She pulled out the keys. 'You do it.'

Karl took the key ring, looked at the fob, and smiled sadly. 'I bought her this,' he said. 'In San Francisco.'

'Where the bridge is?'

'That's right. It's not really a key ring.'

'Oh? It makes a very good one. Is it for napkins or something?'

'No. No, it's a . . . a . . .' Karl seemed uncharacteristically bashful.

'Is it something rude, Karl?' Shirley helped him out.

'Yes,' he said, grinning. 'Very.'

'Well that's nice,' she told him. 'She must have liked that.'

'She did.'

As Karl turned to unlock the door, Shirley looked at the swinging hoop again, unable to stop herself wondering what on earth such a thing could be used for that would not be extremely painful. He opened the door and she followed him in.

'Good carpet,' she noticed aloud. Shuna had liked carpets as a child, had spent hours rolling around on them as she read or watched television.

'The rent's paid until the end of the month. We've been paying it for her while she was too sick to work. So it's not a problem.'

'You and your guardsman friend?'

'No, no.' He smiled. 'The charity.'

She nodded, beginning to take in her surroundings, the calm colours, the lack of pictures or ornaments, the single, big potted palm behind the sofa. Arthur had been right – it was little more than a bedsit – but it was a very comfortable, well decorated one. Shirley now felt the presence of her grown-up daughter intensely and was shy before it.

'It's very tidy,' she told Karl in a stage whisper, as if Shuna were just around the corner. 'She never used to be tidy.'

'Oh, er, I've been cleaning for her.'

'That's kind of you.'

'Not really. I like to clean.'

'You're very good at it. Shall I make us both a cup of tea?'

'Yes. No. You sit down. I'll do it. Oh God.'

He had paused, his hand on the kettle lid, and quite suddenly was overcome, hunched over the fridge. Shirley touched his shoulder gently. He turned and she drew him to her.

'I'm sorry,' he stammered. 'It suddenly hit me.'

'Don't,' she said. 'It's all right.'

He cried heavily for about ten minutes. It came over him in waves, little surges of grief that she could feel in the tightening of his arms about her. He smelled of leather, soap and man; she liked that. Apart from his brief hug in the hospital, she had not held anyone in years. She did not think she had ever held someone in a leather jacket. She let her fingers stray over its rich, studded surface and stroked the back of his head, where his hair was cut so short she had glimpsed a little strawberry mark underneath it. When he felt better and pulled gently away from her to blow his nose, she felt as relieved as if she had wept too.

'Sorry about that,' he said. 'I should go.'

'Must you?'

'I ought to pop into work, just to check on the mail and things . . . Can I pick you up later?'

'It's okay,' she said. 'I'll probably find my own way to the station when I'm ready.'

'My number's by the phone there, in case,' he said. 'You can take it with you and ring me from home, if you've a mind to.' He kissed her softly on the cheek and left. Nice boy.

She made herself a cup of tea. She explored the flat. She lay on Shuna's bed, even slipped between the sheets for a few minutes. She ate some chocolate biscuits from a tin and played a tape of strange music that was in the machine by the bath. Then, feeling she should do what bereaved relatives do, she reluctantly opened the big fitted cupboard, found a suitcase, and began folding clothes to take to the local charity shop. Shuna had developed a good eye for clothes, that much was swiftly evident, a good eye and expensive taste. They were of a size, and Shirley tried on a jacket and coat or two, wondering whether she would ever dare wear something with a famous Italian label and run the risk of Arthur's guessing where it had come from. Then she took out a hanger with the strangest garment on it she had ever seen.

It was black, and so glistening that Shirley though at first it was a black plastic dustbin liner draped to protect something precious. Then she realized that the black plastic was the thing itself; the dress, garment, whatever. It was quite thick, almost like leather, and shiny as a taxicab in the rain. It appeared to be a kind of all-in-one or catsuit, not unlike the things she had seen ice-skating men wear on championships televized from Norway. It had long sleeves and long legs. It was shaped with reinforcements to form a pointy bosom and, strangest of all, had built-in pointy boots and long-fingered gloves. Shirley could not resist putting one of her hands into a sleeve and into the empty finger pieces. It was extraordinary. The plastic clung to her, seeming to become an extra skin. There was not a breath of air inside. It fitted her arm exactly and shone so, even in the dim light from the window on to the area steps, that it was a surprise not to feel wet. She turned to look in the mirror, fascinated as she flexed and turned her fingers and forearm this way and that. Then, as she pulled her arm out, the garment gave off a sudden scent that might have been Shuna's very essence. With a little gasp, Shirley dropped it on the bed as though it had stung her. She stared at it for a moment, then tried to resume her packing, but its gleaming blackness burned a hole in the corner of her vision. It *would* not be ignored. At last, it proved too inviting and she found herself stripping entirely naked. One could see at a glance that this was *not* a garment for sensible underwear.

Shivering with anticipation, she slipped first one foot then the other into the leg pieces and down into the boots, happy that she and Shuna had shared a shoe size, then her arms, then her shoulders were encased in the sinuous, clammy stuff. She slowly fastened the big, black zipper that ran up its front from groin to neck, marvelling at the way it caused the contours of the thing to reshape her own. She had always been proud of her trim figure but no one could withstand age and gravity entirely. As the zip reached her chest, she let out a sigh, feeling her breasts first clasped then lifted upwards and outwards by the curiously pointed cones. Something was stuck in the neck, though, forming an unflattering bulge at the back. Wincing, she reached in over her shoulder and tweaked out a thing that looked like a cross between a matronly black bathing cap and the balaclava helmet she had once knitted Shuna. She hesitated for a moment then saw herself in the mirror, saw how her body had been taken over, transformed and her head left grotesquely unaltered on top. Taking a deep breath, she pulled on the headpiece, grimacing at the queer pull of the plastic on her cheeks and she tucked in the loose strands of her short, grey hair.

Now she looked back in the full length mirror and was afraid at how easily she had become something else. 'Oh, Shuna,' she breathed. 'Shuna, my dear.' But she was exhilarated too. The leg pieces squeezed and caressed her thighs in a way Arthur had never done. The new silhouette it gave her was entirely flattering. Astounded, she drew nearer for a closer, more critical look and saw how the mask had hidden her lines, emphasizing instead the best features that remained, her deep blue eyes, her strong little nose, her still full lips. Lipstick. It needed lipstick. She sat at Shuna's dressing table, pulled open the drawer and found some expensive French stuff and smeared a rich, true crimson about her mouth. Then she stood up, wandered around the flat a little and wondered, sadly, why time could not be frozen for a while, to postpone the mournful necessity of packing up and hurrying for a train.

Exhausted by her sleepless night, her grief and her confusion, she sank onto the sofa and, almost at once, fell into a deep sleep. When the telephone rang, she jumped up from the cushions like a surprised thief. She hesitated then, deciding it would be either Arthur or Karl, answered.

'Hello?'

It was a woman's voice. Cultured. Like a voice announcing symphonies on the radio. 'Time to work, my pet?' it asked.

'Er. No. Sorry. I think you've got the wrong number.'

The woman sighed. 'Come on, darling. Wake up. Are you free to play?'

'Oh,' Shirley stammered, confused. She wondered how much she should tell. Any caller who still knew nothing could hardly be counted an intimate. 'Shuna isn't here. This is her mother.'

The woman laughed. 'Oh *come* on, lovey! I haven't got all day.'

'No, honestly. It really is.'

'Listen. He's a really easy number. One of our regulars. The Wimp. Straight up and down for you. Whang, whang, no bang and you're laughing.' The coarse words sounded doubly suggestive in such a plummy mouth.

'No, you don't seem to understand. Shuna is . . . Well, she's . . . This really is her mother.'

The reply came quick as a blade. 'You're wearing the suit, aren't you?'

'I . . . I . . .' How could she deny it? 'Yes,' she boldly confessed. 'I am. It's lovely.'

'He'll be up in a couple of minutes, darling. It never takes long. Then we can talk.'

The woman hung up. Shirley stared at the telephone receiver for a moment then began to panic. She hurried over to the wardrobe and continued throwing things into bags. This was insanity. She had not slept. She was in shock. She was hearing things. The telephone probably had not rung at all. She would finish packing, catch the train home and make herself a nice cup of hot, frothy malted milk.

The doorbell sounded. Shirley choked a cry then stifled her fear with common sense. There was nothing for it but to be totally honest. She would answer the door and tell the man it was all some grotesque clerical error. He would take one look at her in any case and *see* she was only somebody's mother. It was only when Shirley tugged wide the door and saw the immediate look of terror on the face of the burly, balding man before her that she remembered she had not changed back into her own, reassuringly motherly clothes.

'I'm sorry,' he said at once.

'What?' she asked. 'No. Honestly. Please listen. I'm the one who should apologize.'

'It's not safe out here, love,' he muttered in an undertone and darted past her in to the flat.'

'Now, please! Look here,' she began. A woman was pushing a pram past on the pavement, leading a little girl who peered down into each basement as she passed it. Horrified, Shirley swiftly shut the door and turned to find her caller cringing on the carpet before her.

'Please, no,' he said. 'Please don't hurt me! I'll do anything. Anything!'

'Get out,' she said, deciding that firmness was the only way to handle such an impossible situation. 'Get up and get out.'

'I'll try to be good next time. I promise. Please.' Grovelling he reached out towards one of her shinily booted feet and grasped the ankle. Without thinking, she kicked out and struck him on the chin in self-defence.

'Oh. I'm so terribly sorry,' she began but he was reaching out for her feet again and she stamped on his hand. He gasped then cried out with what she now realized was pleasure. So she stopped apologizing. Too her disgust she saw that, though still on all fours, he had reached down and was rubbing a hand between his legs.

'Stop that,' she said. 'Stop it at once!'

He looked up, his face pink and as unappealing as Arthur's when he had been drinking and began to tell off-colour jokes.

'Make me,' he said, and the challenge was half a plea. He was still playing with himself. Shirley felt sick and slightly faint. The suit was becoming intolerably hot. It was out of the question for her to run out into the street asking for help dressed as she was.

Then it struck her. She did not need to run because she was not afraid. The man was pathetic. The suit itself seemed to lend her power. She smelled again her daughter's scent in her nostrils and her mind cleared. She knew, with a sigh, what she had to do. It was laughably simple. Letting the man's piggish grunts and whimpers feed a clean anger that had begun to burn in her clutched and moulded bosom, she strode back to the cupboard, picked up the thick, black riding crop she had noticed hanging in there and turned to face him. His face lit up with pleasure.

'Please,' he begged her. 'Please, no!'

'Oh shut up,' she said, and smacked him across the back, very hard. He yelled.

'Don't make so much noise,' she spat. 'What will people say, you disgusting little man?' and she hit him again. He was a big man, like Arthur, and could have killed her quite easily with his fat, hairless hands had he wanted to, but he cringed and whimpered, utterly in her thrall as she struck out again and again. She hit him for the years of white Crimplene cardigans, for the decades of watching Arthur mow the lawn, for her wasted bloom and her vanished joys, hit him for Mary Dewhurst, hit him, hardest of all, for the way he and Arthur and stupid men like them had taken away from her the only person she had ever really loved.

It took only two minutes, three at the most. In the brief span from her first smack across his back to his subsiding in muffled ecstasy – 'Don't you dare dirty the carpet!' she hissed – Shirley Gilbert travelled further from the certainties of 66 Hollybush Drive than Saint Christopher could ever have safely carried her. By the last smack, she had stopped being angry and begun to enjoy herself.

Tired with her effort, she sat on the sofa arm, watching her visitor closely. He slowly lurched to his knees, and onto his feet. His face had cleared. He no longer looked beseeching, merely drained of necessity and she realized with a shock that she had made him comfortable. She was obscurely proud.

'Thank you,' he muttered. 'Thank you so much.' His voice was no longer wheedling but almost manly and she felt a pang of apology rising in her breast. Then he reached into his wallet, took out several bank notes, put them on the table and left without another word. No sooner was the door shut than she ran after him, shot the bolt on it and set about feverishly tugging off the catsuit. She washed her face and hands, patted herself dry with a fluffy white towel, then finished packing the suitcase. She repaired her face and hair, dabbed on some scent and tried to ignore the riding crop and mound of sweaty black plastic at the foot of the bed.

Then the doorbell rang again.

'Who is it?' she called out, querulous.

'It's all right,' said the plummy voice she had heard on the telephone. 'It's me. Ange.'

There was a spyhole in the door. Frowning, Shirley peered through it and saw it was the towering siren who had visited the hospital. She opened the door. Angela was dressed almost quietly, in a beautifully tailored linen suit and scarlet blouse.

'Hello,' she said. 'You'd better come in.'

'Thanks,' said Angela, poised as an air stewardess. 'Mind if I sit? My dogs are killing me.' She coiled her impressive length onto the armchair and kicked off her bright red court shoes.

'Well?' she asked.

'Well what?' Shirley asked her back.

Angela languidly gestured towards the heap of notes. 'What did he leave you?'

Shirley counted the notes and was astounded. 'But . . .' she stuttered. 'He must have made a mistake!'

'No mistake, darling,' Angela said, eyeing the money. 'You must have been good. Now listen. I'm sorry I was short with you earlier but his need was pressing and –'

'How did you know I was in that –'

'Mind if I smoke?' Angela cut in.

'Not at all.'

'Shuna smoked all the time. Even on the job. Sorry.'

'That's all right.'

'Anyway. The choice is yours.'

'I'm sorry?'

'The choice. You have a choice. Either you take that suitcase, leave the suit of course, and disappear off to the remainder of your quiet little life and are never heard of again, or . . . or you take that suitcase – if the suit fitted you, her other things will – *and* you take the suit then you come with me and start your new life. Either way, you get to keep the money. You earned it, after all.'

'I don't quite –'

Angela seemed oblivious to Shirley's confusion, holding her cigarette between the long, wonderfully manicured fingers of one hand and patting at her chic blonde chignon with the others. The woman was a mistress of disguise.

'You'll have to leave the flat, of course,' Angela went on. 'I'll have one of the girls torch it, make it look like a dreadful accident, to cover your traces. You'll get a new place, somewhere a little more gracious than this for you, I think, lovey. And a new ID. Car, too, if you want one. I could tell you'd be good the moment I laid eyes on you. Just like her. A natural. Have you ever worn riding stuff? Jodhpurs and so on? The strict, tight-little-hacking jacket look?'

'I'm fifty-five, for God's sake.'

'Age, as you've just so admirably demonstrated, is no bar to a perfect technique and a satisfied clientele. Did you enjoy it? Just a little bit towards the end maybe?'

Shirley froze for a moment then nodded, purse-lipped. Angela smiled lazily.

'Thought so,' she said. 'Easiest money in the world in that case. And they never even touch you. Whatever, darling, I don't have much time so what's it to be? Suburban Slavery, Arthur and *Gardeners' Question Time* or power, liberty and danger?'

Angela stood, towering over Shirley, and seemed to be waiting. She batted her thick eyelids slowly and it struck Shirley that she might not be altogether female.

Shirley felt she was standing on the brink of a precipice but had just been told she was free to fly if she wanted to.

'The other?' she whispered, and bit her lower lip.

'Sorry?' Angela asked.

'The other. The . . . The second thing you said.'

Angela smiled a huge, generous smile. 'Good,' she said and reached into her crocodile clutch bag for a gold fountain pen and what looked like a piece of parchment. 'I sign here.' She scrawled a large A with a flourish and a little x. 'And you,' she placed the pen in Shirley's trembling fingers. It was heavy, good quality. 'You sign there.'

Shirley scanned the old-fashioned manuscript. The words swam. They might as well have been Latin. Perhaps they were.

'Shouldn't I sign this in blood?' she asked.

Angela playfully slapped the back of her wrist.

'Naughty!' she said. 'I can see *you*'re going to be fun.'

Patrick Gale

Facing the Tank

A writer visits a quaint English Cathedral town and discovers its goings-on are stranger than fiction.

When Evan J. Kirby, an eminent American expert on Heaven and Hell, arrives in Barrowcester to do some research, he finds the community in a less than blissful state. There is the bishop sharing his doubts with the confirmation class, while his mother feeds marijuana cookies to Evan's landlady to unleash her psychic powers. Then there is Emma lurking in her father's study waiting for love; Dawn sitting naked in a deckchair at midnight waiting for the Devil, and Madeline seeking refuge from a carnally inclined Cardinal. When Evan delves into the true origins of the local saint, a macabre and romantic sequence of events begins to unfold.

'The sheer funniness of *Facing the Tank* made me laugh out loud.'   *Sunday Times*

'The close world of The Close is tea-cosy warm. But not for long, as Patrick Gale speedily unleashes his merrily black mischief. The uncovering of the sadness behind the doilies and twinsets is in the best traditions of black humour.'

Observer

'Original and amusing, Patrick Gale is an elegant, witty writer with an engagingly bizarre imagination.'

Sunday Telegraph

'A commendably intelligent, entertaining and, at times, moving novel.'   *Times Literary Supplement*

ISBN: 0 00 654545 9

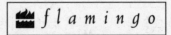 *flamingo*

Patrick Gale

Little Bits of Baby

No one knew why Robin abandoned a brilliant university
career to start a new life at an eccentric island monastery, but
it was thought to have something to do with the surprise
engagement of Candida, Robin's childhood playmate, and
Jake, their mutual friend.

Eight years later, Robin's return to the less spiritual world of
London has far-reaching effects. Much has changed: his
father has left the City to run a progressive kindergarten in
Clapham; Candida is now a household name as a presenter
on breakfast television; and Jake is a successful advertising
executive. When Robin falls in love at the christening of
Candida's baby, he has little idea of how extraordinary the
consequences will be.

'A richly comic novel about the equilibrium of urban lives
and loves upset by an outsider. Affectionate and perceptive.'
Mail on Sunday

'Writes like Iris Murdoch on pep pills. Savage, satirical, often
very funny. Love, death, the decay of friendship, the triumph
of love – all the big themes are here in small doses, cunningly
plotted and skilfully interwoven.'   *Daily Mail*

'His discreet exploration of love between the generations and
the sexes is by turns poignant and humorous.'   *Vogue*

'A wonderful modern comedy of manners, neatly crafted and
full of compassion for all its most foiblesome cast.'   *Company*

ISBN: 0 586 09060 6

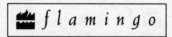

Patrick Gale

Tree Surgery for Beginners

Lawrence Frost has neither father nor siblings, and fits so awkwardly into his worldly mother's life he might have dropped from the sky. Straightforward, honest, and a doting dad, he can be a difficult, taciturn husband – but he's the last person one would suspect of being a killer.

Waking one morning to find himself branded a wife-beater and under suspicion for murder, his small world falls apart as he loses wife, daughter, liberty, livelihood and, almost, his mind.

'Don't miss this corker of a novel. Terrific.'   *Woman's Journal*

'This book starts out in the world of Joanna Trollope, strays into the gilded realms of Noel Coward, and finally ends up in the reflexive New Age sequoia groves of Christopher Isherwood's California. Bright and breezy, Gale is a master of the deceptively light touch.'   *Mail on Sunday*

'Gale is at his most insightful in his descriptions of characters, both of individuals and of the Frost family as a whole. His heroines are as startlingly believable as his hero, and Lawrence manages to be unforgivable on page one and pitiful enough to be forgiven by the end.'   *Observer*

'High in the drama, wit and immodest romance which will be all too familiar to his regular readers.'   *Independent*

ISBN: 0 00 655074 6

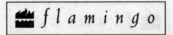 *flamingo*

Patrick Gale

Ease

A novel about downsizing from a life of ease and upgrading to one of sleaze.

Many people would kill to be Domina Tey. She's one of life's successes: an award-winning playwright living in a beautiful house with an equally celebrated writer. A lucky woman. And she knows and appreciates it. But she isn't happy. Life is too easy. It's becoming stultifying, negating her creative force.

Domina decides upon a spell of sleazy living to give both her work and her soul a spring-clean – and elopes with her typewriter in search of just a hint of degradation. She finds it in Bayswater. Safe in bedsit land, she immediately sets about getting to know her neighbour, a candidate for the priesthood half her age.

'Patrick Gale writes with the understated fluency that is the hallmark of contemporary British fiction, and with the irony that usually accompanies it. Like William Boyd and Martin Amis, he skilfully blends the light and the dark, moving unobtrusively from comedy to drama without losing narrative momentum or integrity.'   Book World, US

ISBN: 0 586 09147 5

flamingo

Patrick Gale

The Cat Sanctuary

Judith and Deborah are sisters driven apart by traumatic events in their childhood, but thrown back together again when Deborah's diplomat husband is accidentally assassinated. Judith's lover, Joanna, the instigator of this awkward reunion, finds that as the sisters' murky past is raked up, so too is her own, and the three women become embroiled in a tangle of passion and recrimination.

'He writes about difficult emotions with delicacy, perception and a rare ferocious charm.'   *Guardian*

'Powerful and moving novel in which the darkness is often lightened by the author's deft touches of comedy.'
Sunday Independent

'Gale is a charmingly idiosyncratic writer who could not write a cliché if he tried. Spiced with mischievous irony, this engrossing story contains some interesting aperçus on the process of novel writing.'   *Daily Telegraph*

'A book with claws.'   *The Times*

'Like Gale's previous novels, it's an elegantly menacing, enjoyable read that starts as it means to go on – dynamically. It's a deep and moving book; highly recommended.'
New Woman

'Gale's writing is marvellously entertaining, and there is a compelling sense of biting deep into the core of the bitter truth.'   *Cosmopolitan*

ISBN: 0 586 09061 4

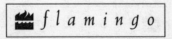